MAKEOVER

MAKEOVER

BARBARA LORNA HUDSON

First Published in 2019 by Fantastic Books Publishing
Cover design by Gabi

ISBN (ebook): 978-1-912053-50-6
ISBN (paperback): 978-1-912053-49-0

ACKNOWLEDGEMENTS

Top of my list again is Dr Vera Baraniecka

I would also like to thank:

- for feedback on parts of the novel: Leke Adewole, Dr Lynette Bradley, Lindy Castell, Michele Connor, Dr Keith Crook, Prof Nora Crook, Ursula Crook, Chris Gawor, Dennis Hamley, David Shufflebotham. Also Fleur Kinson, Jonathan Saunders, and other members of Writers at Blackwell's.
- for an enlightening course on The Modern Novel: Dr David Grylls
- for advice on legal issues: James Sandham and Dr Colin Roberts
- for advice on women's refuges: Jan Gullachsen, Laurie-Mo Gullachsen, and Refuge
- for medical advice: Professor Richard McManus

The Oxford Editors advised on an early draft and Cherry Mosteshar has been supportive beyond the call of duty.

* * *

The memoir that inspired and moved Lucille is *After You: Letters of Love, and Loss, to a Husband and Father* by Natascha McElhone, Viking, Penguin, 2010.

CHAPTER ONE

A Sunday in Oxford

Walter Farquarson's wireless was playing Mozart, the first act of *Cosi fan Tutte*: the aria "Un'Aura Amorosa". He felt a rush of yearning for Sarah, which took the form of a flashback to those sweet lazy Sundays not so long ago when they'd lain in bed till noon listening to music and making love. He realised he had a physical longing, painfully strong—and was ashamed. But then he touched himself through his clothes and went up to his bedroom and brought himself to a climax. And after that he cried.

Their splendid high-ceilinged bedroom seemed uncomfortably large for one person alone, and he wondered if moving to another room might help—this one was so full of memories. Walnut bookshelves, dusty but still glowing, ran the length of one wall; the books they'd owned in common were here, and their two armchairs, each with its own reading lamp on a delicate wrought-iron stand. On the door hung her robe of white embroidered silk. They had chosen it in Chinatown, San Francisco, while he was on sabbatical. If you touched it you could catch a memory of Chanel Number Five. Her empty scent bottle, a little glass swan, the first present he had ever given her, still stood on the chest next to a line of framed photos: holding their babies, receiving an award, tending her roses, the bride at the wedding. Sarah Scott.

That pretty, two-person rosewood sofa in the bay window, where they used to sit side by side and laugh at the antics of the squirrel family and the great spotted woodpeckers in the sycamore tree. He never sat there now. The double bed was unmade. His bedside cabinet was cluttered; a stack of books, a box of tissues, a bottle of pills; the one on Sarah's side was bare and veiled in dust. Although the bed was all his now, he still kept to the right-hand side. He'd left clothing draped over the chairs and the linen basket overflowed. A bulb in the large central light had failed but he could make out spiders' webs swinging from the ceiling and across the corners of the room. I ought to ask the North Oxford Cleaners to come back, he thought. It was a mistake to tell them they were no longer needed.

Walter returned to his drawing room. *The Fire in the Clearing* by Sarah Scott. *The Toy Library* by Sarah Scott. *The Ungentle* by Sarah Scott ... The rows of novels by Sarah Scott—hardbacks, paperbacks and translations—filled a tall bookcase; his armchair was placed where he could see them constantly. He'd moved all photos of Sarah into the bedroom, because the sight of them made it hard to turn his mind to anything except his loss. If he absolutely had to have a glimpse of her, he could find her smiling face on the jackets of her books.

Every day Walter Farquarson looked at these books and ran his fingers along their spines, and remembered Sarah Scott. His wife. She hadn't changed her name to his, not for feminist reasons, but because she was already a published writer when they married and it was simpler to stay Sarah Scott for everything. The only times he'd minded had been when people assumed they weren't married, for being married to her was the thing he was most proud of. I suppose I'm a vain man, he thought—I wanted everyone to know that this warm-hearted, brilliant person chose *me*.

This Sunday Walter planned to spend a few hours preparing his lectures for the week ahead. Then he would press on with fund-raising for the women's refuge: begging letters and calls to people he might persuade. And his daughter or his son would probably telephone—this was the highpoint of his weekend.

But first he scanned the columns of the dating agency in the *Independent*, looking at the advertisements from women aged forty to fifty years old. Sarah had been forty-seven, only forty-seven; she had been dead nearly two years and he was that same age now. "I'd never want anyone to take your place. But dearest Sarah, you'd understand, wouldn't you?" he asked the silent books.

* * *

They waltzed on golden sunset sands. There was a sort of glistening sheen, so perhaps it had been raining, and perhaps more rain was expected, for the maid and the butler—*The Singing Butler*—stood by with big black umbrellas. The gentleman wore an evening suit; the lady wore a slinky scarlet gown and she had bare feet and long scarlet gloves. Lucille wished she could be on that beach, in that dress, with the wonderful man and the two servants. All she needed was a lucky break, a chance to meet the right man. He'd have to be rich. And kind to her—that went without saying. She'd like him to be posh, too, with a plummy accent and gentlemanly manners. In pride of place above her fire of realistic logs, this picture was her comfort and her inspiration. A house-warming gift to herself, it cost her nearly a hundred pounds at that classy little shop in Henley.

Perhaps she should try to sell her other picture, *The Green Lady*? Long, thick, dark hair, rather like her own; warm red lips; flared nostrils—a little horsey-looking, as were hers, unfortunately. She loved the golden collar and the exotic gown. The picture was clever and striking and it had belonged to her mother, one of the few nice things her mother had owned. But the green/blue face could seem a bit unhealthy, even scary. Maybe she should replace it with something encouraging, more like *The Singing Butler*, some artwork that fitted in better with the lovely silk orchids and the glittering display of bottles and glasses on the sideboard.

Lucille looked round her lounge and took stock of her life. She'd finished paying for the off-white three-piece suite and the floor-length satiny curtains and the deep-pile fitted carpet. Soon she'd be able to think about making her kitchen and bathroom more state-of-the-art. The kitchen was crying out for granite worktops and a shiny double oven. The bathroom was an even more urgent case—it still had avocado fixtures dating back to the 1980s; she cringed when her guests required the toilet.

But the mortgage was manageable and it made her smile to think she was now a Homeowner. That made her middle-class. Once she would not have dreamt she could come so far. If her mother could see her now, she'd be over the moon.

The only thing missing was the man. She called herself the Merry Divorcee but she got frightened when she thought, What if I lose my job? What if I get ill? Then who is going to take care of me?

Lucille stood up and stared into her large, gilt-framed mirror, and took stock of her face. *'My face is my fortune, sir,' she said*—wherever did that come from? Good skin still, veiled in a light tinted moisturiser—perhaps this was nicer than the concealing product she wore on work days?—and just a hint of colour on the pouty lips. The less said about her nose, the better. Her eyes were her best feature; her ex-husband, Jason Brown, called them "bedroom eyes". They were big and seductive even without the false eyelashes that she couldn't resist, though today was Sunday and nothing in her diary. You never know who might come calling, as her mother used to say.

Lucille looked like a Lucille all right. She had hated being called Mary, the boring name her mum and dad had saddled her with, and she was dead grateful to her friend Jillie, who said, "You can call yourself whatever you like, Mary." Such a pity she hadn't thought of it earlier.

Her latest surname, Brown, wasn't alluring, either. Perhaps she should change it by deed poll? Go back to one of her previous surnames: Higgs, or her maiden name, Carter? But neither of these was much of an improvement on Brown. Maybe it was best to wait till she found that husband number three.

The phone rang. She snatched it up, forgetting yet again that the caller's identity was shown on the little screen.

"Hiya, baby," said the voice Lucille had grown to dread. She smashed the receiver down without speaking.

* * *

"Walter, can you come to supper next Sunday? We've asked two of my colleagues and their wives. I want to make them feel welcome—they're new to Oxford. Marcia hasn't seen you for ages, and this is a chance for you and me to have a quick chat about the women's refuge. Not ideal, I know. But you'll get a good meal—it's Marcia's turn to cook—and we can sneak off to my study for half an hour."

"To be honest, Mike, I'm not sure … You know, I haven't felt much like socialising since Sarah …"

"I can imagine it must be hard, especially when everyone else is in couples. But we intend to ask another single person as well."

"A woman?"

"Well, yes. But—"

"No matchmaking, I beg you."

"We wouldn't be so crass. And anyway, Marcia says Lucille's a nice woman, but she's certainly not your type. Just think of it as a meal and some company and a chance to make progress with the refuge. If you want to leave early, we'll understand."

Walter felt obliged to accept the invitation. Unsettled and unhappy, he did something he often did these days—like a child reaching for its security blanket, he thought—he leaned across and chose one of Sarah's novels at random off the shelf and looked at her photo on the jacket. *Afterword*—it was her last book and the title evoked a bitter smile.

This was the one whose proceeds Sarah donated to a domestic abuse charity after a visit to the refuge where their cleaning lady had found sanctuary. He recalled how distressed Sarah had been when she returned. The officer in charge had made Sarah promise to keep the address a secret. "Otherwise they get men coming to beat the women up again or attack the staff," Sarah told him. "And another awful thing: the refuge has to turn away women every week for lack of space."

She put her arms round him and stood on tiptoe to kiss his mouth. "Walter, I'll never forget how lucky I am to have a loving husband like you. And it is just luck."

6

"No, my darling, it isn't. I love you because you're so love-able."

"It *is* luck. I'm no more loveable than those poor women. How fortunate we are, you and I. So it would be nice to give something back—no, that's not the right way to say it. You know what I mean?"

Walter had tried to soothe her, for she was close to tears. "It's not like you to be lost for words, my darling. But, yes, I know what you mean."

Walter went into the study and switched on his computer. He printed out his notes from the last steering meeting, the letters of support, and the record of donations received and promised. Soon they'd have to calculate how much was needed and he'd decide what he should contribute from Sarah's estate. He knew it was sensible to take this opportunity for a meeting with Mike to get on with plans for the new refuge. And, besides, making himself a hermit wouldn't bring her back. Nothing would. For their children's sake he had to go on living in the world and find some purpose and interest beyond his work; otherwise there was a danger he'd turn into a boring dried-up academic and an over-possessive parent. "And an over-possessive cat owner," he said to his cat Prissy, who had wedged her fat body between him and his computer keyboard.

* * *

Once more Lucille's phone rang. This time she checked—it was him again, her second ex-husband, Jason Brown. She didn't pick up the receiver. But she remembered. When was it? Two years ago. A month after their wedding. The first time he'd hit her.

Lucille trembled with helpless anger. How could he find the nerve to ring her and call her "baby" after what he had done? "Unreasonable behaviour" didn't come close. She'd heard his car sales business was minting it in, but she didn't get a penny maintenance. She had been too ashamed to claim. And after she left him he'd shacked up with that slapper Sallyanne. Now he wanted her back for a little bit on the side.

It was Jason's fault she had to work for peanuts as a personal shopper at Richley's. This was a job that brought her into close contact with well-to-do, beautiful people; yet she had no hope of ever becoming one of them. A job that rubbed her nose in it. And she'd had to use all her savings for the deposit on this flat, and give up the car and do without holidays and worry about her future.

The phone rang again. No name on the screen—and a voice she didn't recognise. It was her colleague—not a friend exactly—Marcia Johnson, the Human Resources Adviser at Richley's, a rather stern lady with a small bust and enviably long legs. To her surprise, Marcia invited her to dinner.

"An informal supper party really, rather than a dinner," said Marcia. "Mike—my husband—wanted to ask some people from his department."

"Your husband works for the social, doesn't he?"

A hint of irritation. "No, he's a probation officer. We've asked two of his colleagues and their wives—one wife's a teacher and the other one's a social worker—it's awful—I can never remember which is which. Oh, and we've invited that lovely man Walter Farquarson, the one who lost his wife a year or so ago, the novelist Sarah Scott. He and Mike are old friends from university and now he has approached Mike for help with this project of his—Sarah left instructions for him to set up a women's refuge and he obviously hasn't a clue how to go about it."

"What does he do, this Mr Farquarson?"

"*Professor* Farquarson. He's a historian. Fellow of St Nicholas' College. And it seems he's tremendously busy with Sarah's estate. She must have left an absolute fortune—her books have been on the bestseller lists and I'm sure the royalties are still pouring in. He wants to use some of it for the women's refuge in Sarah's memory."

Lucille said, "I'd love to come. Thank you for asking me."

"I've been meaning to have you round for ages."

Lucille thought, No you haven't. You're scraping the barrel. You want a single woman to make up the numbers. Human Resources usually think they're too grand to mix with personal shoppers. Oh well, it's an excuse to buy a new outfit. I've got to put myself about a bit. It's sensible to accept every invitation, however unpromising.

You never know: even women and married couples have unattached men friends and might introduce you; married men might soon be available again. As for widowers—if they've had a happy marriage they soon start looking round. You have to be quick, before they're snapped up. What's more, as well as being rich this Professor Farquarson might turn out to be a very nice man.

CHAPTER TWO

Supper at the Johnsons'

After two slow bus rides and an uncomfortable hike on her killer heels, at long last Lucille found her way to the Johnsons' in deepest Cowley. The house was a mishmash with annexes, a conservatory and a roof extension; it took a while to locate the front door and to reach it she had to struggle up a flight of steep stone steps. A small grey-haired man who she guessed must be Mike Johnson let her in, said, "Hullo and welcome. You must be Lucille. You can put your jacket here," and disappeared. The hallway was narrow with a small room on the left that seemed to be an office, where the guests were to leave their coats, and on the other side the kitchen. Two teenaged boys came out carrying plates of spaghetti and galloped up the stairs. The whole place stank of garlic.

Though tired and flustered, Lucille felt good in her new black satin bubble skirt and low-cut yellow top. She stopped at the hall mirror to refresh her lipstick. Two couples came in without ringing the doorbell, dumped their coats and walked into the kitchen. She could see them in the mirror as they passed. The women's clothes worried her: one wore navy linen trousers (the teacher, she guessed) and the other artificially faded jeans with designer holes in them (the social worker, surely?).

"Come this way when you're ready." Marcia looked out from the kitchen. She wore jeans, too, and had on a pink top with the words "très cool" across the front. Of course! Marcia had told her it was just an informal supper. She'd got it wrong again. At least she'd stand out from the crowd.

Professor Walter Farquarson arrived. It had to be him, the only man on his own. She fancied him right away. A tall, good-looking man, a bit like an older version of Hugh Grant in *Love Actually*, he had greying hair, nice hair though overlong and straggly. His shirt was frayed at the collar and his tweed jacket and corduroy trousers had seen better days. Worried, she glanced down at his feet and was relieved to see that he wore ordinary shoes and not the awful socks and sandals combination she'd noticed before on university men, though Walter's shoes were scuffed and old-fashioned. He'd been neglecting himself, but there was nothing that couldn't be sorted.

He introduced himself. "How do you do?"

"Hiya, I'm Lucille." She smiled, and then added, "How do you do?" because that was what he had said. She smiled at him again, tilted her head a little, lowered it and gazed up at him wide-eyed—her Princess Diana look. Her mother said it was sly, but Lucille was sure it was sexy and endearing. And not easy to pull off successfully; she'd had to practise it a lot.

* * *

Walter was dreading the supper party and having to make conversation with people he didn't know; apart from college meals, this was his first social outing since Sarah died. Had the other guests been warned that he lost his wife not long ago? In that case, they'd be nervous of him. Or perhaps they hadn't been told, and he might be obliged to explain about being on his own

11

and about losing Sarah. He wished he'd asked Mike which it was likely to be.

Now he just wanted to linger in the hall, but here was this brash, colourful woman with a northern accent and rather obvious cleavage putting on make-up in public and looking at him in a peculiar way. Marcia was right—she certainly wasn't his type. And he observed that she was wearing a tiny, incongruous gold cross on a slender chain, dangling towards that ample bosom. Could she be religious? It didn't fit with the rest of her. But anyway, what did it matter to him?

He didn't wish to be uncivil, so he made an effort at conversation while she stowed her paraphernalia back into her capacious, rather sinister, crocodile handbag. She closed it with a snap.

"How do you know Mike and Marcia?"

"Marcia and I are colleagues."

"So you're another human resources person?"

"Not exactly. But I work at Richley's too."

Yes, I know you do, you've just said so, he thought. "Do you live around here?"

"No. North Oxford. Beyond the ring road."

"Uh-huh." He'd been reading about the scandal of the 1930s Cutteslowe Walls, erected to separate a council estate from some new middle-class housing. Some people said the ring road served a similar purpose nowadays. "Have you lived there long?"

"I bought my flat a year ago." He could hear pride in her voice and this puzzled him. He was unable to think of a suitable comment and said thoughtlessly, meaning it as a joke, "Halfway to Birmingham!"

Lucille retorted, "No. Halfway to Bicester Village." He noticed she was suppressing a smile. This lady can give as good as she gets, he thought.

"Bicester Village?"

"It's a retail outlet. You can find brilliant bargains in designer clothes."

Walter frowned. He tried a different tack. "Do you like living in Oxford?"

"Oh, yes. Such a good bus service, and I love the cheerful atmosphere thanks to all the tourists and all the nice young students."

Walter thought, And *I* like Oxford because it has world-class libraries and at least two restaurants bearing the name of a celebrity chef. But he merely replied, "Yes, I believe there's no better place to live in England."

"We ought to join the others, don't you think?" she said.

He followed her through the kitchen and into the conservatory beyond.

* * *

The meal was something of a strain. Lucille concentrated on picking politely at the calorific pasta in a strange creamy sauce that featured olives. She separated out the ugly little black lumps and hid them under a neat pile of pasta on the side of her plate.

Meanwhile, the others talked of old French films at the Phoenix, Shakespeare plays at Stratford-upon-Avon, and a novel everyone except her had read. It was called *Bring Up the Bodies*, which sounded like one of those enormous snakes (a python?) being sick after it had swallowed too many rabbits.

Bring Up the Bodies had won the "Booker" last year. The teacher insisted on calling it "The Man Booker"—a funny name for a book prize awarded to a woman.

And somehow they got on to changes in the Probation Service, and then to schools called faith schools and free schools. Marcia changed the subject. "That's enough about politics." She brought Lucille into the conversation. "Come on, Lucille, tell us what's new in your department."

She couldn't understand why they seemed amused when she told them about the latest fashion trends: bubble trousers and skirts, and geometric patterns. And she felt worse when they seemed to sense her discomfort and pretended to be seriously interested.

"What exactly does a personal shopper do?" asked one of the probation officers.

"Some stores call it 'fashion styling' or 'image consultancy'. We help our customers to discover their own personal style— sort of set it free."

"Men as well as women?"

"Well, yes, but I don't do gentlemen."

"Really?"

Marcia broke in. "Now, then, Mike, don't tease."

Lucille felt herself blushing.

A brief silence. Then Walter said, "I'd like to hear more about it," and several others chimed in: "Fascinating!", "All new to me!", "Please go on."

The teacher asked what qualifications you need to become a personal shopper.

"Well, retail experience in fashion is a must."

"You mean selling clothes?"

"Yes."

"No courses or exams?"

"There's a Diploma in Personal Styling but I haven't got one."

"How much do you charge for a session?"

"Some stores require a booking fee—but we don't, and you don't have to buy anything. The customer gets a free consultation, and we provide complimentary coffee in our private suite, while I hunt round the store and fetch the garments I think will suit her."

"What happens in the consultation?"

Would the woman never stop quizzing her? "We take measurements. And I try to find out about the person. The kind of life they dream of, the celebrities they admire, whether they want to look younger. And practical things—are they happy to wear high heels? will they be driving? and any no-no's."

"No-no's?"

"Things different people rule out. Fur. Angora. Wearing white when you're a guest at a wedding. Showing cleavage. Short skirts. That sort of thing."

"I suppose a lot of them are shopping for an outfit to wear at a wedding?"

"Yes, or a garden party or a christening. I once helped a lady who was going to meet the Queen. Occasion wear. And quite a few seem to be after a complete makeover and I refer them to a beautician and the hairstylist and often to our bra fitter as well."

"Not to a psychiatrist?" said Mike.

What an odd thing to ask, she thought, but then she realised he was trying to be funny and decided to punish him by treating it as a serious question. "Oh, no, not to a psychiatrist. It's not my place."

Walter said, "My wife Sarah's publisher suggested she should have a makeover before all those book-signings and literary festivals. She nearly went along with it but I persuaded her she was fine as she was."

"You were right. She didn't need any of that. Sarah was Sarah. She was her own woman," said Mike. Lucille wondered what he meant. She sensed no one was interested in hearing any more from her, and she was relieved.

Walter had said very little, but he kept nodding politely. He brightened when Marcia asked about the women's refuge he was setting up.

"Yes, we've found premises at last. We can take over the old Deaf Centre. And the donations are pouring in," he said. "I wish Sarah could have lived to see it. She'd have been so pleased ..." He faltered, but then he went on to talk about the steering committee and their plans.

After supper, Lucille sat down next to Walter on a small couch, so that they could have a private conversation.

"I understand you lost your wife not long ago?"

"Marcia's told you, then?" There was a note of relief in his voice.

"Yes. Sarah. What a pretty name!"

He stared at her. "Is it? I'd never thought ... well, yes, I suppose it is."

"Do tell me about her."

"I wouldn't know where to begin ..."

"You must miss her."

"Yes, naturally."

"Of course you do—an awful shock, I expect?"

"It wasn't really a shock. We knew, we'd time to prepare."

"No doubt you felt angry ..."

"No. Why would I be angry? It was nobody's fault."

"Sorry. I shouldn't have jumped to conclusions. I know many people do feel that way. When I lost my mum I blamed the doctor and the hospital and then I blamed myself."

He seemed bewildered. "But Sarah had cancer—everyone did all they could. The only person to blame would have been God." Lucille realised she was out of her depth and that she had probably been hurtful rather than helpful. She was deeply sorry. She decided to change the subject.

"Your wife was a brilliant writer."

"Oh, have you read her novels?" He sat up straighter, seemed eager to hear what she had to say. She'd once tried to read a Sarah Scott. She'd given up after a few pages—too heavy-going; she was just not clever enough and it was so long she knew she'd lose the thread of the story before she got to the end.

She told a white lie. "Yes, of course. I loved her latest—I mean, her last ... oh dear, the title's suddenly gone out of my head."

"*Afterword*. What did you like about it particularly?"

"Um ... the writing. So elegant. Every word seems just right. And the characters, of course."

"Which characters did you like?"

"Well, the main character. And the others, too. They're all so real." Walter nodded, smiling.

Time to change the subject again. "But tell me about Sarah as a person. Was she like any of her heroines?"

"She resembled some of them, I suppose, but no one in particular. Sarah was modest, quiet, caring. A family person, really. She loved our pets and our garden ... She grew prize-winning roses." Walter went on and on, praising Sarah to the skies.

17

Rather to Lucille's relief, Mike came over and said, "Forgive me for butting in. I'll have to take Walter away. We need to talk business for a few minutes."

* * *

In a tone Walter found irritating, Mike said, "You two seem to be getting on well."

"She was asking about Sarah."

"But you don't fancy her? Not your type, eh?"

Walter suddenly felt sorry for Lucille and resisted making witty, unkind comments although several sprang into his mind. "She's well-meaning and kind-hearted, I think. But, frankly, nobody's 'my type' as you so vulgarly put it. And we're not students any more, Mike. Please don't talk as if we were."

"She reminds me of the barmaid in the King's Head—you know, the pub next to College? All bosom and a miasma of cheap perfume."

"Mike, you're a walking contradiction—one minute all professional and socialist and caring, the next minute you're one of the biggest snobs I know."

"Even a probation officer can speak his mind when he's off duty."

"That's enough, and by the way, that isn't cheap perfume she's wearing. Now let's talk about finances. Are the grant applications in? And what's on the agenda for the next meeting?"

When they joined the others, Walter kept as far away from Lucille as he could. He noticed she was left out of the conversation for much of the time, and he felt guilty. He moved back to the sofa to sit next to her and was about to try to make amends when Marcia saved him the trouble by asking Lucille about famous people who'd come into the store. "After all, a lot of writers live in Oxford and the Cotswolds: Colin Dexter, Jillie Cooper, A.S. Byatt, Philip Pullman, Brian Aldiss, Pam Ayres, P.D. James …"

Just as Marcia was running out of names, Mike joined in and enquired if Lucille had "personal shopped" for any of them. "Not Dexter, Pullman, or Aldiss of course—we know you don't do gentlemen."

"Sorry, I can't tell you. It wouldn't be right to talk about our customers. Confidential, you see," Lucille said, and Walter admired her for that. Here was her chance to impress with a piece of celebrity gossip and she hadn't taken it.

* * *

Lucille didn't want to be the last to leave. She put on her jacket and stood in the doorway to the conservatory and asked loudly if anyone knew a taxi phone number. She had several numbers stored in her mobile, but this was a neat way to get an offer of a lift. It worked exactly as she'd hoped: Walter offered. But so did the other guests, and they politely competed for the pleasure of driving her home. Walter won. Unfortunately, it didn't mean he was keener than the others. In fact, his face didn't match his words—he looked distinctly *un*keen. It was just that he was the only one who lived in the city; the rest were from villages outside Oxford.

On their way to the car, Lucille caught a heel in a crack between the paving-stones and grabbed his arm.

The car was a disappointing Honda Jazz. She'd hoped for a Jaguar at least. "What a coincidence," she said. "Your car's the exact same colour as my top." She opened the buttons of her coat to remind him, but he didn't seem to want to inspect her top and just said, "Mmm …" in a polite but not interested sort of voice.

"I love yellow cars," Lucille went on.

"Do you? Actually, we would have preferred grey or silver, but this was a nearly new ex-showroom vehicle."

"Oh." She was disappointed again. She'd thought they had a shared colour preference that would make him like her better. She had been about to tell him yellow was one of the "in" colours, but decided against.

In the car they talked a little about the supper party, the food and the company. Lucille was careful to say nice things about everything and everybody. She made no mention of the olives and she didn't say how much she disliked the overpowering bookcases and the depressing pictures. Nor how she'd sometimes been ignored—people had held long discussions across her as though she was an empty space rather than a real person sitting between them. And at times she'd felt patronised; no one was genuinely interested in her work—not even the women, although every single one of them would have benefited from her services.

When they arrived at her block of flats, she knew better than to ask him in for a nightcap, and it would be pushy to give him her contact details or ask for his. He didn't suggest it either. But he did say, "It's been a pleasure to meet you," and he did wait to see her safely in through the front door.

Back in her flat, she found the answering machine had a "3" flashing: three messages, from Jason Brown again. She deleted them quickly.

In bed—her queen-size double bed that she'd bought in a fit of optimism when she moved here—she simply couldn't sleep, her mind so busy with thoughts of Walter Farquarson. She got up again and stayed up for another hour. She used the time to write a polite thankyou card to their hostess. When she was a little girl her mother always made her do this after she had been to a friend's house for a sleepover. A very old-fashioned custom, but Marcia would like it, and it might just get her invited again. Next, she took a sheet of scrap paper and practised some signatures and read them out loud to hear how they sounded: *Lucille Farquarson, Lucille Brown Farquarson, Lucille Farquarson Brown.*

* * *

Lucille's flat was near the cemetery where Sarah was buried. Walter passed the tall iron gates and was glad they were locked for the night; whenever he went by and saw them open he felt guilty for not wanting to visit the grave. If only he could forget the burial. No sooner was it done than he'd wished he'd had her cremated; then he could have scattered her ashes and would never have had to focus on one spot and think appalling thoughts about the body—Sarah's body—decaying in the earth.

He drove slowly back towards the city centre. Was this what his evenings out would be like in the future? When Sarah was alive, what magnified the pleasure if they were good, and redeemed them if they weren't, was the nightcap when he and Sarah got home, and comparing their impressions of people and conversation—the "post-party post-mortem" they called it.

Mostly they saw things the same way. But Sarah was far more observant than he was. More forgiving, too; she did not like him to criticise their hosts or their fellow guests. If he'd commented unkindly on the Lucille woman in the yellow top, the personal shopper, no doubt Sarah would have scolded him for intolerance and snobbery. And she'd have noticed little things he had overlooked, to make a fairer assessment of Lucille Brown.

He tried to think like Sarah. He'd noted Lucille's ethical stance as regards gossip about celebrities. And, yes, there were Lucille's bewildering but no doubt well-intentioned attempts to be kind about his bereavement, her interest in Sarah and her novels, and her lack of resentment at being by turns left out of the conversation or patronised. But Marcia was right: Ms Lucille Brown was definitely not his type. "Undeniably common" his grandmother would have said—or, even nastier, "a nobody". Not that he himself would ever use words like those, but even so …

Restless, and displeased with himself without knowing precisely why, he went into the drawing room and took up *Afterword* and looked at the photograph on the dust jacket. "Dearest Sarah," he said aloud, "if you could have stayed with me for longer you might have succeeded in turning me into a good person. All the same, I'm better for having been your husband."

Seeking distraction, he checked emails and answering machine, in the hope that John or Rosie might have left a message. Nothing. But then the phone rang. It was Rosie.

"I've been trying to get you all evening, Dad. Where've you been? Sunday's not your college dinner night." She sounded peeved and that made him want to laugh.

"Out to supper."

"Oh Dad, that's brilliant. You've got to get out more. John and I do worry about you, you know."

Walter smiled broadly, wishing Rosie was there with him. "You mustn't worry. Any news your end?"

"Nothing. Just phoned to say hullo. I'm in the middle of an essay crisis."

"I know what it's like. I've got to lecture tomorrow at nine."

"What about?"

"My favourite subject. I'm doing a series on the seventeenth century. We've got to 1649. The King has been beheaded and the Levellers are laying out their demands. They're asking for religious tolerance, equality before the law, and manhood suffrage."

"What about votes for women?"

"Precisely what I'll be asked tomorrow. I never mention it in the lecture because then I can be sure that when I invite questions at least one female student will find the courage to speak up."

"Manipulation in a good cause, eh? It's nice to have a feminist for a father."

"Clever girl! The answer is: women didn't come into it. And servants and paupers were omitted as well."

"The equal opportunities society was centuries away. Can't think why you've got so obsessed with the Levellers."

"Shall I tell you?" He never gave up trying to interest his children in his work.

"Not tonight thanks. No offence, but I'm afraid I haven't time."

"All right, then. What's your essay about?"

"*Emma* and *Pride and Prejudice*. The significance of social class in Jane Austen."

"I can't help you with that, I'm afraid. Not my period."

"Oh well, love you, Dad."

"Love you, Rosie."

He fell asleep in the middle of chapter four of *Pride and Prejudice*.

CHAPTER THREE

Dinner at Lucille's

What should you do when the iron's hot? Ah, yes, you should strike. And if an attractive eligible man doesn't give you his number, there are ways of finding it. Lucille found Walter's by simply looking him up in the phone book. At the same time she noted his address: Summertown, North Oxford. He lived among the older academics who'd been in the area for ages and the high-earning London types who moved in around the turn of the century after large North Oxford houses reached the million-pound mark, even semis as well as detached. Some were quite ordinary and others quite weird, with turrets like pretend fairy castles, and churchy stained glass and dark bits of wood stuck on to the walls to make the houses look as if they'd stood there since Shakespeare's time. Either the Farquarsons bought their house many years back, or else they'd bought recently with the fortune from Sarah's books. She glanced round her own little flat. Walter's place was only ten minutes' drive from here, but Summertown seemed like a foreign country.

The challenge now was how she could get to see Walter again. And soon, before he'd forgotten who she was. The obvious solution was to give a dinner party. She would include a couple and another single person so Walter shouldn't feel cornered. But she'd ask him first; the other guests could be invited once she knew he could come.

She waited a week. Then she sat down with a cup of tea and a chocolate digestive to boost her courage. "Walter. Hiya. Good evening. This is Lucille Brown. You may not remember me. We met at the Johnsons' and you kindly gave me a lift home. I'm a friend of Marcia's."

"Of course I remember you. What can I do for you?"

"I'm giving a dinner party on Friday the tenth and I wondered if you'd like to come. If you happen to be free on the tenth, that is."

"I'll have to check my diary." After a moment he spoke again. "Yes. I'm free. How very kind. Anything I can bring?"

"Just yourself." Oops, that sounded wrong. She tried again quickly. "I mean, there's no need to bring anything, and I'm so glad you can come."

* * *

After the call was over, Walter pondered its implications. The poor woman had sounded terrified. He'd asked what he could do for her; as soon as he'd said that, he'd realised it must have come across as professional, unfriendly. Ditto his remark about having to consult his diary. That was perverse, for he'd known full well his diary was blank; he had stayed in his armchair and hadn't even bothered to check. But he wasn't eager to trek out to that other world of tatty, character-free housing on the outskirts of Oxford to have dinner with a personal shopper and her friends. If only she had emailed him—then he could have waited for a credible excuse to occur to him before responding. As it was, she'd caught him unawares.

He'd accepted so as not to hurt her feelings. The woman

hardly knew him—why on earth had she asked him? Then he thought, It must be to make up the numbers. This stupid "equal boys and girls" rule—as if we gather to copulate rather than converse and share a meal. And there's always a dearth of single men. His friend Paul, also a widower, had warned him that this would happen now he was on his own—all these unexpected dinner invitations. Except Paul didn't mean it as a warning. Paul thought the invitations were a great consolation: "It gets us out of our own boring company and all the bother of cooking for one."

Paul was ten years older than Walter and had lost his wife Elizabeth some five years before. An ebullient, warm-hearted character, he loved to be invited out. He too was a social historian—more social than historian, he joked. Rosie said Uncle Paul reminded her of a Labrador puppy—"but in a good way."

Oh Sarah, thought Walter, it feels so sad and strange to go out to dinner without you. But then he smiled a little; he could see one advantage: whenever the children rang in the evening and got no answer it pleased them to think he was out seeing friends. Rosie even said, "Dad, you need someone—I mean, you need people." Dear, silly girl … yet perhaps she had a point.

"You do your best, Prissy, but you're not a person," he said, and he picked up his cat.

* * *

Lucille was delighted Walter had accepted her dinner invitation. Now she just needed to nail some more dinner party guests. The couple: her friend Helen Chambers and Helen's husband Rod would do very well. Rod had been to university and worked in a bank. Helen, like herself, had only been to the University of Life, but she was a senior secretary, now called an administrator, in the University of Oxford. She considered inviting Marcia and Mike Johnson as well, since she owed them a meal. But her dining table was too small for seven people.

Next she cast around for the important fifth member of the party. Preferably a woman, someone who wouldn't rival her own attractions, but who would be good at conversation and also act as proof that this wasn't meant to be a couples evening. None of her friends from work would fit in; Lucille realised she didn't know anyone remotely suitable.

As she was collecting her post in the entry hall, the solution to her problem appeared: puffing slightly, red-faced, the smiley elderly woman who had moved into the flat above. They'd met a few times, but only briefly, coming home or going out. Lucille glanced hurriedly at the name over the pigeonhole next to hers: Dr J Wilson.

"Oh, Dr Wilson," she said cheerily. "I've been meaning to invite you for ages. Would you be free to come to dinner next Friday?"

"Why, thank you … er …"

"Lucille. Lucille Brown."

"Why, thank you, Lucille. And do please call me Joan. And yes, I'd be delighted." Joan seemed surprised, but very pleased. Poor old thing. Lucille had her down as a lonely lady don. She was often laden with books and files, and out every Wednesday evening till ten—no doubt at a dinner in her college.

Lucille prepared as much as she could ahead of time. It was never easy to entertain on your own: answering the door, introductions, cooking, serving, talking. Not that Jason had been much help even when he was sober—except for the talking: he was good at that.

The dinner would be elegant but not showy-offy. Simple dishes with perfect ingredients. Nothing difficult to present or needing last-minute fuss. Last time she'd tried to impress with her cooking there had been not one but two disasters. First, the zabaglione had refused to thicken. Jason had been annoyed and then drank all the liquid zabaglione for the sake of the Marsala wine in it, and threw up noisily in the kitchen sink just as the guests were arriving. And their first course, her pretty individual cheese soufflés, had collapsed into soggy little heaps. This evening's recipes came out of a cookbook with a "*suggested menus*" section at the back: French onion soup, roast lamb, and sherry trifle. Then real coffee and Ferrero Rocher chocs. She decided to open the Limoncello she'd brought back from Italy and saved for a special occasion. She bought two bottles of red wine and hoped someone would provide extra. She half-regretted telling Walter Farquarson he didn't need to bring anything.

Walter had told her about Sarah's love of animals and roses. She looked out two photos of herself: as a child, holding Chips, her multi-coloured collie cross, and in Spain two years ago, perched on a huge white horse, trying to look brave; put them in silver frames in place of the photos of her two weddings, and set them on the mantelpiece. She arranged red roses in her best vase on the coffee table. Even small roses cost £1.50 each in the Covered Market, so she could only bring herself to buy four.

* * *

To Lucille's delight, Walter noticed the roses right away. "They're little beauties," he said. "My late wife taught me a lot about roses. Let me see … I think this variety is called 'Upper Class.' They come from Ecuador."

Lucille said, "Roses are my favourite flower."

"Ours too," said Walter. "Did I tell you my wife Sarah grew prize-winning roses?"

Helen said, "Real roses! Good heavens, Lucille, what's come over you? Or are they a present from some secret admirer?"

I wish I hadn't invited you, thought Lucille, and answered, "No. I just love roses. Surely you knew that?" Helen shrugged.

The last to arrive was Joan Wilson. Walter and Joan looked delighted to see each other and both turned beaming to Lucille.

"You didn't tell me you knew Joan."

"You didn't tell me you knew Walter."

Joan said the last time they'd talked had been at Sarah's memorial meeting. They were both in the History Department and they'd known each other for years.

"But we shan't talk shop," said Walter, smiling at Lucille.

"No, of course not," said Joan.

"And how do you come to know Lucille?" Joan told Walter she was Lucille's upstairs neighbour. She'd decided to "downsize" because her house in Summertown was just too big for one person at her age, and these little flats, though they weren't exactly architectural gems, were so blissfully easy to run.

* * *

Walter and Joan were both scrutinising Lucille's living room. Lucille followed their gaze and Walter could see she was hoping for compliments. He did his best to oblige. He showed particular interest in the electric fire. "So lifelike!"

"You've made the room very cosy," said Joan. "Lovely thick carpet," she added, after a pause.

"Yes, indeed," Walter agreed, wishing away the huge gaudy flowers that were prominent in the design.

Walter tried not to look at *The Green Lady* and *The Singing Butler*. Instead, he turned his attention to the other guests, Helen and Rod Chambers. They struggled to find common ground, and eventually succeeded: Oxford University, and Rod's memories of his own university, Leeds; Walter's children, John at York University and Rosie at Bristol; how student life had changed; change in the life of the academic, too. "Nowadays you administration people hold the purse strings and all the power," said Walter to Helen.

"It doesn't feel like that," said Helen. "It's more like being nanny to some very spoilt children."

"Touché."

"Present company excepted." Everyone laughed except Lucille, who seemed confused.

* * *

Lucille managed to guide the dinner party conversation on to cultural topics—the latest film at the Odeon, the musical at the New Theatre, the French Impressionists in the Ashmolean Museum.

She knew that Walter would want to talk about his women's refuge. When there was a pause, she asked if he had any more news. Walter said the steering committee were in the process of choosing an architect to redesign the Deaf Centre building. "I never knew it took so much to give an old place a makeover."

When she was little, Lucille had seen her mother being knocked about and vowed she would never let it happen to *her*, but then it did—first with Luke Higgs and again with Jason Brown. So she knew more about family violence than she let on. She asked one or two questions about the refuge and tried not to say the wrong thing. Walter seemed surprised when Joan asked his opinion on whether some women unconsciously ask to be abused. This idea didn't make a lot of sense to Lucille, but she'd definitely read that somewhere, or maybe it was something her mother's social worker had said. Walter confessed he had never heard of this extraordinary notion. In fact, Lucille began to suspect he knew rather little about the subject. She offered to be a weekend volunteer when the refuge was up and running. He said it was most kind of her, but that would not be up to him. He obviously didn't believe it would be her cup of tea.

Taken as a whole, the evening was a success. The only difficult moments were when Helen and Rod spoke of Sarah's novels—several had just been reissued as e-books—and Joan joined in, but Lucille was unable to contribute.

More worrying: Lucille was afraid Walter didn't fancy her. He didn't look into her eyes or make flirty remarks. Nor did he touch her accidentally on purpose, and it wasn't as though he was one of those "don't touch me" sort of people—he hugged Joan enthusiastically when he left. Lucille's greatest fear was that before she could find rich Mr Right she'd lose her sex appeal, and now this appeared to be happening. But it wasn't giving-up time yet. Surely Walter would be duty-bound to return her invitation?

CHAPTER FOUR

Supper at Luigi's Italian

Walter had to admit to himself that he'd quite enjoyed the dinner party at Lucille's. It was a pleasant surprise, and something of a relief, to find Joan Wilson there (odd, though, that she had downsized so far down), and Helen and Rod Chambers were a friendly, unpretentious couple. Lucille ... well, she was plainly unsure of herself despite the brash exterior; good-hearted; not unpleasant to look at in spite of all that make-up; shapely beneath those garish clothes; and such disturbing eyes.

The problem he now faced was how to repay Lucille. He asked Paul for advice. Paul maintained this wasn't necessary; single men were not expected to reciprocate—donating their valuable presence was enough. Sexist twaddle, thought Walter. But to give a dinner party was a step too far down the road to competent, contented singledom. How could he deal with the logistics without Sarah? Cookery was not his forte; and even if he managed to produce a half-decent dinner, how to cope with letting people in and coats and drinks and introductions and small talk, whilst at the same time trying to dish up the first course? He'd have more hope of learning to juggle burning brands like that annoying beggar in St Giles.

And to ask Lucille to his house on her own would give the wrong signals. No, he'd have to invite her to a restaurant. But it ought to be lunch, not dinner; going out to dinner had romantic connotations and he didn't want that. After a week of mulling it over, he phoned her.

"This is Walter Farquarson. Thank you again for the dinner party. It was very pleasant. And now may I invite you out for a meal? I suggest lunch any day next week except Sunday."

Lucille replied in a rush. She sounded anxious. "Oh, I'd love to but I'm never free at lunchtime—working girl, you know. Quick sandwich in the staff canteen."

Walter said, "What about a Saturday?" A pause. She's thinking up an excuse, he thought happily.

Sure enough. "On Saturdays I sometimes work mornings or afternoons and I've a regular arrangement with girlfriends Saturday lunchtime. I'm free on Sundays though."

"Oh dear, this is awkward. I usually see one of my children on Sundays. I go to York or Bristol or they come home." This wasn't true, but he did prefer to keep his Sundays free, in order to get their phone calls and to put finishing touches to his Monday lectures. Anyway, she probably didn't want to accept.

Another pause. Lucille said, "I could manage an evening."

Thwarted, he conceded defeat. "What about dinner, then?"

* * *

Lucille was overjoyed and punched the air the way people on the telly did when they had won something. She hadn't had much occasion to punch the air in recent times. Now she had got herself a date, a proper date, with Professor Walter Farquarson. A couple of weeks ahead, which suggested he wasn't all that eager, but even so. She'd handled the conversation pretty well—she just regretted using the expression "working girl". As soon as she'd said it she'd thought, Oops, didn't that have another meaning?

He'd invited her to one of those chic Italian places in George Street. Not too fancy, lovely food, intimate, plenty of atmosphere.

There was a tap on her door. It was Joan Wilson from upstairs. "Would you care to come up for a coffee and sample my panforte? This is the first time I've made anything like it."

She was interested to see inside Joan's flat. It was like Blackwell's Bookshop, only worse. Books hid every wall—no room for pictures—and you had to avoid wobbly towers of them all over the floor, as well. "Untidy" didn't cover it. Joan even had to move two enormous dictionaries off an armchair so that Lucille could sit down. But Joan's coffee was as good as Macdonald's and the panforte was delicious, and sort of Christmassy. "What's in it?" she asked and Joan listed all the ingredients, so many that it took her several minutes, and went on to give exact details of quantities and timing. It would have been quicker if she had simply handed Lucille the recipe to read. Lucille had already noticed that Joan answered every question with a short lecture.

"Don't you love baking?" she said, when Joan paused for breath. "You take these things that don't taste nice at all and when you've finished out comes something amazing and yummy, like your panforte. It's a kind of magic, isn't it?"

Joan seemed puzzled and did not reply.

After that their conversation was as sticky as the panforte. "What a lot of books. Have you really read them all?" asked Lucille. "And will you want to read them again? I never want to read the same book twice. The way I see it, life's too short. Anyway, once you know the ending it isn't any fun, is it?"

"They're the tools of my trade," said Joan. "I do need to

consult them and reread them sometimes. I stupidly didn't realise how little book space there would be in this flat."

"You should buy a Kindle. I'm saving up for one, so as not to have a lot of books cluttering up my shelves."

Joan smiled, and changed the subject. "What a pleasant surprise it was to see Walter Farquarson at your dinner party. Since his wife's death he hardly ever comes into the department, though I hear he's as conscientious as ever about his teaching, and his lectures are always packed."

"I can imagine," said Lucille, though she couldn't really.

"He's had me to lunch at his college—terrific fun—such a lot of fascinating philosophers, and scientists who are doing weird and wonderful research—I was enthralled. And such a pleasure to meet Richard Dawkins. Charming. Not in the least like they depict him in the media. We talked about faith schools."

Not faith schools again, thought Lucille.

"And Walter has invited me to a seminar-plus-drinks-party next week. So we're catching up, thanks to you."

Lucille felt herself go red, and coughed and pretended the panforte had gone down the wrong way. *She* would never get an invitation to a college lunch or a seminar-plus-drinks-party, or a chance to meet Richard Dawkins. Joan was giving her glimpses of a world that excluded the ordinary citizens of Oxford—the world of high tables and gowns and servants and clever talk. Not that she was jealous of plain, elderly Joan. Not in that way. Rather, she was starting to fear that she herself could never be part of Walter Farquarson's life. Was it really worth persevering? She didn't tell Joan about their date at the Italian restaurant. Walter would not want his university colleagues to know that he was going out with someone like her.

* * *

On the evening of their date, Lucille dressed in figure-hugging jeans, very high heels and a glamorous Italian silk blouse. She was early; she was always early. In the past she had tried to train herself out of her anxiety by being deliberately late, but this hadn't worked. She was afraid of keeping people waiting, of stealing their time.

Now she occupied herself by examining the unusual items that decorated the restaurant entrance: two giant bottles stuffed with preserved fruit and vegetables in improbable bright colours: apples, oranges and pears in one and yellow, red and green peppers in the other. She was about to ask a waiter whether these were real when Walter arrived, exactly on time. She noticed he was wearing brown cords and a grey tweed jacket; he almost certainly hadn't changed before he came out. No doubt the date with her wasn't that important to him.

After the fun of studying the menu—she pretended ignorance and got him to help her choose—the real test began. It reminded her for some reason of the O-Level French conversation exam, which she had failed. Lucille tried to keep to topics they would both know about and to move the talk along when they seemed about to dry up. They discussed holidays in Italy, and the weather in Oxford, and skimmed over the week's news headlines.

* * *

Walter reassured himself that this wasn't really a "date" (surely that meant going out with a potential romantic or sexual partner?) But still he felt ill at ease; he wanted their meal over even before it began, and he found it hard to concentrate on the conversation. Lucille had been to Italy, but hers was not the Italy he and Sarah knew well, with its glorious buildings and paintings and statues and mosaics. Lucille talked about a cheery pizza maker in a village near some seaside resort he'd never heard of, and about an elderly Catholic priest who had found her sobbing in his church and tried to comfort her even though he could not speak a word of English. The latter story embarrassed Walter and though he tried to show some sympathy, he didn't like to ask why she had been crying.

All through the meal, his mind kept flipping back to his first date with Sarah, a punt ride with a picnic on the river bank. A pair of swans followed their boat, and Sarah told him that swans practise long-term monogamy. Sarah wore a plain summer dress, the same shade as the clump of bluebells nearby, and he noticed her eyes were that colour too. They talked about books and lectures, and regarded it as a special omen that they were both drawn to the seventeenth century: Sarah to John Milton's poetry and he to the Civil Wars. It was their second summer at Oxford. He bought her a little bottle of scent in the shape of a swan, and within weeks they were engaged.

* * *

By the time they got to dessert, Lucille could see Walter had started to listen in to a party of students at a nearby table who were having a loud and bad-tempered discussion about King Richard III; they argued over him as if he had only just been killed. She could think of one sure way to refresh Walter's interest in the conversation with her: mention Sarah Scott or ask about the women's refuge, or both.

"Now tell me. What news of the Sarah Scott Refuge?"

"The Sarah Scott Refuge?"

"Isn't that what you're going to call it? In her memory."

"Well, I suppose we could call it that. We haven't decided on the name yet. And you're right—it makes sense. Except that Sarah wouldn't have wanted it; she wasn't that sort of person. My own suggestion is 'St Frideswide's Centre' after that Oxford princess who stood up to wicked men. We certainly won't call it a refuge for battered women. Though that's what we'll focus on first, providing a place of safety. But we hope to widen the scope, so that it becomes more than just a refuge."

"How do you mean?"

"Mike suggests we branch out and offer extra skills training for women, new learning opportunities: self-esteem, assertiveness, literacy, that kind of thing. We'll add projects one by one as we assess what works and what's needed. Mike has psychologist friends who are doing meta-analyses on the various types of intervention."

"Oh." Lucille thought, How good it would have been for Mum to get some help with self-esteem and assertiveness. And for me as well. Too late now. She nodded, and smiled at Walter. She considered asking what a meta-analysis was, but she was afraid she might not understand the explanation. "What lovely ice cream! The Italians are the experts, don't you think?"

* * *

Mission accomplished, thought Walter. He was glad to be home and he planned to look up the latest article on the Richard III controversy: did the discovery of that twisted skeleton in the Leicester car park have anything to add to historians' debates about the king?

It was only ten o'clock. He found a message from Paul asking him to phone back and he did so immediately, pleased to have someone to talk to.

"You've been out?" Paul sounded envious.

"Yes."

"Aren't you going to let on what you've been up to?"

"Italian meal."

"With …?"

"With Lucille Brown. You know—the woman who had me to dinner a couple of weeks ago. You said it wasn't necessary, but I felt I ought to return her hospitality."

"And?"

"And nothing."

"So that's why you're back so early … Listen, Walt, I've had a thought. What about the Galapagos Islands?"

"What about them?"

"There's an Oxford and Cambridge alumni trip at the end of August. If I can afford it, you bloody can. I've been wanting to brush up my Darwin ever since I joined the Humanists—he's the nearest thing we've got to Jesus."

"Won't a library book do the trick? Or a lecture by Richard Dawkins?"

"Absolutely not. And there's all the strange birds and beasts. Or, as Darwin put it, 'endless forms most beautiful and wonderful'. Imagine little Mr Blue-footed Booby doing his courting dance in front of his great big lady love."

"I can't." Walter could see himself turning into a real old curmudgeon, but he seemed unable to stop it.

"And we can go snorkelling in blue equatorial waters and frolic with the baby sea lions."

"You win." It sounded quite different from any holiday he had taken with Sarah. Perhaps he might not miss her as badly as he had that Easter in Florence.

Walter looked up the details of the trip and next day he and Paul booked their places. Afterwards, they had a coffee in Walter's college room. Walter confided that he saw this holiday—at least partly—as a strategy for getting some space away from Lucille Brown. "Isn't that how you say it? Or do I mean putting some clear blue water between us?"

Paul said, "I get the picture. Is she after you? And you've been doing a mating dance, haven't you? And now you regret it?"

"None of the above. But I don't want any misunderstanding."

* * *

Lucille rang Walter. First, she thanked him for the meal. Then she added, trying to sound casual, "I do hope we can do it again soon."

"Yes." His voice was flat, quiet, unenthusiastic. But she decided not to take the hint.

"It'll be my treat next time. When would be convenient?"

"Actually, a friend of mine has persuaded me to go away with him in the vacation. And I've got proofs to check and deadlines to meet before then."

She ignored the mention of proofs and deadlines, being unsure what that might mean, and tried to sound interested in his holiday. "That's nice. Where are you going?"

"The Galapagos Islands. Ecuador."

She knew the Galapagos were in Ecuador. She'd seen advertisements; those trips cost thousands. Golden sands like in her picture. And a huge ugly tortoise called Lonely George. The poor old creature was without a mate, like her and Walter.

"Well, give my love to Lonely George," she said, hoping to impress with her general knowledge.

"Lonesome George is dead," said Walter. "He died a year ago. Old age and heart failure."

She felt foolish. "Oh, I'm sorry. I didn't know."

Walter laughed. He seemed to think she had intended to make a joke, whereas she had simply put her big foot in it once again.

CHAPTER FIVE

Lucille's Holiday

"So he's off on holiday, is he? Pretending to be too busy to see you? I would forget about him, pet. There's plenty more fish in the sea. You deserve to get away too, have a holiday of your own." Lucille's adviser was Marigold Robson, a large saleslady nearing retirement age. Always impeccably well-groomed, she still kept the big hair that she'd gone in for in the eighties, and she loved Poison perfume. She looked nothing like Lucille's mother, and yet she reminded Lucille of her mother when she talked in that friendly Geordie accent, and was kind and understanding—comfortable, motherly.

Lucille had been telling her troubles to Marigold and her other special friends, Jillie from Cosmetics, and Annette, a personal shopper like herself. They sat at their usual table in Richley's staff canteen. The three younger women were having salads, and Marigold was having her favourite macaroni cheese with a hefty slice of garlic bread.

"You know I met my better half on a villa holiday in Greece?" Marigold continued. "1970-something. You should try a villa holiday. And go somewhere hot. A chance to get a tan and meet people."

"You mean men?"

"Of course I mean men. The organisers try to keep the numbers equal."

Lucille gazed gloomily round the canteen—only half-a-dozen men to be seen, and all of them already taken. "I'll look into it."

But it turned out that the villa parties of Marigold's youth no longer happened. When she got home, Lucille googled "*villa parties*" and all she could find were pictures of large houses with swimming pools, for families or groups of friends. You had to have a family to bring, or collect up your own group of friends; the travel company wasn't offering to do it for you.

"Well, try a singles holiday," suggested Jillie next day. Over lunch they searched on Jillie's new iPad.

They found several companies that offered group holidays for people aged thirty to forty. "Perfect," said Jillie. "Anything younger would be cradle-snatching."

"I'm nearly forty-three, remember. But I suppose I could pretend to be under forty." They assured her that she could.

"Hang on. What if our Lucille fancies a toy boy?" said Annette.

"And what about a good old-fashioned sugar daddy? No chance of finding one of those either," said Marigold.

"Thirty to forty is fine," said Lucille. She didn't want a toy boy—couldn't afford one anyway—and though she needed security she hoped to find it with a nice man of her own age rather than a sugar daddy.

"And look! Here's ten days on a Greek island. Champion!" Marigold sounded almost weepy with nostalgia. "So sunny. Warm sea. The Greeks are the kindest, honestest people in the world. You can leave your luggage in the town square overnight and nobody would dream of stealing it. And if you can't find a place to stay, the locals will take you in. And so safe. You can walk anywhere after midnight and sleep on the beaches."

It was embarrassing. Marigold had brought in two faded colour photos of herself and her husband Bill. The first was taken in Greece. Seventies-style flares, a pretty-pretty Laura Ashley flowered dress, and an awful lot of hair. The second photo, produced with a flourish, showed the two of them after their wedding at the registry office. They wore matching white three-piece trouser suits with extremely wide flares. "A-a-ah" was all anyone could think of to say.

Meanwhile, Lucille was considering Sunfriends' prices. Oh, well, it's cheap compared with Walter Farquarson's holiday, she thought, though this didn't alter the fact that she couldn't afford it. The single supplement annoyed her. "I'm not paying that. I don't mind sharing."

"You'll mind when you ... ahem ... meet someone and want some privacy." Annette was always so practical.

"No. I won't meet anyone. I just know it." Her three friends shook their heads in disbelief.

"Hadaway!" said Marigold.

"You've got to. That's the whole point of the holiday," said Annette.

* * *

Walter was surprised, and not pleased, to receive another phone call from Lucille Brown. He thought he had put her off, tactfully but firmly, with the vague information about his holiday and his deadlines. He half-admired her persistence, though he was puzzled by it.

"You haven't gone on holiday yet? Just wondered if you fancied a break from your work. After all, you have to eat. I'm planning another little dinner party."

Walter repeated what he'd told her before. "I really can't take any time off. I have to submit my paper to the journal by the end of the month and I've got the proofs of my latest book to deal with. Then we're off to the Galapagos. And besides, my son and daughter are here."

"What a pity. I'm going away soon, too. To Greece. Singles holiday with Sunfriends." He'd never heard of singles holidays or Sunfriends, but he could guess what it would be like.

"I hope you have a nice time." He also hoped she'd meet someone on her singles holiday and leave him alone. Probably she would meet someone, for she'd look gorgeous in a bikini and she'd make friends easily, especially with the men.

* * *

Heathrow Airport. It's like every special place you rarely go to, thought Lucille, you think back to all the other times you were here: who you were with, and what was happening in your life at that time. Lucille had been abroad three times. A week's honeymoon in Portugal with Luke; a weekend in Spain with Jason; and two weeks in Italy with Jillie, soon after leaving Jason. She thought about these in turn. She'd enjoyed every trip, but none had lived up to her silly expectations. Each time, she had hoped she would come back a changed person with a new outlook and a shiny new love life as well—with Luke Higgs, her first husband; then with Jason Brown, her second; then with some rich, handsome stranger who might just possibly become her third husband. Today she was less optimistic. She looked at her fellow singles. All were younger than her, and attractive and confident. And there were many more women than men; she wondered if anyone had ever used this as grounds for demand-ing a refund from Sunfriends.

During the flight the captain announced they were going through an area of turbulence. You're telling me, she thought.

Her roommate said she was "an assistant commissioning editor"; she was pleasant, but clearly had more in common with the other singles—it turned out they were all from London; several of them were in publishing, and one was a journalist, and they were soon exchanging shop talk and gossip with quite a lot of bitching and laughter. No one showed any interest in retail or the fashion industry. Soon Lucille was wishing she hadn't come.

The resort hotel was near the sea. Golden sands, as promised. And on the clifftop stood an old castle or temple, but it was in ruins. The countryside was parched and unappealing; no grass, just a sprinkling of dusty little bushes. There were shops close by, crammed with things she didn't want or couldn't afford, and pushy salespeople came out on to the street and pestered. Lucille decided this would definitely have to be a beach holiday—there was nothing else to do—and on the first day she joined the rest of her party on the sands. As she lay on a sunbed, slippery with oil, wearing her new white bikini, she wished her body wasn't so pale—it was almost as pale as the bikini; she was sorry she'd decided to save money by doing without an artificial tan. Jillie had told her about someone who came to your home and set up a little tent and sprayed you with a magic chemical.

So passed the first eight days of the ten-day holiday. She wasn't unhappy or bored, exactly, but though no one was nasty to her she was not really part of the group. She felt inferior to the other women, who were all of them closer to thirty, better-looking and more interesting than her. She noticed a small flurry of curiosity when she let slip she had been married twice, but if anything this seemed to make the men wary and the women disapproving. They probably wondered what was wrong with a person who had failed twice. Before they judge, they ought to try living with Luke Higgs or Jason Brown, she thought, but all the same she was afraid there might be some truth in it.

By day eight she could no longer delay the postcards she had promised to her friends. She had hoped to send news that would make them envious. She couldn't honestly do that, but she bought cards with stunning views of sand, sea and cliffs and little white houses and ancient ruins. The challenge of selecting the cards and composing the messages kept her occupied most of the morning: they had to be different and yet consistent with one another in case Annette, Jillie and Marigold brought them to Richley's and passed them round. They also had to fit in with whatever she decided to tell her friends when she got back.

To Annette and Jillie, two variations on the same theme:

Beautiful place. Perfect weather. Don't you wish you were here? Nice hotel. Lovely beach. Hot! Hot! Hot!

And to Marigold:

Thinking of you. Hope this reminds you and Bill of romantic moments. I don't imagine these beaches have changed.

On day nine a tall, dark and nearly handsome young Greek crouched down beside her sunbed. She was surprised and flattered that he had selected her. After all, he had plenty of choice. He had strange, hooded eyes, and a serious expression. His conversation wasn't original, though. A lot of stock questions: "Where do you live? Do you like Greece? Have you a car? What is your job?" His name was Yannis and he said he was a geography student on vacation from Athens University. He came from a nearby village and helped at his father's grocery store.

"I have moped. I show you most beautiful beach."

At last something was happening that she could talk about when she got home. And his look of admiration and the way he stroked her forearm after he had helped her to her feet made her feel a little more desirable and desired. She was up for an adventure after eight days of stewing and moping in the sun.

She tied her scarlet sarong over the bikini and picked up her bag.

They went by moped to an empty beach, over which towered a huge half-built hotel with no sign of builders. Yannis flipped her little chain with the cross attached. "Pretty! Is real gold?"

"Yes. It was my mother's." She tried to put thoughts of her mother aside. She was going to have sex with a man she'd only just met and who was young enough to be her son. Her mother would have advised against.

Yannis took her hand as they walked to the water's edge, and they kissed. Lucille untied her sarong and let it drop on to the sand.

"Now we swim." But they didn't. They waded into the warm water and when it was up to their waists, he ran his hands down from her neck to her breasts. Then down farther. He poked his long fingers clumsily up through the legs of her bikini. Then groped inside again from the waist, and wiggled his hand down to her pubic hair. Then quickly—quite expertly—he dragged the bikini pants down over her hips and legs and feet. She made a half-hearted grab for them. He said, "It OK. I got it safe. No lose," and threaded an arm through the pants.

Next he fished into the top of her bikini and squeezed her nipples—a little too hard. Like following a recipe: *Three pinches of nipple. Then stir vigorously.* And so he did, finishing with a brisk rub. And was inside her. Sex in the sea—a strange new sensation. A sensation she liked. She looped one leg around him. The gentle lapping of the waves made her skin thrill to their touch. The blinding white of the hotel, the unreal blue of the sky with just a few fluffy clouds scudding about and making her dizzy, the postcard-coloured blue-green of the sea. The beauty of the world and the joy of sex—the thrills you never tire of.

But in the midst of all this pleasure came a down-to-earth thought: thank goodness she was on the pill. It occurred to her that he hadn't asked.

And he hadn't used a condom. Did he imagine the salt water would protect them? Annette had warned her, "Be careful you don't bring back more than a piece of pottery and a few wooden spoons from Greece." Annette had once met a genito-urinary specialist who told dreadful tales that ought to have deterred even the most sex-starved woman from having sex with the Yannises of a Greek holiday island. Lucille had laughed off the warning and she suddenly recalled it now. But only for a moment. She shut out these worries, but she couldn't climax and he made no attempt to help.

Afterwards they did it again behind a rock on the beach. Again she did not have an orgasm and the thought of their stupidity, and the realisation that he didn't care about her in the least, intruded more than before.

In silence, she towelled herself dry and put on sarong and cardie, and he pulled on his jeans.

His moped was locked, she noticed. So this was not the law-abiding Greece Marigold had gone on about. Instead of returning to the hotel, he took her to a little café in his village and bought her a very small, sickly-sweet black coffee and a single pastry, a rather stale nuts-and-honey confection. Not supper, although it was suppertime. A gang of schoolchildren in their early teens passed by. Several called and waved to Yannis. Among them was a girl wearing earphones; she had a ponytail and a very short skirt. "Innes. I marry her when she grows up," he said.

"Oh."

The moped had run out of petrol and the garage was closed. Lucille panicked. She hadn't enough cash for a taxi. And she hadn't been invited to stay the night. Marigold told tales of Greek hospitality—things were certainly different now.

"No worry." Yannis flagged down a lorry with crates of fizzy drinks and fruit in the back. Mingled with the diesel fumes was a delicious scent of oranges. Her mouth watered.

"He's my cousin and he'll take you."

The cousin was a beefy, sweaty chap with glistening black hairs poking out of his tee shirt and a chunky gold chain round his thick neck. She did not catch his name.

"*Milate anglika*?" she asked nervously.

The lorry driver did not speak English.

"No worry," said Yannis. "I explain him where to go." He said something to his cousin and gave a mysterious wink. The cousin smirked and hauled her up into the cab. Yannis, giving her some help from below, pushed his hand between her legs as he did so, and against her will she felt another surge of sexual excitement and hoped he had not detected it, and was cross with herself.

The sky was nearly dark but it seemed polite to gaze out of the window and pretend to admire the scenery. Besides "*Milate Anglika?*" Lucille knew only a couple of phrases in Greek. "Greece is a beautiful country," "*Orea!*"

She said the two phrases.

The lorry driver pointed to her crotch. "*Orea!*" he repeated with an ugly grin. A gold tooth glinted.

She ignored him and stared into the darkness.

Then, driving more slowly along the twisty coast road, he said "*orea*" again and lunged across and fumbled in her lap with his right hand.

"No!" she shouted.

"Yes!" he replied. So he did know some English after all. And he sounded annoyed. He slowed down more, and she grabbed her bag, leapt out of the cab and ran off into the scrubby bushes and hid in the dust, clenched into as small a ball as she could manage. She could smell the wild herbs crushed by her body.

The lorry stopped. She heard the handbrake scrape. Then shouts. She tried to keep her breathing silent.

The lorry did a many-point turn in the narrow road; the headlights swept the bushes. And at last it went back the way they had come. She waited till the sound had died away and began to trudge towards the resort village, terrified he'd change his mind and come after her. It was dark and scary. The only noise was the loud chorus of crickets—did the damned things never sleep? The sea was somewhere far below and for a moment she thought she could hear that too, but it was the pounding in her ears. She could just make out the pale winding road.

She heard a motor approaching. She dived into the dusty shrubs. It might be a harmless car driver who would give her a lift, but it could be him again. She dared not risk being seen. A taxi appeared and passed by, and she ran back on to the road and waved, hoping the cab driver would catch sight of her in the rear-view mirror. It did not stop.

An hour later she heard the first faint plunks of bazouki music from the bar on the edge of the resort. And soon she reached the hotel and climbed wearily up the stairs. She was hot, and sticky with that sweat you get from anxiety. She tiptoed into the bedroom without turning on the light, but her room-mate woke up. "Oh, it's you at last." She sounded curious rather than worried. "What happened to you?"

"Lovely outing with Yannis. I've seen some of the real Greece," she boasted. She was glad the room was dark because she was sure her face would have given her away.

"Well, good for you!" said the roommate sleepily, in a sarcastic tone of voice.

She forgot about supper till it was too late to get anything to eat, and anyway, she wouldn't have dared disturb her roommate again. She spent a hungry, restless night.

Next morning Lucille was sitting by herself enjoying a late breakfast and feeling back to normal when Yannis turned up again. She complained about his cousin's behaviour. His English was not good enough for him to grasp the meaning of "assault"; so, unwilling to do an embarrassing mime, she had to use words like "impolite" and "rude" and "frightened". It wasn't certain he understood, or perhaps he didn't want to. He didn't look surprised and he didn't apologise. He just said, "You come out with me again?" He squeezed her thigh under the table and gazed at her affectionately with his dark hooded eyes.

She refused to return to the beach with him. "No, I have to

pack. We're going home this afternoon. I have to say goodbye now."

But he followed her upstairs. "We say proper nice goodbye," he pleaded. Outside her door he stroked her neck and when she found her roommate was out—it was nearly lunchtime by now—against her better judgement she let him in; and they had sex again, in a hurry.

Over coffee and pastries—lunch was over—they sat in the dining room with nothing left to say and she wondered how to persuade him to leave.

Yannis took the last baklava. "Your address, please? I send postcard."

Too polite to refuse, not quick-thinking enough to give a false address, she wrote it down on a paper serviette. She did not include her phone number or email.

"You write to me? Yes?"

She smiled non-committally and took his address. Then she gave him her hand and said goodbye, hoping to sound polite and firm at the same time. He stood up, gave her a long wet kiss and went away at last.

Lucille looked round at her fellow singles. A group of them were at a nearby table, and they had kept glancing at her and Yannis between bursts of laughter and chatter. She hoped they were impressed—she was the only one who had found herself a holiday romance. Not bothering to lower her voice, one of the women said, "He'll be back on our beach when the next batch of singles arrive." And the sole man among them whispered, loud enough for Lucille to hear, "They pick out the older women—the desperate ones."

* * *

During the return flight Lucille tried out in her head several souped-up versions of her Greek romance. She might have put on her beautiful cream linen dress with the designer label, which she had bought specially for the trip and never worn; taken a taxi to the grand hotel in the next village; lounged elegantly beside the pool; met a handsome, rich, sophisticated Greek writer, and swept him off his feet. And they would have had fabulous sex in the sea and again in his luxury suite before a heartbroken parting (because being a fundamentally decent man and a devout Greek Orthodox Christian, he had no choice but to return to his glamorous but cold-hearted wife). This was the best version. On the other hand, a slightly sanitised account of the episode with Yannis and his obnoxious cousin might be just as entertaining, as well as being nearly true and therefore easier to tell.

At Heathrow, most of her holiday companions had someone to meet them. Envious, Lucille scanned the crowds in Arrivals, as if by magic some friend or relative would materialise. She felt awfully alone. She thought of the film *Love Actually* and its catchy theme song about love being all around at the airport. So not true.

Two weeks after her return came a postcard from Yannis with a picture of some green fish. She was surprised. What she could make out from the scrawl said, *You buy car? Can I come visit? When you come visit again?* She did not send a reply. She had thrown away the serviette with his address, and in any case she had nothing to say to him.

But soon she had another souvenir of Yannis, less welcome than his postcard—a worrying lump in an embarrassing place.

She'd never expected to have to visit this sort of clinic. You didn't need a referral letter, or an appointment; it was all very discreet, yet this was the most humiliating experience in her life. Anyone could be in the waiting room. It occurred to her that if someone she knew came in they'd be as scared of being recognised as she was; the embarrassment would be mutual, but none the less horrific for that. She sat in a corner and tried to hide behind a copy of the *Oxford Times*. She felt a jolt of fear when her name was called and she had to put the paper down and walk to the consulting room at the far end, in full view of least a dozen people.

Two female nurses or doctors introduced themselves by their first names and read the form she'd filled in with the details— where and when, and who with; she was ashamed she didn't have an address or even a surname for her so-called "partner". After that she had to undress and open her legs. She closed her eyes and tried not to cry, but the tears did start when they said the lump was only a wart. They took swabs and some blood and said they would do all possible tests. And they painlessly froze the wart off there and then.

By the end of August Lucille knew she was all right. A letter in a brown envelope marked "*strictly confidential*" announced that her results were negative.

The singles holiday was a write-off, but she cheered up and continued to laugh with her friends about her Greek adventures (the true but sanitised version), and wondered whether it was worth ringing Walter Farquarson again. But then she remembered that about now he was off to the Galapagos Islands.

CHAPTER SIX

Walter's Summer Vacation

Walter raced through the proofs of his latest book, *Seventeenth Century Rebels: reformers ahead of their time.* His editor suggested they might enter it for the Charles Hudson History Prize. "Whatever you think best," he replied without enthusiasm.

Throughout the rest of July, he worked on his journal article about the Levellers imprisoned in the church at Burford in 1649. At first, they were told they were all to die. It wasn't clear when they knew who would be executed and who would be spared. In the event only three were shot and the others were forced to watch. Walter wrote a speculative piece about what might have become of the survivors, what they would experience in the rest of that remarkable century, and what the three who died would miss: the very partial fulfilment of their idealistic aspirations, and their ultimate disillusionment. So much happened that they could never have imagined.

This was becoming a recurrent, futile preoccupation of his— the life unlived, all the things the prematurely dead would never know. More years of history, of course, and their family story too. The dead Levellers would not experience the Great Plague, or cease to celebrate Christmas, they might even have welcomed the return of King Charles II … and they would not see their widows remarry or else stay single and mourn their husbands till their own death.

Sarah had not seen Rosie and John leave home for university, and she would not see them find partners and become parents themselves. And she would not see him remarry, if indeed he ever did.

Once his article was submitted, Walter applied himself to the reading list from the professor who would accompany the Galapagos tour. He hoped the holiday preparations would distract him from an inexplicable, lingering temptation to contact Lucille Brown. Last time they'd spoken she said she was going to Greece on a singles holiday. With any luck, she would have met a decent man with whom she could live happily ever after. He did not expect to see her again.

It would be good to have Paul's company, and this trip was an opportunity to learn more about Darwin's ideas, and zoology, botany and geology. He was looking forward to it.

* * *

In Departures, while declaiming about how Darwin was recruited to join the expedition on the *Beagle*, and inveighing against the privileges of the rich in the nineteenth century, Walter dropped some travel documents from an overstuffed trouser pocket. Paul picked up a passport and said, "What's this, Walt? You're holding one already. Why have you got two passports?"

There was nothing for it but to confess his foolishness. "It's Sarah's." Paul made no comment. He nodded and handed the passport back.

* * *

The alumni party stayed at a small hotel on Santa Cruz and boarded their day yacht every morning to sail to other islands. Each evening, their Galapagos expert gave a lecture. She had a tendency to overrun her time, while the hotel staff stood ready to start serving and the smell of dinner wafted in from the kitchen.

During these lectures, Walter sensed his non-scientific brain struggling, bit by bit relaxing, and finally shutting down. It only woke up again if there was mention of Darwin's agnosticism and his philosophical arguments with religious friends and opponents. Unlike himself, Sarah had an open, eager mind—though her degree was in English literature she was keen to learn everything she could about the natural world. When she was with him, his brain strained and kept pace. Now he was on his own, he enquired less and cared less about new knowledge outside his own field. As a result he had doubtless become boring—but it didn't matter, since he no longer had a significant other to bore.

Paul noticed Walter's indifference on their first day. "You're not even trying to see that finch, Walter." It was a little brown shadow skulking in some bushes.

"I can't bring myself to care. Why do you bird-watchers expect everyone else to share your obsession?"

But the spectacular beauty and the astonishing inhabitants of the place broke through his apathy: the big white birds with long, lacy, impractical tail feathers—the red-billed tropicbirds; the magnificent frigate birds with their vast scarlet pouches inflated to tempt the females; the Disney-coloured cartoon fishes; and all the trustful creatures who didn't know what human beings were capable of.

At islands with beaches they made wet landings, which meant slithering over the side of the craft into the warm, clear water. Snorkelling gear and flippers were issued; and braving the roars of the Beachmaster, the sea lion pater familias, they would duck under and turn their masked faces downwards. Walter was a poor swimmer but each time he would snatch a brief glimpse of a bizarre, beautiful underwater world before a wave interfered and dragged him towards rocks and he floundered to the surface again. On the second day he gave up and discarded the mask and flippers. A playful young sea lion swam towards him and they circled around and chased each other, and he could not remember when he had last experienced so much simple fun.

When they returned to the yacht Paul made a point of talking to Liz and Peter Corwood, and Walter reluctantly joined them. The Corwoods were too frail to disembark. She so patient, so devoted; he so agitated if she left him for even a moment; yet with his wife beside him Professor Corwood gazed around with an expression of astonishment and delight.

All that science, all that research, but no answers to help Peter Corwood, a distinguished scientist himself. Walter had never had much to do with an Alzheimer's sufferer. Meeting Peter made him thankful his parents had retained their faculties, though it had been terrible to lose them both in their sixties. He recalled that two Fellows of his college had become vague and later confused; one of them had taken to hugging female undergraduates and the other kept losing his way in the college gardens. Walter had avoided them as much as he could. They ceased to lunch in College and rumour had it the Master had asked their wives to stop them from coming in. Absorbed in his career and his own close, happy family, Walter had not given them another thought. Getting to know the Corwoods reminded him that he had no idea what became of those two once-brilliant colleagues. He had never even asked the Master for news, let alone telephoned their wives. It was too late to do so now without embarrassment all round.

"Come and see us when we're back home. We don't get out much and we love having visitors," Liz Corwood said, and they exchanged phone numbers.

They broke the homeward journey on the Ecuador mainland, in Quito, the capital. In the central square, swarms of street children surrounded them, pleading to clean their shoes. Walter's sandals didn't need it, and, embarrassed, he paid the children to go away. He noticed that Paul gave them money, too, but Paul chatted with them, and tried to find out more about their lives. Walter would have felt awkward doing that, although he had more Spanish than Paul.

In the Church of St Francis, he looked up at the painted wooden sculpture on the high altar, the *Dancing Madonna*. She wore a mantle of deepest blue, and she had unexpected little silver wings on her shoulders and a chained dragon at her feet. She captivated him; and as he stared at her, he was reminded of Lucille Brown: the rounded cheeks, the small, pretty mouth and the long dark hair framing her face. His college held a dinner dance in December and if he could bring himself to attend he would need a partner ... He would love to see Lucille dance.

When Paul joined him, Walter said, "Fascinating, don't you think? That blend of traditional indigenous art and the Spanish Catholic iconography. The history of a people in one exquisite object."

"Don't you find religious images repellent?"

"Come off it, Paul. Just because we're non-believers doesn't mean we have to cut ourselves off from religious art. Try to forget your prejudice and look at that statue for a moment."

Paul conceded that it was beautiful.

Walter bought a postcard of the *Dancing Madonna*, and posted it off to Lucille with the words, *Look forward to seeing you when I get back. Walter.* Perhaps he ought to see her at least once more. He hoped she would still be interested.

In the shop at the museum of the great Ecuadorian painter, Oswaldo Guayamín, Walter again thought of Lucille. They sold silver jewellery designed by the artist himself, and Walter picked out a simple pendant on a broad torque, which he knew would appeal to Rosie. A piece like this would complement Lucille's slender neck and look perfect with those low-cut tops she favoured, much better than her silly little cross. He brushed the notion aside—buying jewellery for Lucille was a foolish, dangerous idea. He thought of Sarah—a minor, very minor, sadness was that he would have loved to choose necklaces for her, but Sarah did not care for jewellery, except for her two rings.

When he opened his wallet to pay for Rosie's necklace, he felt as usual for the small inner slot in which he carried Sarah's wedding ring.

At Heathrow Airport, by force of habit he scanned the crowd in Arrivals, seeking Sarah's smiling face. When he returned from conferences abroad, she'd never failed to meet him.

Paul said, "Stupid, isn't it? I half-expect Elizabeth to meet me at the airport. After all these years."

"No, it's not stupid," Walter replied.

* * *

Paul and Walter hired a taxi from the airport. They drove to Paul's house first, a little two-up, two-down, terraced cottage in a narrow side street on the edge of Jericho. Paul insisted Walter come in for a whisky. Though it was almost midnight, he claimed the night was young and the holiday not yet over. Walter accepted. John and Rosie had gone back to university, and he did not relish the prospect of returning to his empty house.

"I could have sworn I left an upstairs light on," said Paul. "The bulb must have died." When he inserted his key, the front door opened of its own accord. He switched on the light. Every drawer and cupboard was open, the television and the computer were gone, books and papers were scattered all over the floor, and among them lay several empty wine bottles. Cigarettes had been stubbed out on the hearthrug. At the opposite end of the long open-plan room the French windows to the garden stood ajar. There was a stink of alcohol and tobacco, and some turds in the downstairs toilet. "At least they didn't do it on your carpet," said Walter.

He told Paul to call the police, but Paul froze and stared at the empty shelf beside the fireplace. His face crumpled. He turned and rushed upstairs. Walter hesitated, and then followed.

Paul was in his bedroom, slumped on the bed and running his hands over the bedside table. Walter realised Paul was crying. Horrified, he tried to offer some comfort: "You're insured, aren't you?" Paul nodded.

Walter continued, "Well then, it could be a lot worse. Now come downstairs and phone the police."

Paul composed himself and complied. While they were waiting for the police Paul said, "Shall I tell you what has really upset me?" Walter was curious, but at the same time he didn't want to hear in case Paul started to cry again. Before he could reply, Paul told him—his favourite photos of Elizabeth had been stolen for their silver frames from the shelf in the living room and the bedside table. They were all taken before the advent of digital cameras and he hadn't got the negatives. Paul began tearfully to relate the story of each lost photograph: the occasion, the setting and who was behind the camera. At a loss for what to say, Walter was relieved when the police arrived.

After the police had gone, Paul remembered a bottle of whisky left in a plastic bag after his last supermarket shop. The burglars had not found it. He poured them a tumblerful each and they drank and talked till morning. They spoke of Elizabeth, and also of Sarah.

"One of the worst things about being widowed," said Paul, "is that your wife is the very person you long to share your grief with."

Walter struggled to his feet, his mind confused, his words slurred. Paul was dropping off to sleep and, besides, the talk of Sarah had made Walter want selfishly to get away from Paul and Paul's problems and return to his own home.

Walter walked unsteadily, trundling his suitcase through the still dark streets of North Oxford. The rumble of the suitcase wheels worried him and he wondered how many sleeping residents he had disturbed. But then he thought, Why should I care?—they can just cuddle up to their partners and go straight back to sleep.

The damp breeze refreshed him, and sudden anxiety caused him to quicken his step. He recalled that North Oxford was burglar country—more so, indeed, than Paul's part of town. Then he remembered Sarah's engagement ring; he had it in a drawer in his bedroom. Though he would always keep the wedding ring, he meant to give the engagement ring to Rosie, but he kept vacillating. The memory it evoked was just too precious, and he had an irrational fear of parting from that memory along with the ring.

I must tell Paul to install a burglar alarm, he thought, as he entered his house, kicked his way through the jumble of mail on the doormat, and punched in the alarm code. He checked all the rooms and everything was as he'd left it. In his bedroom he took out the diamond ring and contemplated it for a while, twisting it under the electric light the way Sarah used to do, to make the three diamonds sparkle and flash, and replaced it in its little velvet box at the back of the drawer.

CHAPTER SEVEN

Autumn: dates and makeovers

Two hours after his return home, Walter was awake again, with a dry mouth and a headache. He drew the curtains and gazed out at his wet, colourless garden. A gloomy autumn morning. A small bright gap opened in the grey depressing sky, but it soon clouded over again. It was too early to ring Paul; he hoped Paul was sleeping off the whisky and the shock and distress.

He wanted to set out at once to fetch Prissy from the boarding cattery, but it was too early for that as well.

Though he had checked the night before, he looked again into his children's bedrooms. Rosie's bookshelves were bright with birthday cards; she'd had her twenty-first in July. A collage of cuttings featured Virginia Woolf and Jane Austen and a crowd of other female faces he couldn't identify. Paperback novels were piled on the floor and the dressing table, and he made a mental note to discuss extra shelving or whether she would like to take over a second room. Sarah would have approved of this idea. Rosie could take her pick of the two guest bedrooms which were hardly ever used, or the little downstairs room they called the parlour where the television had once been, in the days before it was allowed into the drawing room. He looked forward to talking about this next time she phoned.

John's room was crowded with "gear"—little hammers and trowels, and rucksacks, and a heap of old jeans and shorts and sunhats with an incongruous toy bear perched on top. And souvenirs of archaeological sites—unrecognisable stones and bits of metal and murky photographs of sandy trenches and crumbling fragments of walls. More like a storeroom than a place to live. Sadly, Walter accepted that next year, once John's degree course was finished, his son would be seeking adventure far away.

His cat's company helped a little, but the house was sad and empty and silent after the summer with Rosie and John, and their friends who filled the place with laughter and terrible music. "Aural torture", he called it. Rosie and John tolerated the thumps and yowls, though they still preferred classical music, thank goodness.

Walter tried to concentrate on his work, but he kept remembering the impulsive postcard he had sent to Lucille Brown. How ridiculous. Just because the *Dancing Madonna* in Quito had reminded him of her, that was no reason to pursue her acquaintance. He wished her well, but there was no future in it. Yet with the postcard he had committed himself to at least one more meeting. Assuming, of course, that she had not already been snapped up. He was unsure whether or not this was what he hoped.

For two weeks Walter checked the weather forecast regularly. He wanted a fine Saturday so that he could suggest a country walk before Lucille's regular lunchtime engagement. In this he was disappointed—two dry weeks were each followed by a wet weekend, and he could postpone it no longer. He telephoned to propose another evening arrangement and they went to see the film *Philomena*. Since he had not invited her to a meal beforehand, Walter felt obliged to suggest a drink afterwards, at the

Jude the Obscure pub. He hated these new pub names in place of the old, historic ones, and scowled at the inn sign which showed a crude, cartoon Jude, like an illustration in a children's fairy story, with a knobbly staff in his hand, a crowd of towers and domes ahead of him, and a wooden post saying "*Oxford*". Whoever painted that sign could not have read the Thomas Hardy novel.

* * *

Lucille said the name of this pub reminded her of the amazing book with the same title. "I saw the film when I was in my twenties. The stars were Christopher Ecclestone and Kate Winslet. I loved it so much I bought the book. I can't remember who it was by."

"Thomas Hardy. A lot of *Jude the Obscure* is set in Oxford."

"Are you sure? I seem to remember the town was called something else."

"Yes, Hardy called it Christminster. Poor old Jude dreamed of studying at the university but of course in those days people like him weren't eligible. It's different now."

"How is it different?"

"Well, anyone who's at all bright can go to university nowadays. Ever since—let me see, the nineteen-forties—what with all the scholarships and now the student loans as well."

"Oh. I thought they wouldn't accept Jude because he was working-class."

"That too, I suppose."

Nearby, an obnoxious gang of students were shouting and shrieking with laughter and downing expensive drinks in large quantities. Does he think I was too stupid to get into uni? she wondered. Perhaps he does and perhaps he's right about me, but in his position he ought to understand that lots of clever kids from poor families can't afford it and are scared to take on those huge debts.

Instead of arguing, she said, "The bit I remember best is when Jude finds his three children dead. The oldest one has hung the two babies and then himself and left a note saying '*done because we were too many.*' That made me cry."

Walter laughed. "Really? Most people think that passage is ludicrous. Especially the spelling in the suicide note—*m e n n y.*"

* * *

Walter recognised he had been tactless about Jude and his tragedy, and dropped the subject. He asked Lucille's opinion of the film *Philomena*. He had been surprised to find they seemed to enjoy the same films, though they were interested in different aspects. Whereas Lucille focused on the characters and their experience, he analysed directorial style and cinematic technique.

He had seen tears shining on her face during *Philomena* and, yes, he too had found the story moving.

"How unforgivable of those nuns. To have her son adopted without her consent, and then to prevent them tracing each other – outrageous."

"But they thought they were doing it for the best."

"That's the Catholic religion for you. I can't fathom why the woman remains a believer after what they have done to her. No reasonable person would forgive them."

"She's a good Catholic and she forgives them because that's what Christians should do."

He glanced at the little gold cross that Lucille always wore. He was tempted to ask her its significance, but he restrained himself.

He went on labouring to convince Lucille of the evils of religion till he was interrupted, somewhat to his relief—and probably to Lucille's relief, too, he realised. "Walter Farquarson, what are you doing in my local? And in its new 'secluded garden' at that! Aren't you frozen?" Without waiting to be invited, Paul dragged a stool over to their table, beamed at them and helped himself to an olive from their "sharing platter".

Walter was obliged to introduce them.

"You're welcome to all my olives," said Lucille.

"Thank you." Paul took a handful and went on talking with his mouth full. "Walt and I go back a long way." He jumped up. "My shout. What'll you have?"

Walter demurred. "I've got a lecture to write and I think Lucille wants to catch her bus."

Lucille shook her head at this, and Paul, his round pink face radiating goodwill and glistening with olive oil, protested that he needed some company, and aside from that, he'd been longing for an opportunity to meet Lucille. Walter was annoyed: Paul had no right to let Lucille know he had been talking about her. Grudgingly, he agreed to another glass of wine and Lucille asked for a diet Coke.

After that, the conversation he'd just had with Lucille seemed to get recycled. Lucille spoke about *Jude the Obscure* and Paul agreed with her that the death of Jude's children in their little house in Jericho—"a house just like mine," said Paul—was heart-rending and believable, not ludicrous at all. Paul had seen *Philomena*, and again he agreed with Lucille more than he agreed with Walter. Walter could see Paul liked Lucille and found her conversation interesting. This made Walter a little relieved. But he was also a little annoyed, and he could not understand why—it surely couldn't be jealousy, for that would be absurd.

Paul said his insurance company had settled up, and they told Lucille about the burglary.

"I hate the expression 'sentimental value,'" she said, "but did they take anything of that sort—photos, perhaps, or jewellery?"

She was the only person who had asked him that, Paul said, and he told her about the photographs, and talked about Elizabeth till Walter interrupted and insisted it was time to say goodnight.

Paul thanked Lucille for listening and added, "I do hope we meet again soon. Don't let this fellow monopolise you."

Walter was disconcerted by his own reactions to Lucille. He couldn't help being attracted to her—physically—and he saw more and more to admire in her character too. Or was he just trying to pretend it would be acceptable to bed her? Seeking excuses? Was he drawn to her because he was just an ordinary lonely man who missed his wife and needed a sympathetic woman friend? Or was it because he was frustrated and sex-obsessed? Either way, he concluded, he ought not to take advantage of Lucille's obvious vulnerability and her anxiety to please. He was no philanderer, he told himself. But he had no wish to enter a committed relationship, and certainly not with a woman like Lucille with whom he had precious little in common. What he needed was the company of a woman with

MAKEOVER

a similar background to his own, and some sex without commitment.

When they parted, he kissed her chastely on the cheek and pressed his hands stiffly to his sides, because those lovely breasts were attracting them like a pair of magnets tugging at paper clips.

* * *

Frustrated after nearly a month of failing to attract Walter, Lucille decided to pull out all the stops and have a makeover. On her day off she went in to Richley's and made full use of her staff discount. First stop was the hairdresser's salon on the top floor.

"Your usual?" asked Jean-Pierre. He sounded more like a British barman than a French coiffeur.

"No, I want a complete change. A new cut. A bob. But first I need a more interesting colour."

Jean-Pierre lifted a dark brown lock and sighed. "What's wrong with this?"

"Boring. Come on, Jean-Pierre. Think of something."

"A lighter brown, maybe?"

"But I want to be noticed."

"Don't we all, Lucille sweetheart, don't we all?"

Jean-Pierre consulted the colourist. "OK, we could take you from brown to chestnut." When they'd finished, her hair had the rich sheen of real chestnuts new out of their shells, plus a hint of violet just for fun, and her luxuriant fringe swung back and forth, flirtatiously hiding one eye and then the other when she tossed her head.

All aglow from Jean-Pierre's blow-dryer and sheer glee, she

hurried to the lift. The doors were just closing and the people inside were jabbing at the buttons to keep them open for her. Someone hit the wrong button and her arm got crushed between the doors.

When she arrived at Jillie's counter in Cosmetics on the ground floor, she was examining the sore arm, worried about the bruise she knew would soon spoil the look of her short-sleeved dress, but she was still smiling. While on duty in her white uniform, Jillie was usually serious and professional-looking, almost like a dentist or a nurse, but when she saw Lucille's hair she clapped her hands and gave a most unprofessional whoop. "Wow! Jean-Pierre has excelled himself. You're going to charm the pants off that stuffy professor of yours." Jillie hadn't met Walter, but she had formed a none-too-flattering opinion of him. Because of that, Lucille absolutely refused to introduce them.

"He's not stuffy and he's not mine," Lucille retorted. "And you shouldn't be so familiar with your clients. Now do your job, woman. I want a complete makeover."

Together they selected a softer beige foundation, and Jillie insisted on banishing the false lashes in favour of a clever thickening and lengthening mascara. The lipstick was the latest shade, a subtle, fetching plum.

In the afternoon she had her eyebrows threaded, rather publicly, in the middle of a shopping mall. A place where teenagers came in threatening hordes to chill out and annoy people rather than to shop. The meaty smell of hot Cornish pasties fought with assorted sickly aromas from enormous lumps of soap. Lucille hated pasties, and she hated cheap perfume even more— if she couldn't afford the real thing she did without. The eyebrow threader had a booth amongst stalls selling plastic handbags and cut-price phone covers, with a sex shop on her right and an optician's on her left. Many shoppers stopped to stare. She felt like one of those poor freak show people at the St Giles Fair in olden days. Luckily, she saw no one who knew her. And it didn't hurt much, and anyway, she didn't dare wince, being on public display like that.

Finally, she went to the fancy so-called clinic, in the street with all the posh unaffordable dentists. She had her lips plumped up with collagen and the single worry line between her brows smoothed with Botox, all at considerable expense and more discomfort than she'd been led to expect.

During her lunch hours later that week, she applied her own expertise to herself. She splashed out on two complete new outfits which featured higher hems, higher heels and a higher bosom. (As she often told the customers, it may cut into you, but a well-engineered underwired bra does complement an elegant blouse.)

When she passed them next day on her way to the bus stop, the builders in her road seemed to notice the change. The wolf whistles were definitely louder and when she tried to look stern and pointed to their sign saying *Considerate Contractors Scheme*", they only whistled the more. Ogling and leering she didn't like, but whistling and even the occasional "phwoar!" was rather nice.

Her work colleagues were impressed as well. Yet when she next met Walter he seemed not to notice any difference. Was he really so unobservant? Or was he just playing hard to get? Even men did that sometimes.

The following Sunday she plucked up courage and examined

her finances. She had begun to run up debts on her credit card. Normally she paid the debt off at the end of the month and avoided interest charges. This month she did not have enough in her current account to cover it. With a quavery sensation in her stomach, she raided her savings. It was easy enough to transfer the money across, almost too easy. Only a couple of little mouse clicks. After all Mum had gone through to keep them out of debt and all Mum had taught her about paying your bills on time and never borrowing, had she got herself on to the road to real trouble? Never mind, the mortgage was the main thing; the rest didn't matter so much, so long as she kept her flat. And she had her job, no worries there, money coming in every month; people would always need personal shoppers. She would just have to be more economical and the kitchen and bathroom would have to wait a bit longer for *their* makeover.

If Walter Farquarson were to fall in love with her, she would never have to worry about money again. But what if he still held out? What if it had all been in vain? Then where would she be?

* * *

Much as he hated the chore, Walter studied his monthly bank statements. There had been large deductions from the dedicated refuge account. Walter was relieved to see the money put to use at last—allowing it to sit in the bank earning so little interest displeased his zealous and intimidating financial adviser.

Along with Mike and the rest of the steering committee, Walter was pleased with their choice of architect, a woman with experience of such conversions and who seemed to have a genuine interest in their aims, and plenty of practical nous as well as aesthetic sensibilities. Mike had obtained a plan of the refuge Sarah had visited, and they studied this beside a plan of the Deaf Centre building as it was now. While the professionals debated and grew overambitious and then lowered their expectations again—the floor space forced limits upon them—and the architect pontificated about "acoustic privacy", "visual privacy" and "inclusive design", Walter had allowed his mind to wander. As instigator and chief benefactor of this project, it was fitting that he should play a leading role, but the nitty-gritty of walls and floors and windows was beyond his ken and his interest, and he was no expert on finance, either; he just wanted these poor women to be given sanctuary, and, most of all, he wanted to commemorate Sarah.

Next day, when he looked again at the architect's plans for the transformation of the Day Centre for the Deaf into the new women's refuge, he was bewildered.

He went round to Mike's and asked Mike to explain the proposed design all over again. "I'm hopeless at this technical stuff. I thought I'd grasped what the place was going to look like, but now the plan has switched back into a lot of squares and rectangles on a big sheet of paper."

"What it is that you don't understand?"

Walter spread the plan over the desk in Mike's study and embarked on his catalogue of questions.

What were the two small squares?

The smaller one was the interview room, Mike replied, and the other was the office. Of course. In fact, when he looked closely he could just make out the tiny signs to that effect.

The rectangle marked "*kitchen*" was enormous. "Isn't this a mistake?" he asked. "Nobody needs a kitchen as big as that."

Mike explained that they required several cookers and sinks and microwaves, because several women would be preparing meals at the same time.

"What an odd arrangement."

"And at least three industrial-size fridges, so the residents can have a section each."

Until then, Walter had not realised there would be no chef and no communal meals.

"All right. But why such huge bedrooms?" They were nearly as big as Walter's own—far too big for one person.

Mike explained that many of the women would bring their children with them.

Walter had not realised they would have children in the refuge. "Won't the children be cared for by the Council in foster homes?"

"Really, Walter, you're like somebody out of a Dickens novel."

"Sorry, sorry. Remember, I'm not a member of the caring professions ... Though I didn't think probation officers were, either."

Mike refused to be provoked.

By contrast to the bedrooms and the kitchen, the bathrooms seemed to Walter to be too small.

"They are for showers, not baths."

"But surely most women would rather have a bath?" Sarah had preferred a shower, but he assumed the average woman liked a long soak with perfumed bubbles (or was it oils?)

"Perhaps. But showers are quicker."

Walter thought, Would it matter if others had to wait? But he said nothing.

"A woman with small children wouldn't have time to *run* a

bath, far less take one," Mike continued. "And showers waste less water." Walter had never considered that sort of thing.

Then Walter noticed the interview cubicles were to have CCTV cameras, their position marked on the plan in minuscule writing. And there were to be security cameras in several other locations. "Whatever for? And what about people's privacy?" He hoped to prove to Mike that he was not really so insensitive and uncaring.

"Security cameras are for security." Mike had to explain this, too. Among the residents there might be a few women who would lash out, distraught, angry not just with their violent partner but with anyone who seemed to represent Authority or the System. Such a convoluted idea would never have occurred to Walter. It seemed to him that someone in trouble would hardly be likely to lose their temper with the very person who was trying to help them. However, he chose not to argue—Mike was the expert, after all.

"And the larger rooms?"

"Group work. And this space is a play area for the kids."

"And the one big room? You said they wouldn't have communal meals."

"Multi-purpose, but mainly for community meetings. And the architect suggests room dividers, so it can be made into three smaller units if need be."

This all seemed reasonable, and Walter raised no further objections about the interior layout of the building. But he was vehemently against the garden being paved. He insisted lawn was more attractive, with perhaps a large rose bed in the middle. He had just granted permission for a new variety of white rose to be named "*Sarah Scott*" in her memory. Mike struggled to convince him, pointing out that paving stones would stand up to all the traffic whereas grass would just be churned into a mess of mud.

"Traffic? What traffic? We should simply put up signs like we have in College: *'Keep off the Grass'*."

Mike snorted. "And what about the children?" Walter had forgotten the children.

A high fence was to be built round the yard. Now this Walter could understand—it was important for security. "Yes, of course. We'll need anti-climb paint, too. We have to make sure that if the partners discover the address they won't get in and assault the staff or have another go at the residents." Mike seemed impressed that Walter knew this at least, and they concluded their discussion just before suppertime. Marcia's beef lasagne was big enough for three and Walter considered he had earned his meal.

* * *

Lucille's company was a diversion from the tedious practicalities involved in the funding of the refuge and the transformation of the Deaf Centre. Walter was glad of a companion at films and plays. He hated to go alone, particularly to the theatre, where he felt conspicuous and irrationally ashamed, sitting by himself with no one to talk to in the interval. Lucille appeared to approve all his suggestions. He was unable to persuade her to express a preference, though he tried to remember to consult her every time.

She only gave her opinion when it came to restaurants. She never wanted to eat at the better ones. Wherever they ate, she often skipped a course, chose the cheapest items and refused wine, claiming to prefer tap water. He felt some slight irritation, for this detracted from his own pleasure in their meals. And some guilt as well, because they divided the bill equally between them although invariably he had dined far more expensively than she had. It was some weeks before he grasped the connection between Lucille's self-restraint and preference for cheap meals, and her insistence on "paying her way" as she called it. Even when he understood this connection, he could not think what he could tactfully do about it, short of eating and drinking less himself.

In spite of these concerns, Walter always found a good reason for eating out before the film or the play. He hated cooking now he had no Sarah to guide him and keep him company in the kitchen, and he believed that after a hard day's teaching, one deserved to be cooked for rather than have to cook.

As often as he could, he persuaded Paul to join Lucille and himself. Paul was—how could one put it?—"good with Lucille". Whenever Paul was with them, they had plenty of laughter and some agreeable and quite interesting discussions about people, and Oxford (the city, not the university, of course), and local politics. It came as a surprise to hear Lucille call Oxford "a city of inequalities", and back up her assertion with statistics about people living below the poverty line and the differences in life expectancy between Oxford districts.

Most important was the reassuring notion that this was a night out with friends, not a date with a girlfriend. Afterwards, they would escort her to her bus stop together. With Paul present there was no danger of being tempted into kissing or romantic talk. Sometimes Paul would try to leave them, but

Walter always pleaded with him not to break up their convivial threesome.

When the two men met without her, Paul often commented on how charming she was, but if Paul suggested Walter and Lucille ought to become "an item", Walter snapped at him. Once Walter said nastily, "If you like her so much, Paul, why don't you ask her out yourself?" and Paul answered that being ten years older than Walter he was far too old for Lucille and, even more to the point, he had an off-switch where friends' girlfriends were concerned. Walter shrugged and did not reply, but he recognised in himself an illogical sense of relief, even though Lucille was not, of course, his girlfriend.

And so the autumn turned to winter without any of the "development in the relationship" that Paul advocated and Walter was afraid Lucille expected. No doubt "development in the relationship" was Paul's euphemism for sexual intercourse.

CHAPTER EIGHT

Winter

In early December Walter received his invitation to the St Nicholas' College Christmas dinner dance. He collected it from his pigeonhole in the porters' lodge before setting off for the Jude the Obscure to meet Lucille and Paul. Instead of the incorrect and upsetting "*Professor and Mrs Farquarson*" it was addressed to "*Professor Farquarson and Guest*". He tossed it straight into the recycling bin. Then he fished it out again.

Paul caught sight of the gilt edges and the top line of the invitation poking out of Walter's jacket pocket. "Is that your grand dinner dance invitation? Are you going this year?"

Lucille was listening. Walter wished he had time to think it over properly, but that was not possible. So he answered, "No. John and Rosie will be here." He avoided looking at Lucille.

When Walter and Paul were next alone together, Paul apologised. "Poor Lucille. I just assumed you would be taking her to your dinner dance. I suppose I shouldn't have put you on the spot like that."

"No, you shouldn't have."

Paul asked when Rosie and John were coming home, and Walter had to confess that it wasn't till after the dance. And he had to acknowledge that their presence in Oxford did not prevent him from going out in the evenings.

"I thought not. They're past the age for needing a babysitter.

It was the first excuse you could dream up for not inviting Lucille Brown."

Walter shrugged. "There wasn't time to think of anything better."

"All right. Now, please can I have Lucille's phone number?"

"What do you want it for?"

"I intend to ask her to our Kingston College do instead. Sort of make it up to her."

"And will you be partnering her?" Walter tried not to let his annoyance show.

"It depends. I had thought of taking my sister-in-law Nancy—Elizabeth's sister—she will be over from New York on her own, staying with our niece in London."

"And what, precisely, does it depend on?" Walter knew what was coming.

"Whether you will consent to be my guest as well, and partner Lucille yourself. Then we could go as a foursome."

Walter was caught in a trap. He disliked the idea of Lucille dancing the night away with Paul; he also disliked the idea of having to accompany her himself. Then he recalled that Paul's college was different from his own. She would fit in more easily there. And if she did make some social gaffe and let him down, well, it wouldn't be quite so bad as it would at St Nick's, an altogether more traditional place, and in front of people he had to work with every day.

Paul was regarding him with an amused, quizzical expression which meant these ponderings of Walter's were all too predictable and had in fact formed the rationale for Paul's strategy. Paul was just too clever by half.

"All right, Paul. You win, you cunning, interfering old devil.

And you don't have to tell me: I haven't forgotten my manners—
I am the one who ought to invite her."

* * *

Lucille consulted Helen Chambers on what to wear to the
Kingston College dinner dance. Helen was surprised—as a personal shopper, surely Lucille was the expert? But university
types hardly ever used personal shoppers, Lucille explained, and
she had never been to an Oxford college function.

Helen invited herself over and riffled through Lucille's
crowded wardrobe. She advised something evening-ish but not
too dramatic. "This isn't the Oscars. And they're a conservative
lot, these dons." By the time they had taken out every item of
party wear and held it up and Helen had sighed and shaken her
head again and again, Lucille was close to tears. She could not
afford a new outfit, even with her Richley's staff discount, and
anyway, knowing their stock so well, she realised that the sort
of dress she needed could only be found at a certain upmarket
boutique in the High Street. She told Helen she would have to
phone Walter and cancel.

Helen said, "This isn't like you, Lucille. You don't usually give
up so easily," and went out to her car and returned with a carrier
bag. The name on the bag was the name of that very same boutique on the High. "What about this? I brought it over just in case.
I bought this dress in November, and I've only worn it once." It
was a nearly floor-length, long-sleeved dress of palest green lace
over a dark green taffeta lining. It fitted almost perfectly.

Lucille was so pleased and grateful she could hardly speak.
"I can't tell you how much this means to me."

"So don't even try. Just see if you can alter it a little. You are going to be the belle of the ball."

Lucille made a few tucks at the waist and down the side seams, so that the material followed her curves without overemphasising them.

* * *

Walter was relieved when he saw Lucille coming down the stairs from her flat. She was wearing a dress that reminded him of fresh spring leaves, no jewellery except her little gold cross, and dainty shoes with small, neat heels—Rosie had a pair like them—"kitten heels", he'd heard them called. He caught a faint waft of an expensive musky perfume.

In the car she hardly spoke, but as they walked towards the college hall she said, "I've never been to a college dinner before."

He sensed she was afraid she would let him down and he felt a rush of guilt for having feared that she might. "I do hope you enjoy it."

It occurred to him later that he ought to have complimented her on her appearance, but he knew Paul would pay her enough compliments for both of them. He was embarrassed when she complimented *him*—it was as if she had never seen a man in a dinner jacket before.

Paul had arranged for the four of them to sit together. Also at their table were two scientists and their scientist wives. Kingston's atrocious acoustics prevented a general conversation and they talked to people opposite and on either side. Walter overheard Lucille giving her neighbour an animated account of *Philomena* and then she went quiet while the zoologist explained the latest theory on the evolution of the domestic cat. A little later he heard her say something about the shortage of good dress shops in Oxford and inform the women that she had borrowed the green dress from her friend. He need not have worried about possible social gaffes; not only was Lucille enjoying herself, it was plain that everyone else was enjoying her conversation. He found himself growing impatient for her to turn round and talk to him.

No sooner had Walter got her attention and begun telling her and Nancy about the Cutteslowe Walls, which had been built near the site of Kingston College, than they heard a commotion at the other end of the dining-hall. Then a shout. "Someone's choking. Is there a doctor present?" No one moved. Everyone peered around the company as though trying to winkle out a medic in hiding.

"Any first-aiders?"

Lucille jumped up and ran towards the speaker.

"Good grief!" muttered Walter.

There was a hush in the dining hall. A few people took another furtive nibble of their Beef Wellington, while others whispered and looked solemn and let their beef grow cold. Walter stood up and tried to see what was happening, but his view was blocked by a group of diners from the Master's table, who encircled Lucille and the person in trouble.

Two ambulance men ran in, and Lucille returned to her place. "No need to be quite so surprised. Richley's offered time off to anyone who would do the Red Cross training programme. I reckoned it might come in handy, and it has."

The Master banged the gavel to get attention. "The Senior Tutor took ill. Thanks to the lady who came forward to help, it seems he will recover all right. Please go on with your dinner."

"Well done, Lucille," said Nancy.

"Yes, well done, Lucille," Walter echoed.

"We're proud of you," said Paul.

"Nice of you to say so, but it's no big deal."

"What happened?"

"The poor old gentleman swallowed a big lump of meat without chewing it properly and it blocked his windpipe. I carried out a Heimlich manoeuver." Walter nodded, and made a mental note to google "*Heimlich manoeuver*" when he got home.

After the meal, a small band struck up and they started to dance. Lucille twirled and smiled and managed to look entirely graceful while she performed energetic, confusing and sexy nightclub moves that Walter couldn't master. Walter recalled the *Dancing Madonna* of Quito.

Because they had drunk too much wine, Walter and Paul and Nancy decided to leave the cars at the college and go home on foot. Walter summoned a taxi for Lucille. She thanked both him and Paul profusely for a wonderful evening, but he thought she appeared a little sad as she climbed into the taxi and said good-night.

"What a lovely person," said Nancy.

Paul agreed heartily and Walter remained silent. It had not occurred to him to pay for the taxi and he was sorry when it was too late. After this evening his feelings towards Lucille were more muddled and conflicted than ever.

* * *

In the taxi Lucille wondered why Walter had not come with her. Even if he was not going to stay over, she would have expected him to see her home after such a special evening. She had felt like Cinderella at the palace ball, loved every moment—the meal, the conversation, and especially the dancing. It was a bonus that she had been able to help out with the choking gentleman. She wished she had someone waiting at home to tell about her evening, and who would listen while she talked through the disappointment at the end, when she had to return alone.

And there was the Christmas question. Walter had asked, "What are you doing for Christmas?" and for a short, joyful moment she thought he was on the brink of inviting her to spend it with him. But he went on to talk about the trials of cooking the dinner for his son and daughter, and how this year the three of them were going to a hotel in Cornwall. He hadn't waited for her reply, and then he realised and said, "What about you?" He had only asked because it was a conventional question at this time of year.

She was going to spend Christmas alone and she felt ashamed of this, so she had made up a story about having a jolly get-together with her neighbours. She had said the same to the friends who *had* invited her to join them, to Jillie and Marigold and Helen and Annette, who all had family celebrations planned and insisted that one extra person would be no trouble. Her pride got in the way. She was afraid they were asking her out of charity. And apart from that, though she knew it was a long shot, she'd wanted to be available in case Walter should happen to invite her.

* * *

On Christmas morning, Lucille put a small chicken in the oven and began to steam her Christmas pudding. "*Serves two*" it said on the wrappers, but she intended to eat it all herself. She tried to read, she switched on the television, but she couldn't settle to anything. She decided to have a good clear-up. When she went to the dustbins, she came upon Joan Wilson also taking out her rubbish.

They exchanged a "Happy Christmas" and suddenly Lucille burst into tears. Afterwards she tried to think what brought that on and decided it was the thought that year by year she was turning into a lonely old lady who never had anywhere to go for Christmas.

Joan lifted up her arms as if she intended to hug Lucille, but dropped them again and said, "Oh dear. Are you not feeling well? Is there anything I can do?"

"Not really, but thank you … unless … if you're not going out, why don't you come and have some dinner with me?"

"I'd love to."

They returned to Lucille's flat and Lucille dried her eyes and brought out the sherry. She was grateful to Joan for not asking why she had been crying.

"If I'd known you would be on your own I'd have invited you properly," said Lucille. "I've told people I'm spending Christmas Day with my neighbours, so it would have saved me having to lie."

Joan laughed. "You know, my dear, I've been telling that very same lie every December for at least twenty years."

Lucille raised her sherry glass. "To no more lying!" She prepared some more carrots and sprouts and potatoes and made a white sauce to go with the pudding. Joan fetched a bottle of wine from her flat.

They talked and laughed about Christmases past and their best-ever presents—the little puppy Chips was Lucille's and a subscription to a magazine called *Girl* was Joan's—and after their dinner they watched the Queen's speech and argued enjoyably about the Royal Family. At teatime they staggered up to Joan's flat to sample the tiny Christmas cake she had made, and Joan disappeared into her bedroom and returned with an unopened bottle of *Je Reviens*, a present from her Banbury niece who she never saw and who did not realise that she never wore perfume. "Merry Christmas, my dear. And thank you."

They had some cherry brandy and then Joan fell asleep in her armchair and Lucille went back to her own flat. Alone again, she thought more sadly about Christmases past, and wondered what Walter and Rosie and John were doing. She looked up the weather in Cornwall, and saw that it was raining and hoped the sun would come out for them tomorrow.

CHAPTER NINE

A Trip to Darwin's House

Walter's children came home from university the day after the dinner dance, and furnished an excuse for him not to see Lucille until they were gone again and the new term began.

He still kept Sundays for himself in the hope of hearing from Rosie and John, and to prepare his teaching for the week ahead. But on Saturdays Lucille was now free, as she had apparently given up the regular lunches with her girlfriends. Walter began occasionally to invite her for a Saturday walk—she had told him how much she missed the countryside now she was without a car, and he took pity on her. He tried to ensure that other people would be with them, but he rarely succeeded.

During a spell of mild weather in early spring, Paul proposed a Saturday expedition to Down House, Charles Darwin's home in Kent. The perfect sequel to their holiday in the Galapagos, he said. A Mecca for humanists. "We can see his journals and his study where he wrote *On the Origin of Species*. The gardens are magnificent, and an expert guide takes you round and explains how Darwin's experiments were done."

"All right, all right, you've convinced me. But I've already arranged to go for a walk with Lucille. So I'm afraid I can't join you."

"Bring her along. I'll ask Joan Wilson too. I can wander round with Joan if you want twosome time with Lucille. And you can sit in the back seat of my car with her. It's a hundred miles from Oxford."

Walter grumbled that he wasn't a love-struck teenager, had no desire to canoodle in the back seat, and doubted whether Darwin would be of interest to Lucille.

Paul said he suspected Lucille would be interested in whatever Walter was interested in. He added, "Even if she's never heard of evolution, I bet she'll grasp the theory like a shot. Sometimes you and I conflate education and intelligence, you know. I reckon your Lucille is one smart cookie."

Walter was glad to hear that, but he just said, "All right, all right. I suppose I can ask her. And by the way, she's not 'my Lucille.'"

"Methinks the gentleman doth protest too much."

Walter phoned Lucille to ask if she'd mind the change of plan. As Paul had predicted, she turned out to be very interested in Darwin.

When they arrived at the flats to pick up the two women, Walter got out. He found the front door open and went into the entrance hall. From the bottom of the stairs he saw Lucille before she saw him. She was standing in front of the full-length mirror on the landing outside her door, checking her lipstick, and fluffing up her hair with her fingers. He saw her wide, anxious eyes reflected in the glass, and he noticed that her hands were trembling. When he called hullo she squared her shoulders and came down to meet him. That sexy walk. That confident, sexy smile.

Next, behind Lucille, Joan Wilson came clumping down the stairs. She was kitted out for the excursion in her usual nondescript skirt and jacket, but with the startling addition of a sort of baseball cap in camouflage colours. She must have sensed their surprise, for without being asked, she explained that the cap was useful for keeping her hair tidy in the open air. Lucille said it was a shame to cover such pretty hair; even if it got a little out of control it was far nicer than any kind of hat.

"Do you really think so?" Joan beamed and went pink, and delayed them while she puffed back up the stairs in order to replace the baseball cap with a rather pointless wisp of pale blue chiffon.

"Would you mind going in the back, Lucille?" said Paul. "There's more leg space for Joan in the front." Walter inched as far as possible along his side of the seat, in order to avoid physical contact with Lucille on the journey.

After they had walked round Down House, they took a tour of the grounds. Their guide, an erudite young woman, gave them details of the scientific experiments Darwin had carried out with the help of his children, who acted as research assistants.

A bird flew screeching at high speed over their heads. Paul and Joan got excited and discussed its possible identity.

"A bird of prey, surely," said Paul.

"Those wings with sort of elbows—a falcon of some kind? But what? A hobby?"

"No, a hobby is about the size of a swift."

"A goshawk?"

"Not here."

"A merlin?"

"What does a merlin look like?"

"I haven't the faintest idea."

The bird flew over again, this time displaying its long tail feathers. When it turned at an angle, the sunlight revealed that the feathers were green.

"It's one of those flamboyant parakeet things that have no business in this country," said Joan.

They turned away, looking disappointed. Lucille, however, stared after the bird. "But it's beautiful. That colour—it's thrilling. And the shape, the way the bird's body tapers to a point, is so … so graceful. Aren't we lucky to have seen it?"

Walter noticed that the parakeet was the same colour as the dress Lucille had worn to the Kingston dinner dance.

The parakeet flew back over the huge Spanish chestnut, and over the ancient, propped-up mulberry whose branches used to tap on the windows of the nursery. In that nursery, ten little Darwins flourished—or at least seven of them did. (Three did not.)

Walter said that was how it was in Victorian times; losing one or two of your children was the norm, so it didn't hurt the way it would hurt a modern parent.

Lucille said, "I don't see how we can be so sure," and went scarlet. Then she mentioned something she had clearly just learned that afternoon: Darwin had abandoned religion not as a result of his scientific studies, but because he lost his little girl when she was ten. After her death, he would walk with his wife and family to the village church on Sundays, and leave them at the porch. Walter was silenced. He thought about Rosie when she was ten, and how he and Sarah would have felt if they had lost her then. How he would feel if he lost Rosie now.

She'd been phoning less and less often and never wanted to talk for long, and his emails seemed not to reach her. In another sense, he was indeed beginning to lose his daughter.

On the way home he didn't feel inclined to chat and pretended to sleep.

When they arrived at Lucille and Joan's building, Joan suggested they all come up to her flat for a scratch supper of minestrone soup. He guessed she had prepared this specially, since she emphasised there was more than enough for four. Nevertheless, he cried off and insisted on going home alone by bus. He tried not to mind the looks of disappointment from his three companions.

As soon as he got home he attempted to contact Rosie. He called Rosie's mobile number and found the phone switched off. He rang the porters' lodge at her hall of residence and asked if he could leave a message for Rosie Farquarson. The porter said they had no Rosie Farquarson on their list and he assumed she had moved out. He refused to get Walter a forwarding address.

"Even though I'm her father?"

"Sorry. Security."

On the Sunday morning he received a phone call from John. John was so worried about a paper he had to finish that it seemed wrong to trouble him with questions about Rosie. He stayed in the rest of the day, hoping for a call from her. Finally, before turning in, Walter rang John back to ask if he had any news of his sister and whether he had her new address.

John said he hadn't got her address, either. Then he hesitated and went on, "She's preoccupied. New boyfriend, it seems. My guess is, this Nigel's not somebody you or I would approve of. She was very cagey when I spoke to her last."

Walter wrote to Rosie care of the hall of residence, a brief, careful note asking her to get in touch, hoping she would come home and join him and John in the Easter vacation as usual.

After two weeks came a short email: Rosie stated without explanation that she couldn't make it over Easter but she would definitely come to Oxford in the summer. Then John rang to say he wanted to take part in an excavation in York throughout most of the Easter vacation. Walter agreed that John must seize every opportunity to get experience, hoped John would pay at least one flying visit to Oxford, and told himself that he must stop laying on the guilt and allow his children to live their own exciting, worthwhile lives.

CHAPTER TEN

Early Summer and
a Second Makeover

By early summer, Saturday walks with Walter, sometimes morning, sometimes afternoon, had become a regular arrangement. Lucille had gradually given up her strategies—pretending to need his help over stiles and ditches, or to remove spiders and leaves from her hair. These feminine ploys didn't seem to work with Walter, and, aside from that, their interesting conversation took her mind off any such silliness.

But Lucille was losing hope of ever converting Walter from friend to boyfriend. Her expensive makeover had had no effect whatsoever.

To make matters worse, paying her share of everything was eating into her budget, but she did not want to sponge off Walter—at least, not at this stage. The memories of hardship in her childhood tormented and frightened her. As summer approached and new season's clothes would soon be needed, she worried more and more. Then it occurred to her: the way to a man's heart was through his stomach and dining in was cheaper than dining out. And she still hadn't been to Walter's house. She put these three thoughts together and took the plunge.

"Why not let me cook for us at your house?" He agreed right away. She was surprised, for she'd expected him to raise objections. But then she thought, Why would he refuse a friendly offer like that?

"Would you mind doing the food shopping? I could email you a list." He was happy with that as well.

She arrived ten minutes ahead of time, carrying a selection of spices and herbs in a little basket. Since she didn't want to inconvenience him by coming too early, she walked the length of the road on the opposite side from Walter's house. The houses were detached, and no two were the same. The original owners must have been quite desperate to cut a dash and stand out from the crowd.

Exactly on six she came into Walter's driveway. As well as a double garage, he had space enough to park three cars. The house was red-brick and had stone garlands over the porch and two large ground floor windows. Halfway up, in the middle, was a tall, narrow, stained glass window, which brightened up the front of the building.

As soon as she stepped inside a feeling of inferiority swept over her like a blast of air conditioning. They passed through the high, wide hall into the lounge. She shivered as if the place was draughty. This was only the second time she had been in the home of a university lecturer and as in Joan Wilson's flat she was amazed at the quantity of books—books were everywhere. But it was far tidier than Joan's place, and there were paintings on the walls, though nothing she recognised.

Walter noticed she was looking at the paintings, and said, "We decided to dispose of all reproductions and only to collect original works by artists we knew. Of course, Sarah had lots of friends in the art world. Most of these were presents or bought at private views."

Apart from the walls, the rooms were quite bare, as though apart from books and pictures he didn't have many possessions, in spite of being rich. No fitted carpets, just wooden floorboards and old-fashioned, non-matching rugs. There was a greyness about everything and a mustiness in the air. The place needed dusting and hoovering.

Lucille stopped in front of a bookcase opposite a big arm-chair. All the books in it were by Sarah Scott. She was wondering whether to comment when a plump black and white cat strolled in and twined itself round Walter's legs. She crouched down and tried to make friends with it, but it gave a quiet hiss and raised a paw with the claws out before stalking away again. "Sorry about that," said Walter. "She's getting old and crotchety."

The lounge opened into the dining room through a wide archway. In both rooms she saw photos of Walter's son and daughter at different ages, but not a single one of their mother. On the dining room wall hung a large framed photo, very artis-tic, of a cruise ship taken from high above, nothing but a tiny white speck in a vast blue bay. "Have you been on a cruise?" Lucille asked.

"Yes. The Hebrides. We went in 2010. We hadn't been back since our twenties. Sarah took that photograph from Ben Nevis. The cruise company were good enough to employ us both as lecturers. I talked about the Scots' involvement in the Civil Wars, and Sarah talked about her novels. Two of them are set in the west of Scotland: *The Sea Eagle* and *The Treeless Isle*. We loved the Hebrides but we didn't much enjoy the cruise experi-ence, except for the food, of course. Most people say that, don't they?"

"Mmm." Do they? she wondered. She did not know anyone who had been on a cruise.

"Now take me to your kitchen." On the way they passed the open door to the study. "*Our* study" he called it. Two enormous desks with two proper desk chairs were placed not side by side, but back to back. He must have guessed she found this arrangement a bit odd, for he explained, "We don't—we didn't—want to distract each other."

The kitchen. He seemed embarrassed when she admired the chrome and granite and the butler sinks and all the fancy machines. This was the kind of kitchen she dreamed of. "Sarah loved cooking and she was brilliant at it. So we spoiled ourselves," he said. "We used to prepare our meals together. I was her assistant. But now I'm on my own I hardly ever cook. I do a little when John and Rosie are here, but they don't think much of my efforts."

Lucille unpacked her basket, and inspected the ingredients Walter had bought. "All present and correct. Now go and read the paper or watch telly or whatever. I'll tell you when it's ready. You can set the table." She thought he looked relieved, and she was glad to be left alone, for if he'd stayed he'd be bound to be thinking about Sarah and remembering the times when he and Sarah worked in this kitchen together.

* * *

Walter thoroughly enjoyed the dinner: a refreshing cold soup made from avocado pears, perfectly grilled lamb chops with rosemary and tiny new potatoes and petits pois, and finally, a wonderful, elaborate concoction of raspberries and hazelnuts and cream. And afterwards it felt comfortable and friendly, almost intimate, as they sat in the drawing room and drank their coffee and talked. The perfume of early roses drifted in through the open window.

Some of the things that mattered to him turned out to matter to Lucille too. True, she had never heard of the Levellers (she thought they were a rock band); but she seemed moved by their story and entered into his speculations, his what-ifs. She extracted a promise to take her to Burford and show her the church with the Leveller prisoner's name carved on the font and the plaque in the churchyard where the three executions took place.

She went over to the bookshelf with the rows of Sarah Scott books, and asked if she might borrow one. Before he could answer, she picked out *Afterword*.

Suddenly he was angry. "No. I'm afraid you can't," he snapped. "This is a collection. I don't want a gap on that shelf. And anyway, you told me you'd read *Afterword*."

Lucille looked crushed. Her eyes filled. "Oh yes. Oh Walter, I'm so sorry. That was thoughtless of me."

He was annoyed with himself—for being rude to Lucille, but also for permitting another woman free range of Sarah's kitchen. He wanted to apologise, but the words would not come, even though he could see they were expected and knew they were deserved.

"I ought to be going, Walter … beauty sleep and all that …"

"Of course." Coldly, politely: "Would you like me to drive you home?" The weather had changed, and rain was hammering on the windows.

"No need. Really. My bus stop's at the end of your road. Just walk me to there."

Mean of him—he should have insisted on the lift, but he did as she suggested.

As they left the house the security light came on and she jumped and froze as though she had never seen one before. Like a rabbit caught in headlights, he thought, a rabbit about to be squashed.

The bus stop had no shelter. When the bus appeared and they said goodnight, he noticed she was shivering in her thin jacket.

* * *

In spite of the upsetting end to her visit to Walter's home, Lucille still hoped … though quite *what* she hoped she found hard to spell out.

She had a brainwave. She went to her computer and googled "*Sarah Scott novelist*" in search of some clue to what Walter Farquarson found attractive. She could have kicked herself for not thinking of it sooner.

There were two photographs of Sarah on the Internet. Lucille was surprised at what she found: this handsome man had married—well, she could think of no nice way to express it—a frump. In the earlier photograph Sarah wore an arty velvet coat, open, showing a shapeless tunic over shapeless trousers. Her age in this one was hard to guess—long, straight brown hair, slightly saggy jawline. In the later photo she was clearly over forty and overweight, in old-fashioned spectacles, with untidy salt-and-pepper hair, dressed in an uninspiring skirt and lumpy rather than curvy in her cardigan. It dawned on Lucille that she'd wasted her money—even before her makeover, she'd been miles more attractive than poor Sarah.

101

Now she decided to re-think her look. Careful planning was required. There was no sense in trying to copy Sarah's appearance exactly—the trick was to become just a little bit more like her.

Jean-Pierre, grumbling, washed out the chestnut dye and returned her hair to its original colour, the same dark brown Sarah's had been. She started to wear her glasses again, but, unlike Sarah's, hers had designer frames and the thinnest possible lenses. She toned down her make-up—still effective, but not so much of it. And she bought clothes like Sarah's in that later picture (two sizes smaller, of course): plain over-the-knee skirts and simple blouses and sweaters. Understated, but not boring, she hoped. Surely she'd be a match for Sarah now.

While Jillie put the finishing touches to her new, subtler eye make-up, Lucille explained her strategy. The tiny brush Jillie was using poked Lucille in the eye. "A *match* for Sarah?" Jillie echoed. She sounded shocked.

Lucille said nothing. Jillie was right. It was insensitive and in extremely poor taste to think and talk like this about a dead woman who had been her superior in every way that truly mattered.

Her other colleagues noticed the change in Lucille's appearance. And Annette and Marigold soon found out what she was up to. She now wished she hadn't confessed her failures and schemes to Jillie; though Jillie was loyal, she wasn't discreet.

"Listen, pet. Pretending to be someone you're not never pays in long run," said Marigold. "The only person you're likely to fool is yourself."

Annette added, "And what a waste of money."

Lucille's line manager spoke to her severely. "I know we can't sack you or even discipline you, Lucille. But as a friend, I ask you to consider: in that outfit, do you really think you inspire the customers to purchase fashionable new clothes in our store?"

The line manager was a pleasant enough woman who suffered from having a big bottom that was unconcealable except by facing your public at all times. She believed those old magazine tales about vertical stripes being slimming and had taken to wearing vertical-striped trousers; Lucille wondered if her knickers had vertical stripes as well.

"I'm ever so sorry," she said humbly. "I just thought a change might be nice."

After that Lucille wore her previous outfits and make-up to work, and kept the new look for when she was seeing Walter.

Impossible to tell whether Walter noticed her second transformation. He gave no sign.

* * *

The transformation of the Deaf Centre was almost complete. The builder showed Mike and Walter round. The ground floor was now one vast, dreary space, like a church hall, with side rooms of various sizes and a large kitchen.

"It'll soon be time to decorate your walls and cover your floors," the builder said. "We need to know what paints and materials you've chosen. If you want to get them at trade prices we have to order well ahead."

Walter sighed audibly and the builder gave him a sharp look. "What did you say?"

"Oh, nothing." He addressed Mike. "We ought to be going."

Mike thanked the builder and promised to be in touch soon.

"Oh God," groaned Walter, once they were out of the building. "I hoped we could leave all this stuff to the architect and the builders. And now they've sent these huge awful catalogues and paint colour charts. Who knew there were so many shades of green? It's got to be a pleasant environment but I have no idea what sort of thing would work. We just want a tasteful décor that makes these poor people feel welcome and comfortable … And now I suppose we've somehow got to narrow the selection down and run it past the committee. What a bore."

Mike offered a solution. Before deciding, they would look around another refuge not far from Oxford. But it turned out that this place didn't allow men on the premises. Walter was appalled. Mike explained that they claimed the residents associated men with fear and pain, and needed to be able to relax and recover their confidence. "That's the argument."

Unconvinced, Walter told Lucille about this outrageous policy.

"It's offensive," he complained.

"Whether or not it offends men isn't really the point," Lucille said. "All the same, you'd think they'd want to bring in as many decent ordinary men as possible, so as to remind the residents that not all of you are monsters. Otherwise they'll never be able to settle down happily with another man. We've got to have faith that most men can be trusted."

Marcia went to see the other refuge on Mike and Walter's behalf. She came back with details of the décor, reported on suggestions from the staff and residents, and produced a list of the items she had noticed. The walls were in strong colours; the floors were easy-maintenance, wipe-clean, but not hard (they'd found stain-resistant carpet wasn't adequate). The furniture was versatile—sofas and tables that divided into sections, everything with washable surfaces; lots of "laminate", whatever that was. Nothing in the least tasteful or memorable.

"Serviceable" summed it up. A disappointing contrast to Walter's vision for an elegant and peaceful establishment, vaguely resembling his college senior common room or a London gentlemen's club. Worst of all, from Walter's point of view: the art consisted of popular contemporary prints including *The Singing Butler*, scenes from Bollywood films, and several photographs of Buddhas and of the Royal Family, particular favourites being Prince William and Kate and their baby boy, and the late Princess Diana in her enormous frothy wedding gown.

Walter showed Marcia's list to Lucille and in an unguarded moment told her how naff he thought it was to have *The Singing Butler* on your wall. He tried to bury his faux pas by adding, "It was a bad print of it, Marcia said. But the Royals are the really awful thing."

The angry retort he received took him by surprise. "What is so wrong with being interested in our Royal Family? I haven't got any photos of them myself, but I do have *The Singing Butler*. You may have noticed it. Pictures like that take you into another world—and they can make you happy, even if it is only for a few moments and has nothing to do with your own life."

"Don't they make you feel life is bloody unfair?"

"Maybe it *is* unfair, but it's wiser not to brood about that, and just plan for the future and hope for the best."

"Those images of the idle rich merely encourage escapism."

"A better word for it is 'respite', don't you think? Perhaps people like you who are comfortably off don't need that sort of thing."

Walter stared at her. "Respite" indeed! Not a Lucille word. He dropped the subject, and told her about the other items needed for the refuge: a television set, kitchen gadgets, and all those versatile, practical, ugly pieces of furniture. Lucille reminded him that everything must be sturdy and toddler-proof.

At the next committee meeting, Walter still kept getting it wrong. He favoured linen bed covers, cream tweed sofas, pale curtains; he baulked at washable tiles and paint. But eventually he shrugged and yielded on every point. He was starting to lose what little interest he had ever had in these matters.

Perhaps to placate him, the rest of the committee voted to adopt the name he had suggested, "The St Frideswide's Centre".

Now that the building was almost ready, and the finances organised, the Steering Committee metamorphosed into a Board of Trustees with Walter as chair and Mike Johnson as probation representative. All the others were women—a bank manager, a local councillor, and senior figures from social services and two domestic violence charities.

"You can relax now, Walter," said Mike. "From now on you'll just have a ceremonial role, like a gracious royal patron."

Appointments were made, and experienced professional women took over. They sent out information to potential referrers and there was soon a stream of emails from churches and social workers.

Walter wanted to celebrate the opening and to bring in the press and talk about Sarah. Mike and the professionals now in charge disabused him of that idea.

When they were alone together, Mike explained. "We can't celebrate—it's not a cause for celebration, and we absolutely must not advertise the refuge's whereabouts."

Walter understood and accepted. "But shouldn't I at least go and see round it when it's up and running and the battered women have arrived?"

Mike sighed. "You can pay a visit, I suppose, but only if the staff and residents agree. Please try to remember, Walter, this will be people's home for a while and you will be there as a guest. And please don't call them 'battered women'. These women are survivors."

CHAPTER ELEVEN

Burford and Minster Lovell

June. The loveliest time of the year in Oxfordshire. Walter suggested a walk along the River Windrush to Burford. As usual, Lucille seemed not to know anyone who would want to join them. This was indicative of the problem, he thought—her friends did not belong in his world.

When he proposed inviting Joan Wilson, Lucille pointed out that Joan had arthritis and couldn't manage the distance.

He'd asked Paul, but Paul had gone to Cambridge for a conference on eighteenth-century women. "You never know who you might meet," Paul said with a grin.

"What, another conference? You and your networking! Are you looking for research collaborators? Or another lucrative lecture invitation?"

"Neither. Have you never heard of a conference romance?— like a holiday romance, but classier, more intellectual. I'd like to meet a nice lady historian."

So it was just him and Lucille again. He liked to have company on his walks, but he preferred them not to be à deux with Lucille.

When the spire of Burford Church came into view, Walter recalled his promise to bring Lucille here—a rash promise wheedled out of him on the evening when she had cooked dinner at his house, an evening that had ended badly. Lucille had never reminded him of his promise, but as they entered the village she suggested they go and look round the church. "If you don't mind seeing it again."

"I'd be delighted. As you will have gathered, it's a favourite of mine. But I rather assumed you'd prefer to have a browse through the shops. I believe there are some dress shops you might like. We could split up and meet again later." He had a vague recollection of the wife of a visiting American professor saying she had found some classic British clothes and, amazingly, some unusual and elegant imports from Japan, on the High Street in Burford. He and Sarah had always enjoyed a foray in the antique shops followed by a cream tea at Huffkins'. Sarah had not been interested in dress shops.

Lucille frowned, but just said, "No. I'd like to see the church, if that's all right with you."

Walter gave Lucille his much-practised guided tour of Burford Church, a labyrinthine building with a complicated history, hard to summarise. He began with the Romans, and when he reached the seventeenth century he went into considerable detail about the Levellers, much of it a rerun of what he had told her before.

Lucille ran her fingers over the inscription on the font: "*Anthony Sedley 1649 Prisner*". What had become of Anthony Sedley? she asked. She seemed relieved to hear he had not been executed. "I imagine he was a true survivor—he used the time to dig away into the lead, to make a memorial, while the other poor souls were probably too scared to do anything."

"Speaking of memorials ..." Walter told Lucille the story of the Parliament Speaker, William Lenthall of Burford. "In his will he required that only the words '*vermis sum*' should be inscribed on his gravestone. It's believed that they complied, but now there's no sign of any memorial at all. The awful nineteenth century renovators must have thrown the stone away."

"What does *vermis* … what you said … mean?"

Walter was annoyed with himself. He should have realised Lucille had as little Latin as those Victorian vandals.

"*I am a worm*" or "*I am become a worm*." After he translated it, he became acutely sad. He took out his handkerchief and wiped his eyes.

Lucille continued, "*I am a worm*—I suppose he meant 'worms'. Awful. That's why my mum asked for cremation. I didn't really want it, because I hated to think of her being burned, but it was probably better than having her buried." She was staring at one of those Gothic-style memento mori features still popular in the seventeenth century, a hideous stone skeleton beneath a sarcophagus.

Walter thought of Sarah. He turned away.

Lucille laid her hand on his arm but said nothing and moved to another memorial, on the wall of the church. This featured American Indians, the first depiction of them in England. After a moment or two, Walter regained his composure and resumed his commentary.

A tortoiseshell cat was prowling in the churchyard. Walter called it over to him and crouched down to stroke it. "I apologise. I'm a bit gloomy today," he said. "I keep thinking about our cat. She's off her food and I'm worried about her."

* * *

Before returning to Oxford they went to Minster Lovell. After lunch at the Old Swan, they walked to the ruined Hall beside the River Windrush. Walter told Lucille about its history, but deliberately omitted the ghost story attached to the place. From teenage assignations in spooky places he recalled that any mention of ghosts seemed to encourage females to grab your hand or snuggle up to you. *Then*, he had wanted it—*now*, he most certainly did not.

From the Hall they strolled down to the Windrush. The hawthorn trees were clouds of white and the air was perfumed with it. At the weir they came upon a distressing drama. A mallard and seven ducklings were in the river above the weir. Down below, calling pathetically, swimming round and round, was a solitary duckling which had obviously fallen over the edge. The mother duck was quacking in alarm, aware that one of her young was separated from the group, but unable to rescue it.

Walter didn't stop. "There's nothing we can do. We have to let nature take its course."

"No, we don't." Lucille bent down and broke off a large elder branch heavy with blossom. She took off her shoes and little white knee socks and rolled up her trousers. Holding the branch in front of her, she stepped carefully into the water and inched along the top of the weir. The water was shallow but where it fell over the rim the current was strong. The stone was slimy and twice her foot slipped and she almost fell. Guiding them with the branch, she shooed the ducks out on to the riverbank. The mother duck made as if to fly but could not bring herself to leave the ducklings. She allowed Lucille to herd them all slowly along the bank to the lower level of the river. They needed no encouragement to hop into the water again, and the lost duckling joined them.

Lucille smiled happily as they watched the duck and her family sail away downstream. She crossed back to Walter and steadied herself on his arm. As she tugged her socks over her wet feet, he observed that her manicured toenails were the same bright scarlet as her fingernails.

"That was clever," said Walter. He was impressed, and relieved she had not met with an accident.

"I once lived on a farm," she replied. As if that explained everything.

"So much trouble for the sake of a single duckling. I believe they have a huge mortality rate. I'm afraid rescuing one makes practically no difference in the grand scheme of things."

Lucille grinned. "But it makes an enormous difference to that one little duckling."

Walter said nothing. He half-remembered a similar philosophical pronouncement: something about saving a single baby turtle out of thousands crawling towards the sea. Earlier that year there had been international outrage over the killing of one giraffe at Copenhagen Zoo. The creature's name, Marius, was all over the papers. Walter had not signed the petition to save it. Irrational, sentimental, he thought … and yet indicative of the human propensity to care.

As if she sensed his train of thought, Lucille went on, "It seems we feel the need to help most strongly when it's only an individual animal or an individual human being. The charities know that. It's why they ask us to sponsor a single child even though they use the money to help a whole village. It's the way we're made, don't you think?"

Walter nodded. He agreed with her, but to him his own small family mattered much, much more than the millions of children of strangers. Then he thought, That's exactly in line with what she's saying.

CHAPTER TWELVE

The Award

It was Helen who gave Lucille the hot news from the History Department: Walter Farquarson was on the shortlist for the Charles Hudson History Prize.

"Will you be going to the award ceremony?" Helen asked, and Lucille said, "Oh, I expect so." She'd thought she and Walter had grown closer on that outing to Burford and Minster Lovell, but now she felt less sure.

Her friend must have guessed this was the first Lucille had heard of it and that she hadn't been invited, for Helen went on to mention that ordinary members of the public were allowed to attend the ceremony, and it was to be held in the Sheldonian Theatre, the grandest building in the whole of Oxford.

Lucille saw Walter next day but he said nothing about the prize. No doubt he was embarrassed because naturally he wouldn't want to invite someone like her to the party they were bound to have afterwards. She tried not to mind, and she felt so thrilled for him that she decided to go to the Sheldonian Theatre anyway.

Unable to afford a new "occasion outfit", she dressed in her yellow top with a loose grey jacket and a long grey skirt. She had to sit high up in the theatre on the hard tiered benches. She noticed several of the people around her had brought their own cushions.

These seats were close to a flock of fat painted cherubim with wreaths and garlands—carrying these around for no obvious reason, just frolicking, she supposed, the way some birds do on a warm, windy day. She preferred birds. Huge portraits featured interchangeable gloomy men in gilt frames, wearing white gowns under black or red robes. She stared at some busty ladies with wings, little golden people blowing trumpets, gilded seashells, marble pillars, an enormous organ and two huge lions' heads with arrows poking out of their mouths.

When she spoke to him an older man started, even looked a little scared, yet all she said was "Lovely day". A large lady sat far too close, though there was masses of room. Lucille wondered if she wanted to chat and smiled at her, but the lady paid no attention, even though their arms and thighs were touching, and began to read a strange book with nothing on its cover, not even a title.

No doubt Walter's son and daughter were present, far away on the ground floor, sitting on the elegant pinkish brown chairs that were marked "*reserved*".

Walter came in. For once he was not wearing his cords; he had on a dark suit, a white tie and a university gown, and he carried a mortar board. He looked extremely distinguished and quite out of her league.

She watched him take his place on the low platform alongside the other shortlisted historians, three younger men, all of them bearded and far less attractive than Walter, and two older women. All six were soon smiling pleasantly, nodding to their supporters and chatting to one another like old friends.

* * *

Walter scanned the auditorium and located John and Rosie near the front. He was so delighted Rosie had come that he could hardly think about the award. The chair next to Rosie was unoccupied, and he couldn't take his eyes off it. He visualised Sarah sitting beside Rosie and John and smiling up at him, and he was relieved when a man came and took the empty seat. He looked farther back and nodded to Paul and Joan and other members of the History Department.

On the benches high above he caught sight of Lucille Brown in her vivid yellow blouse. How on earth had she found out about this event? Joan Wilson or Lucille's administrator friend Helen Chambers must have told her. It was good of her to come, he supposed. However, he felt a little disconcerted by her presence, but glad that at least she wasn't sitting in Sarah's place beside Rosie and John.

The proceedings opened with a speech from the chairman, who welcomed the distinguished company and thanked the generous sponsors. Next the competition judge began elaborately to introduce and summarise the books on the shortlist. She praised Walter's meticulous scholarship, and added that with his powerful and lucid writing style he would doubtless find a wide readership beyond the groves of academe. Walter barely recognised his own book and realised the judge—though scrupulously fair in her judging, no doubt—had put a spin on his thesis that he had not intended, certainly not consciously. She said Professor Farquarson had shone new light on the plight of the poor in the seventeenth century, and his work had a poignant message for society today.

He was puzzled, even disconcerted, by these observations, and found it hard to focus on the rest of the judge's remarks. At last she finished her preamble and arrived at the announcement of the winners. Walter tried not to stare at the judge and looked around the theatre. He saw that John and Rosie appeared almost terrified, Rosie clutching John's arm; and that Lucille had her eyes fixed upon him. He hadn't expected to win and up till now he'd thought he didn't care, but in these final moments he desperately wanted to.

The judge gave the prize-winners' names in reverse order. Walter had not got third prize; that was for the biography of a little-known Stuart princess. Nor the second; that went to a re-examination of the Crusades. So he was either unplaced or he was the winner. He prepared his face to smile, whatever the result, and got ready to applaud the winner, unless …

"And the first prize goes to … Professor Walter Farquarson for *Seventeenth Century Rebels*." It seemed to him that Rosie and John clapped louder than anyone in the theatre and he thought he heard a shout from John. He glanced up at the gallery. Lucille had risen to her feet and she was clapping with her hands held high. He stepped forward to shake the judge's hand and receive his cheque. He was unable to take in her words of congratulation. When he next looked towards Lucille's place on the benches, he glimpsed her pushing past the other spectators and hurrying towards the exit.

* * *

Immediately after the ceremony, Lucille went into Blackwell's bookshop across the street from the Sheldonian Theatre. Blackwell's were quick off the mark—displayed on a special table of their own at the front of the store, she found a pile of Walter's books, "*Seventeenth Century Rebels: Reformers ahead of their*

Time. Winner of the Charles Hudson History Prize. Signed Copies." His signature was a distinguished, graceful scrawl. Amazed how easy *Seventeenth Century Rebels* was to read, she browsed through a few pages and she recognised some of what Walter had told her about those Levellers imprisoned at Burford. The book cost £49.99, more than she had ever paid for a book in her life, half the price of a good pair of shoes. She bought a copy with her credit card.

That evening, while she ate her baked potato and cheese salad, with her new book propped up against the teapot in front of her, Lucille wondered where Walter was now. No doubt he was celebrating in grand style with his son and daughter and his university friends. She had agonised throughout the ceremony—should she have tried to catch his attention? But if he had known she was present he might have thought she was stalking him, and if she had joined the crowd who surrounded him afterwards, he might even have pretended not to know her.

She had just put her rubbish in the bin when she saw Joan Wilson coming unsteadily up the road. Joan was in her college dinner outfit, a flowery dress with faded black gown over it and sturdy, clumpy brogues. Lucille hurried back into her flat and hoped Joan had not seen her. A long speech from Joan about the ceremony and the celebration afterwards was the last thing Lucille wanted to hear.

The following morning she met Joan in the hall and Joan said nothing about the award. Perhaps she was being tactful—she must have noticed Lucille's absence from the party.

When she next saw Walter he didn't mention the award either, and she couldn't resist saying, "Oh, by the way, congratulations on winning that history prize."

"Thank you." He seemed embarrassed, or was he just sur‐
prised that she had heard?

A flash of inspiration. "I saw it in the paper." That was nice
and vague—she just hoped it had actually been reported some‐
where.

He surely would have said, "Thank you for coming to the
Sheldonian," if he had seen her there. Not surprising that he'd
missed her—such a huge crowd, and she had been sitting so far
away. Anyway, he would no doubt have been looking for his
children and all his university friends in the reserved seats.

* * *

Why collude with Lucille's pretence that she had not been
present at the award ceremony? Walter couldn't work out his
own motives. He felt uncomfortable, but he reasoned, It was her
own choice to say nothing. And if she had admitted she'd come,
he would have had to pretend he hadn't seen her.

He was rather ashamed that he had chosen not to invite her
to the ceremony and the drinks reception. It was churlish, really.
And on reflection he realised she might well have blended in;
he'd observed that these days she had taken to wearing longer
skirts and less surprising colours. However, she would doubtless
have wanted to tag on to his little family group with Rosie and
John, and that would have given entirely the wrong impression.
As for the formal college dinner afterwards ... he was sure she
wouldn't have enjoyed that at all. Besides, he wanted all the time
he could get with his children, especially his daughter. His plea‐
sure that Rosie had made the effort to come to Oxford
outweighed even his pleasure at winning the prize.

Rosie left early the next morning. There had been no mention of the boyfriend and Water dared to hope that his and John's worries were unfounded. John too had nothing to add and seemed to feel it was inappropriate to grill Rosie on the subject.

Alone again, Walter's thoughts returned to Lucille Brown. By way of recompense—or rather, to ease his nagging conscience—he invited Lucille to lunch before their walk the following weekend. She asked if she could bring anything and he said, "Well … maybe some pudding?" He thought he would ask Paul, too, and persuade him to contribute part of the main course, preferably the meat dish. But Paul was unavailable (doing eligible widower duty at a lunch elsewhere) and Walter was obliged to tackle the preparation on his own.

CHAPTER THIRTEEN

A Visit to the Corwoods

Lucille enjoyed Walter's egg salad, and the summer pudding she'd made was a success. Nonetheless, Walter seemed out of sorts, and to cheer him up, she asked him to show her his holiday photos from Ecuador.

Lots of iguanas—"disgusting, clumsy lizards" Darwin had called them, Walter said—and pictures of the *Dancing Madonna* taken from different angles. The statue on the postcard he'd sent her. She's a bit like my *Green Lady*, she thought, but healthier and more cheerful … a bit like me, in fact. When she asked him to tell her about the statue, he had unusually little to say, muttered "eighteenth century", and moved quickly on to photos of the exterior of the church. Lucille had an "Aha!" moment. Walter must have noticed the resemblance between herself and the *Dancing Madonna*. That was why he had sent her the lovely postcard from Quito. For a few moments Lucille was too happy to concentrate.

When she focused again, he was showing her a photo taken on the yacht, of an older couple, the woman with her arm around the man. The man looked puzzled, and the woman's smile seemed forced.

"Liz and Peter Corwood. We became quite friendly, Paul more so than me. But the husband has Alzheimer's."

"Have you kept in touch?"

"To tell the truth, I haven't contacted them. Though they live just outside Oxford, in Bournbrook. Paul visits them from time to time but I'm afraid I keep putting it off. She's a nice woman, but it's so sad and I don't know what to say to him, or to her either. I suppose I ought to give her a call and go to Bournbrook to see them. I gather they don't get out much."

Lucille said hesitantly, "If you want to visit them, perhaps I could go with you? It'll be easier with two of us. We could combine it with a walk next Saturday afternoon. We should ring to warn them first, of course."

"But what is there to talk about to a person with Alzheimer's?"

"You speak to them like anyone else, just maybe a bit slower, and be prepared to repeat yourself. Using your hands helps too. And talk about what *he* wants to talk about."

"I bet he won't remember the Galapagos."

"Some photos might jog his memory. Why not print a few off and show them to him? But if that doesn't help, I'll keep him company and you and Liz can chat about your holiday."

"How is it you know all this?"

She nearly said, "Because it's obvious," but answered more diplomatically, "I'm not sure. I must have picked it up some-where along the way."

* * *

They planned a walk that took them near the village where the Corwoods lived and Walter rang Liz to ask if it would be convenient for them to drop in.

Peter Corwood recognised Walter but when Lucille shook

his hand, he said he was terribly sorry, he had forgotten her name. Walter laughed. "But you've never met this lady before. She wasn't on the Galapagos trip. How could you be expected to know her name? This is Lucille Brown." Peter looked upset and bewildered, and grasped his wife's arm.

While Liz reassured her husband, Lucille whispered to Walter, "Try to keep it simple." She hoped she didn't sound bossy.

When Liz brought their tea, Walter took out the photos and Liz sat on the couch on one side of him and Peter on the other. Having seen the photos before, Lucille sat opposite the other three. While Liz and Walter talked about their trip, Peter reacted as if it was all new to him. Over and over again, Liz said, "Do you remember …?" and Walter said, "Don't you remember …?" But Peter seemed confused, then tired, and finally distressed. Lucille said nothing at first, but she felt more and more sorry for Peter. She waited for a pause in their conversation. Then she pointed to the garden and asked if Peter would show her around.

* * *

No matter how hard he tried, Walter found himself incapable of holding a conversation with Peter Corwood, so he was relieved when Peter ushered Lucille out through the French windows. He and Liz went on reminiscing about their holiday. Soon they were laughing about the Sally Lightfoot crabs—neither of them could recall the origin of their name—and the blue-footed boobies whose name was so perfectly apposite.

They could hear Peter's and Lucille's animated voices and Lucille's uninhibited giggles and Peter's booming laugh. Liz said,

"It's wonderful to hear him laugh. He hardly ever does that these days. Sometimes he cries. In fact, the doctor is thinking of prescribing an antidepressant." She sounded so very sad that Walter wished he could comfort her, but he could think of nothing to say.

After an awkward silence he said, "Shall we join them?" He and Liz sat down on a bench beside the border of hollyhocks and lavender. Lucille and Peter were standing in the middle of the lawn. Peter was commenting on the flowers and the grass, and Lucille was repeating what Peter said about them: "red ... big ... blue ... no rain ... have to water."

Peter took Lucille's arm and guided her to the pond. "In the water. Little frogs."

Lucille clapped her hands. "Yes, tadpoles. Oh, Peter, how fascinating. I used to catch them when I was a little girl."

"Tadpoles, yes." Peter gestured at the model heron which stood guard beside the pond.

"Does that scare the real herons off?"

"Yes." Peter led her away from the pond and showed her a nest box on an apple tree. "I did it."

"You made it yourself?" Lucille stood on tiptoe to examine the box, running her hands over it and peering inside. "I expect you get blue tits?"

"Yes. Blue tits." Flushed with pleasure, Peter hurried into the house and returned with a large illustrated book on garden wildlife. He handed the book to Lucille and picked some raspberries and offered them to her. She ate them while she and Peter looked at his book together. Walter watched the raspberry juice trickling down her chin. He brought out his handkerchief—perhaps she'd let him wipe the juice away—but she took a tissue and did it herself.

"Lucille is very skilled at bringing Peter out," said Liz. "Better even than your friend Paul. She doesn't torment Peter with questions or correct him the way so many people do. I'm afraid I do that myself sometimes, and I should know better by now. Has Lucille worked with people with Alzheimer's?"

"No. I don't believe so."

"What does she do?"

"Something connected with fashion, I think."

As they were leaving, Peter caught Lucille's hand. "Come again."

She gave him a hug. "Thank you, Peter. Of course I will," she replied.

CHAPTER FOURTEEN

Pets

After their visit to the Corwoods, Lucille's hopes rose again. She felt her friendship with Walter had moved forward a little, entered another phase. But for the friendship to become closer, she now realised, it was necessary to reinvent herself in some other way than just changing her appearance.

How could she become more like Sarah Scott, who wrote books and grew prize-winning roses? She was aware that she herself wasn't clever or well educated. And she knew nothing about gardening. She had plans for a bright floral display on her little balcony when she could afford to buy some bedding plants, but all she possessed as yet was a rainbow-coloured windmill, and three red plastic butterflies whizzing round a stick in a pot next to a tired geranium.

But she could do "animal lover". Walter had mentioned that Sarah loved their pets, and he owned a cat himself.

Lucille saw herself as a dog person. She had sad memories of the only dog in her life. She'd originally thought her father loved that dog. Her father had named her "Chips" because, he said, he liked chips more than anything else in the world. Her mother had said, "Well, I suppose you couldn't call a dog 'Beer.'" When her father was drunk, if he was in a good mood, he hugged Chips so tight that she yelped, and gave her lots of slobbery kisses.

Sometimes Lucille came home on the late bus and if he was still awake and sober, her father walked up the lane to meet her. He always brought Chips and she took the dog's lead and her father carried her school bag on the way back. She had been so relieved and grateful the night he'd turned up and threatened to set the dog on a strange boy who had followed her from the bus stop. The boy had scarpered and she and her father had laughed about how Chips, if let off the lead, would just have gone up to the boy and tried to make friends. Later, she felt sad for the boy when the policeman told them that he had learning difficulties and had run away from a care home in the next village.

But her father changed, and when he dealt out the blows to her mother and to her, he often hit and kicked Chips as well, and caused the poor dog to whine and cower when he came near. Eventually Chips disappeared. Lucille came home from school to find Mum in tears. Chips had been put to sleep because she had bitten the postman, Mum said. Lucille ran out of the room and from the hallway she heard her father say he'd buried that fucking mongrel, never you mind where, and her mother say "I'll report you to the cruelty people, Jim Carter." Lucille rushed back and tried to get between them, but she was too late to stop her father punching her mother in the face.

Two years later, when she was nearly sixteen, she was followed home once again and this time she had neither dog nor father to protect her. That was another dreadful memory.

The next stop after hers was an army base, and on the night in question a dozen or so soldiers got on the bus. There had been a few wolf whistles and suggestive remarks aimed at an older girl who left the bus two stops before. When Lucille got off, one of the soldiers got off too. She hoped it was because he wanted to look for badgers or was desperate for a pee; he didn't seem to be drunk. He followed down the lane, walking just behind her. When she slowed down, he slowed down; when she speeded up, he did the same.

Lucille tried to make polite conversation: "What a dark night … wish I'd remembered my torch … at least it isn't raining." The man said nothing. She played her best card: "My father will be on his way to meet me with the dog." Still she got no answer.

They continued to walk in single file, down the hill, over the beck, along the tunnel of overhanging trees, past the ruined farmhouse, through the small wood. There was no sign of her father. All she could think was, When is the man going to do it? and Will he murder me afterwards?

At last they arrived at the farm gate. A light shone in the cottage window. She fumbled with the chain, pulled open the gate, hurried through and fastened it behind her. The man stayed on the other side. She glanced over her shoulder and saw him turn round and disappear up the lane the way they had come.

She rushed into the cottage. Her mother was sewing at the kitchen table and she could hear her father's snores from the bedroom upstairs. As she told her mother what had happened, she began to shake and sob. Her mother said this was the last straw and promised they would soon move to the village.

Sure enough, they lost the cottage because her father hardly did any work and the farmer needed the cottage for another labourer. She and her mother moved first to a bed and breakfast paid for by the social services and then to a council flat, and her father simply disappeared. "Never mind, flower," said Mum. "Your dad is a bad 'un."

Her mother found a job as a charlady at a surgery in the town. It was the best she could find, she said. She had once been a shop assistant, and charlady was a step down, so when people asked she pretended she was the doctor's receptionist. At the time Lucille thought it was pathetic to lie about your job like that, but when she was older she realised that many people judge you according to your work.

She also came to understand why her mother had lied to her about the death of Chips.

* * *

Much as Lucille would have loved another Chips, getting a dog now would mean more responsibility and expense than she could manage, so her new pet would have to be a cat. She telephoned to consult Walter on the subject of cats and how to look after them. She said he was the only cat owner she knew; this was not strictly true, but nearly. "How do you house-train them? I know about dogs, but cats are different, aren't they? Is it true that cats train themselves?" He explained about litter trays and where to buy one.

She went to the animal rescue shelter and chose a kitten, almost fully grown. The kitten was just a black and white moggy, but she called her Cleopatra after a prize-winning Siamese she'd admired on television, Cleo for short. Within days Cleo was using her litter tray and not long after she was answering to her name. They quickly grew attached to one another.

Still Walter seemed unimpressed. Lucille couldn't work out what was the matter with the man. When she phoned, he sounded distant. He spoke slowly and his voice was flat. She invited him to come and meet Cleo and he agreed politely but without a trace of enthusiasm.

When Walter arrived he crouched down to Cleo's level and did several long, slow blinks, and Cleo did the same. "This is the way to introduce yourself to a cat," he explained. He soon had Cleo playing a chase game with his handkerchief.

As he was leaving, Cleo sneaked out of the flat after him. When Lucille came out on to the landing she discovered the pair of them playing another game—he hid below the stairs with Cleo on the open treads, and poked his fingers through the gaps, and Cleo tried to bat them with her paws. When Lucille laughed and said, "Are you two having fun?" he stopped and looked sheepish.

* * *

A week before that first meeting with Lucille's cat Cleo, the Farquarsons' fourteen-year-old cat Prissy had fallen ill. The vet recommended euthanasia.

Walter thought back to the day they brought her home from the animal rescue centre. How excited the children were, Sarah too. Prissy had been little more than a kitten and loved to play. That week the children spent all their pocket money on cat toys—balls with little bells in them and catnip-filled cloth mice. Homework was badly neglected till Sarah pointed out that a cat, especially a young cat, needed much more sleep than a person, and they were wearing the poor thing out.

Prissy was one more link to Sarah that would soon be lost. He took his cat home again from the vet's. And watched as she suffered. After a day of this, he forced himself to take her back.

Poor Prissy purred on his lap as the lethal injection went in. The vet pronounced the kindly-meant cliché, "This is the price we pay for owning a pet." Yes, it's true, Walter thought, the price of any love is loss. When he got home he sat down heavily in his armchair. His house was emptier than ever. He began to rehearse the phone calls to John and Rosie to tell them what he had done to Prissy.

The phone rang. Lucille Brown. He was glad it was not John or Rosie, because he was not ready to talk to them. Lucille announced that she was getting a cat and she sought his advice. Terrible timing, but of course she couldn't know that. Why *his* advice? he wondered. He told her to go to the shop in the Covered Market and buy litter and cat food, but suggested she should wait till she had chosen her cat before choosing a collar. Typical of Lucille, he thought, half-amused, half-irritated, to be so concerned about what the animal was going to wear.

Later that week, she rang again with further questions and a third time to invite him round to meet her new pet.

He couldn't help thinking there was something special about Lucille acquiring a cat that very week, and when she opened the door to him, beaming, with the cat in her arms—a black and white moggy just like the young Prissy—he experienced a surge of affection and was not sure whether it was for the cat or for her owner.

Later, when he was briefly alone with little Cleo outside Lucille's flat, he was transported back to the days when Prissy was new and the children were young and Sarah had laughed affectionately at the silly cat games he loved to invent. "Stair Monsters" was the favourite.

After Lucille had bundled Cleo back inside, he gave her his usual peck on the cheek and then added a hug which conveyed more than he wanted to feel or to show.

"I didn't intend to talk about it and spoil our evening," he blurted out, his arms still around her. "Our cat Prissy … on Monday I had to have her put down." Lucille hugged him back, hard.

CHAPTER FIFTEEN

John and Rosie

Lucille googled "Sarah Scott novelist" again and this time read a bit more. One obituary concluded, *Sarah Scott's husband Walter Farquarson and their children Rosie and John meant more to her than anything else.*

I've got to meet the kids, Lucille thought. Walter didn't talk about them much, except when Paul was present. Paul had no children of his own and seemed to be a sort of honorary uncle to Rosie and John.

Walter's children were home for the holidays. Lucille screwed up her courage and asked him to bring them to her place for lunch. She did it by phone rather than email, and gave him a wide choice of dates, making it hard for him to refuse. All the same, she was quite surprised when he agreed.

She watched the three of them coming up her road, arm in arm, chattering and laughing. She'd never seen Walter laugh like that. Rosie had no make-up on, and wore faded jeans with a plain white blouse and an anorak—a lovely girl with curly dark brown hair and high cheekbones, but Lucille could see she'd benefit from some advice in the fashion department. John was in jeans, too, and a denim jacket. He'd probably come straight from an archaeological dig—he certainly fitted the part, with dirty trainers and dried mud on his knees. He looked like Walter, or like a younger version of Hugh Grant.

When the visitors came in, Cleo trotted over to them and purred and rubbed against their legs. "She's just like our Prissy," said Rosie, and John asked Lucille's permission to pick the cat up. Lucille felt happy and relieved. This was a good start, and she was sure they would all get on.

There was rock music on the CD player (Lucille had bought one of the latest releases on the advice of a DJ on Radio Oxford). The lunch consisted of burgers and chips followed by ice cream with chocolate sauce. They didn't eat much, but they said it was delicious and they appreciated the trouble she'd gone to.

Conversation didn't exactly flow.

"Been to any gigs lately?" Lucille enquired.

"No."

"Festivals? Glastonbury?"

"No."

"What sort of music do you like?"

Rosie and John exchanged glances. Each seemed to want the other to answer her question. "Well, we're into classical music, really," said Rosie.

"Opera when we get the opportunity," John added. "The operatunity."

"Oh," Lucille said, flummoxed. She'd never learned to appreciate classical music. At home her father always shouted, "Switch that rubbish off" if the radio was playing classical music, even when it was only a short piece on *Desert Island Discs*. And she had never been to an opera. She'd once tried to watch one on television but it made her drowsy, and even though it was in English she couldn't make out the words.

Next, she asked what they planned to do for a living—she nearly said "when you grow up" but stopped herself in time.

Their answers confused her.

John said he wanted to be an archaeologist.

"But I thought you were one already," Lucille said.

"Well, yes, I'm studying archaeology. I hope to make it my profession."

"Cool!" Lucille said, and turned to Rosie.

"Next academic year I'm starting a master's in creative writing," said Rosie.

"I'm not sure what that means."

Rosie explained that the creative writing course would help her improve her style, make her characters more lifelike, and develop clever plots and exciting themes. At least, that's what Lucille thought she said.

Lucille glanced at Walter—he was gazing at Rosie and she guessed he was thinking about Sarah. Rosie put an arm round him and they exchanged a little smile.

"And what do you do in your spare time?" she asked.

Rosie worked on a student poetry magazine and belonged to a writers' group, and John played chess for his university. Lucille struggled to think up intelligent follow-up questions. John and Rosie answered pleasantly and patiently, but she guessed her questions were not quite right and they were finding the conversation awkward.

She smiled and nodded understandingly when the two young people talked about essays to write and books to read for next term, and how they had to go home and get on with their work. She knew next term was many weeks away and this was just a polite excuse, but she felt relieved. She only wished Walter could have stayed behind. At twenty-one and twenty-two, John and Rosie were old enough to make their way back to Summertown without him.

After they'd gone, she tormented herself with imagining what they would say about her and her flat. To blot out these painful thoughts, she found a favourite DVD of her mother's and put it in the player—*Rebecca*. The heroine marries a glamorous widower, Max de Winter. His dead wife, Rebecca, was a great beauty and apparently wonderful in every way, but in the end she turns out to have been an evil bitch. Lucille couldn't help wishing Sarah Scott had been like Rebecca, not to look at, but personality-wise. Unfortunately Walter's late wife was the exact opposite of Rebecca. Sarah was no beauty and she was rather saintly. And another thing—the second wife in the film didn't have to contend with snooty stepchildren.

Although she was fond of saying you shouldn't brood about it, Lucille reminded herself that life simply wasn't fair. Her mother had tried to make her accept this as fact from an early age, when she saw that other kids got things she didn't get. Clothes that fitted properly, for example. Her own were bought with plenty of room to allow for growth and she had to wear them till they were so tight the buttons came off and the seams burst. A lot of them came from manky charity shops. She was the class scarecrow.

And she'd been a laughing stock when the other children heard that the Carters had sugar beet for afters because it tasted like tinned pineapple. She remembered with a pang of shame the time she had brought a school friend home to tea and her mother asked the friend whether she wanted butter *or* jam on her bread, and the friend misheard and said, "Yes please, Mrs Carter." And sometimes her father smacked her for no reason. Once he did it in front of the friend, who refused to set foot in their cottage again and seemed to blame Lucille for her dad's scary, unpredictable violence.

Fast forward thirty-odd years and she still expected life would turn out to be fair after all, and if she tried hard enough she was bound to achieve whatever she longed for (within reason, of course). Because of this expectation, she was not about to abandon her dream of security without a fight. She looked up at the *Singing Butler* and tried to smile bravely.

* * *

"*The Singing Butler!*" said Rosie, the moment Walter had started the car. "Oh, Dad. I couldn't stop looking at it."

"Yes, I know. The painting the critics love to hate. The most popular print ever."

"He's got a retrospective in Glasgow this year. What's his name?"

"Jack Vettriano, I think. They call him the People's Painter."

"And that green-faced woman!" said John from the back seat. "Cringeworthy. Dad, Lucille may well be a kind-hearted soul. Nice of her to invite us—saved us from another restaurant meal or another dose of your cooking. But surely the *Butler* picture sort of sums her up? Fortune hunter. With a touch of the soppy romantic. Shallow."

"No, that's unfair. I don't know her well, but I've already discovered depths in her that I truly hadn't expected to find."

"Hidden shallows, you mean," said Rosie.

Walter's patience snapped. "Rosie, that's enough. It's not like you to be so quick to condemn on so little evidence." He looked at his daughter. He'd thought she was laughing, but he saw she was near to tears, from anger—and sorrow, too, he guessed. "I know, love. You're comparing her to your mother. Maybe you're misinterpreting my ... friendship with Lucille." Rosie did not reply, and Walter was unsure what to say next. He just hoped she would not ask him to further define this friendship, for he himself didn't know what sort of a friendship it was.

They were now in North Oxford proper, just beyond the Summertown shopping district, past bathroom and curtain boutiques, the bookstore, the artisan patisserie, the gourmet deli and the luxury frozen meals place Rosie called the upmarket Iceland. John said, "Dad, is that a new block of flats they're building on the corner? Have they torn down some more of the grand old dons' houses?"

"Houses like ours, you mean?"

"Exactly. The houses of the grand old dons. The barbarians are at the gate." John chortled at his own joke.

"Which brings us back to Ms Lucille Brown," said Rosie.

"No, Rosie. Stop sniping. That's enough," said Walter. "Have your mother and I brought forth an unkind little snob?"

There was silence. Walter glanced across at Rosie, and saw tears on her cheeks.

When they got home Rosie went straight to her room. John followed Walter into the kitchen and helped him to empty the dishwasher, and then he sat down at the table. Walter sat down too.

"I miss Prissy," said John. "Lucille's Cleo is the spitting image of her."

They were quiet for a moment.

John said, "Don't be hard on Rosie. You've got to understand, Dad—to Rosie and me you and Mum were an item, an entity. Now it's a bit like getting to know a stranger. You were baked together like ... like ... one of Mum's marble cakes. You were both here in our house such a lot, back to back in the study, Mum writing her novels and you 'working at home' as you called it. When I was tiny I actually thought of you as *mumand-dad*, with no spaces, like an email address." John paused and looked away. "And now you are another person who dates strange women. Don't get me wrong. We still like you—we love you—but you are new and different."

For a moment Walter was angry. Did John mean to imply that his grief for Sarah was less than theirs, or less than it ought to be? But he said, "I don't intend … I don't want to be new and different. I'm sorry." He saw that his taking up with a woman so unlike their mother had upset both their children. John and Rosie seemed to think Lucille Brown had got her hooks into him.

Within days, Rosie was to return to Bristol and in a week's time John was leaving to join an archaeological dig in Turkey. Next morning Walter made an effort to make peace with them.

He still hadn't got Rosie's new address, though John had confirmed his suspicion that her reason for leaving the university residence hall was to move in with Nigel, the boyfriend. "Rosie, can I have your new phone number, the landline? And the address, if you don't mind. I might need to send post on to you."

She wrote the address down for him. "Sorry, no landline. I don't bother with the mobile much, either, and the computer's not in good shape. Don't call me, I'll call you." She laughed after she said this, but he could tell she meant it. When he asked when her graduation ceremony would be, she said she did not want to attend. "I don't have to collect the degree in person. No offence to you and John, but to be honest, I don't feel like celebrating without Mum."

CHAPTER SIXTEEN

The Kiss and After

After that difficult lunch, Lucille sat stroking Cleo and trying to calm herself down. Cleo at least had made a good impression on Rosie and John as well as on their father. Maybe the pet idea was working—though she now appreciated Cleo for herself and not just as a means to an end. And her feelings towards Walter had definitely changed too. He was no longer just a ticket to security, he was a sweet, vulnerable man she could easily love. She tried to see the bright side—the lunch hadn't been a total disaster and after those visits to Burford and Minster Lovell and to the Corwoods, she had sensed that Walter was warming towards her. Perhaps he was just shy? Did he need a bit more encouragement?

Lucille made a resolution. The next time they were somewhere private, she'd make Walter kiss her properly. She invited him back to her flat for lunch on Saturday after a walk across the fields to Islip.

They talked about Islip, or rather, *he* did—he told her all about Edward the Confessor, who was born there, and she pretended to listen, but she could not concentrate and felt excited and nervous. Eventually he smiled and said, "You seem a little preoccupied." She apologised.

As soon as their lunch was over, he got up to leave, refused coffee, and said he had a lecture to prepare. When he gave her his usual goodbye peck on the cheek, she turned her head so that their lips met, opened her mouth slightly and pushed her body against his. She enjoyed the moment—his hard chest and the sexy masculine smell of him. For a few seconds he responded to her kiss, pressed her mouth open farther, and put his arms around her. But then he pulled away. She didn't know what to say, and neither, apparently, did he. He simply left without saying anything except goodbye. When he had gone she realised they had not talked about another meeting.

After half an hour, her anxiety got the better of her and she went to the computer. She thought to send some sort of apology, try to shore up the damage. But he had got there before her. He had sent an email already, destroying her hopes: *I'm sorry. I'm not ready for a new relationship. It's all my fault. I'm sure a lovely woman like you will soon find another, more suitable man.*

Lucille wondered, Was it that kiss? Had she come on too strong? Or had his kids turned him against her? Whatever— she clearly wasn't good enough for the Farquarsons. Well, that's that, she thought. She finished the wine and polished off the Ferrero Rocher.

She bent down to stroke Cleo. "Just you and me from now on, Cleo."

It seemed to her that Cleo knew something had changed, and for the better as far as Cleo was concerned. She jumped on to Lucille's lap and did her inconsiderate, clawing, settle-down routine. Walter had explained that this kneading behaviour was a hangover from kittenhood, when she would have done it to get milk from the mother cat.

"Yes, Cleo, you are allowed to sit at the table with me now." Yes, Lucille decided, she could relax her standards. No more struggling to impress, no more trying to live up to him and his posh friends and those too-good-to-be-true-butter-wouldn't-melt student children. She took the most recent CD she possessed from its hiding place at the back of her cupboard and put it in the CD player. She turned the sound to loud, jigged about a bit, tripped over the cat and said "Fuck!" and enjoyed saying it.

The rest of the afternoon was spent sobbing occasionally and watching *Love Actually*.

In the evening she cycled unsteadily to Macdonald's and treated herself to a Cheese Whopper and chips and a large Coca Cola. Back home, she settled down to watch an old episode of *I'm a Celebrity Get Me Out of Here* whilst burping the Coke bubbles in chorus with Cleo purring on her lap.

* * *

After he'd clicked "*send*" and sent his hasty email on its way, Walter experienced a mixture of sadness and doubt and hearty relief. It was the right, the ethical thing to do, he told himself. It was not a dreadful mistake he might come to regret. One more kiss like that and they'd have been having sex and then they would be "in a relationship" as it was called nowadays, and there'd be no decent way out.

At least no one had been hurt and now they were both free. Lucille could find a more suitable man and he could find a more suitable woman. He needed an independent woman with a worthwhile career of her own, a companion for cultural pursuits, a charming guest to take to college functions, who would be happy to share his bed two or three times a week, but wouldn't seek to share his life. Someone who wouldn't try to replace Sarah.

Trying to relax in his armchair, he looked across at the bookcase as if seeking Sarah's assurance that he had done the right thing. He began to read a doctoral thesis. Its author was a young man who could be relied upon for original, if sometimes far-fetched, insights into the puzzles of history. Supervising theses like this was one of the perquisites of his job. But he soon found himself unable to concentrate. He picked up the novel he had started to read earlier in the week. The words grew blurry and he couldn't make himself care about the invented people and their ridiculous loves and yearnings and regrets.

He got up and returned to the study and switched on the computer. The only emails were "offers"—bargain romantic dinners for two, bargain romantic breaks, and "buy with one click" novels with lurid, titillating covers. He did some deleting and then visited an Internet dating site. A succession of pleasant, smiling faces appeared, all trying to conceal a loneliness, a neediness, which he didn't want to admit that he shared.

He felt restless and uncomfortable. Their kiss had stirred up emotions and sexual longings that he was unable to subdue.

* * *

Lucille scrubbed away her make-up, what little was left of it after all the crying, and took off her clothes. The doorbell rang. She glanced at the clock: 10.15. It must be Joan Wilson—poor Joan had locked herself out a couple of times recently—though she wasn't usually out so late except on a Wednesday. Lucille threw on her bathrobe and went down to the front door.

Walter. She hadn't expected him, but she knew immediately why he had come.

"I'm sorry to disturb you. Will you …? Could we …?" More like a child expecting punishment than an eager lover.

She nodded. He followed her up the stairs to her flat. Then he opened his arms to her and she came into them and he held her tight. She could feel how tense he was.

"A drink?" She released herself and picked up the whisky bottle and a glass. He shook his head.

She took his hand and led him into her bedroom. She undid her robe, drew him on to the bed, kissed him gently, and guided his hand over her body so that he could know how ready she was.

He made love to her carefully and quietly, with a sort of controlled determination, until his climax came. He moaned as if he was in pain, and finally he called out, "I love you, Sarah." He withdrew immediately and kissed her face again and again and held her close and said, "Oh my dear, I'm sorry, so sorry. Oh Lucille, can you forgive me?"

Lucille sat up in bed and cradled him in her arms. "It's all right."

* * *

Lucille said it was all right. At first, Walter was unable to reply. At last he said, "No, it isn't all right. Not only because of what I said, though that was unforgivable. But to come back again and take advantage …"

Walter knew what he had done was indefensible. He had used and humiliated a generous, lovely woman. A woman who had tolerated his blowing hot and cold, who had listened to his donnish, rambling monologues about the Levellers and Edward the Confessor, and who had loyally attended his award ceremony and entertained his ungrateful children and never asked anything for herself. He thought back to all the times he had spouted on about how wonderful Sarah had been. But he had never offered Lucille a single compliment. Inside his head he had, of course. He admired many things about her, and not only her sweet face and her gorgeous body. But never out loud. It was Paul who told her how much he liked her fashionable clothes and her changing hairstyles, and acknowledged her insightful contributions to their conversation—a case in point was when they talked about Darwin on that visit to Down House.

Best of all, Lucille Brown had a special quality that Walter himself lacked—he saw this clearly now. It was "social"—or should it be termed "emotional"?—intelligence.

Now he was exploiting her again, allowing her to comfort him when it was she who deserved to be comforted. He regarded her sad, lovely face, bare of make-up, and looked away. He moved out of her embrace and turned from her and swung his feet on to the floor.

"Stay where you are," she said. She got up and put on her dressing-gown and left the room.

He was ready to leave when she returned. He noticed she had applied lipstick and tidied her hair. He could not think what he should say to her, but he knew it had to be some form of goodbye. She had brought them mugs of tea and buttered scones. To his own surprise, he drank and ate greedily.

He said thank you and handed back the plate and the mug. Then, with an effort, he stood up to go.

"Lucille …"

"I know. There's no need for you to spell it out. It is really goodbye this time. No hard feelings. And perhaps we can stay friends?"

"Yes, of course. And thank you." He kissed her on the forehead when he left the flat.

As he drove back to his own part of Oxford he forced himself to make plans. Perhaps he could find a pleasant woman who didn't require too much commitment, with a background more like his own. Internet dating might be the way forward, after all; this was something to discuss with Paul. Walter needed some new undertaking to divert him from his prolonged mourning for Sarah and his regret for what he had done to Lucille.

CHAPTER SEVENTEEN

Online Dating: Lucille

"How about Internet dating? Now you've given up on that history man of yours, you've nothing to lose." Lucille had informed her friends she was no longer seeing Walter and refused to tell them anything more.

Lucille was with Annette and Jillie in the staff canteen. Internet dating was Jillie's suggestion. Jillie had been doing it for several weeks and she'd got so many dates she could hardly cope.

"Isn't it dangerous?" said Annette. "You never know who you might meet … a cheating husband, or a fraudster, or maybe even a mad axeman …"

"You could meet any of those at a dinner party in Oxford," Jillie protested.

"Rubbish. You've been watching too many *Morse* and *Lewis* programmes, Jillie. And anyway, how many dinner parties do *I* get to go to?" Lucille caught sight of Marcia Johnson with her clique from Human Resources and Accounts at their usual table at the far end of the canteen. She waved, and Marcia hesitated, then nodded back. Lucille remembered that rare invitation to supper and how awkward she'd felt and yet how excited to meet Walter Farquarson. She'd owed Marcia and Mike an invitation for so long that the idea had to be abandoned. Besides worry about the expense, she hadn't been able to face all the dilemmas—what food to serve, what wine to serve with it, and especially who else to invite.

Look forward, don't look back, she said to herself. She turned again to her own friends. "I've haven't had more than a couple of invites since I left Jason. No one needs an extra female." She paused, and added thoughtfully, "But the idea of being introduced to someone by a computer gives me the creeps."

"Don't knock it till you've tried it. Come round to mine after work and I'll show you the ropes," said Jillie. "And why don't you come, too, Annette? You might be tempted to try it yourself."

"But Jillie, haven't you got a date tonight?" said Annette.

"I'll text him an excuse. A sudden dose of flu."

"He might not believe you."

"So what? As you two will soon realise, there's plenty more where that came from."

They sat in front of Jillie's computer and Jillie demonstrated how to search for a date online. "Easy-peasy." She told the computer she was a woman in her forties seeking a man in his forties or fifties. Up popped rows and rows of grinning faces and little snippets of information: age, job, location, education. And marital status—a few were widowed, but the rest weren't all single or divorced, some were only separated, or even still married.

"Oh dear," said Lucille. "Most of them want a woman ten years younger than themselves. Under forty at least. What a nerve! There's still lots of choice for you two but not much hope for me, middle-forties, middle-aged."

"Yes, well, you may not be a spring chicken, exactly, but you're not that bad for your age," said Annette. "They'd be stupid to rule you out."

"Quite right," said Jillie. "You're well-groomed and well-preserved, so you're entitled to lie. Take five years off. You can get away with it. I'm thirty-five and you don't look any older than me. And here's another clever tip: if you sign in as a man you can find what you're up against by way of competition."

They did another search, this time pretending to be a man seeking a woman. The results came as a shock to Lucille. There were swarms of bubbly natural blondes and they far outnumbered the men.

Jillie wasn't fazed. She continued the lesson. "'*Fun-loving*' means up for it," she explained. "And '*gsoh*' means great sense of humour."

By the end of the evening, Annette had still not been tempted. Lucille, however, summoned up her courage, and that very night filled in the forms, produced an enticing profile, and uploaded her most flattering photo. Surely she'd be able to spot the cheats and the psychos? And she resolved not to take anything her dates said at face value.

Next day at coffee time, she told her friends she'd made a start.

"Please be careful," said Annette.

"Yes. Don't be too trustful," said Jillie. "Usual rules: meet in public places, make sure you can get home without needing a lift, and don't give them your address or your real name till you've met at least once. The dating agency lets you write to each other through their site, and you sign your messages with just your username. By the way, what is your username?"

"*Sue Bridehead.*" They were baffled, and she explained that it just came to her. It was the name of the feisty woman played by Kate Winslet in a film she had seen.

The others failed to get the reference, and she started to tell them the tragic story of Jude the Obscure and Sue Bridehead.

Annette interrupted her. "And why don't you keep us informed. Tell us who you're meeting, and where and when. We'll ring you on your mobile and you can have a code word for 'Not OK'. We could come and rescue you."

"You'd probably be too late to save me," she said, "but I suppose you'd be able to help the police to find my body and hunt down the murderer." Jillie laughed, but Annette shook her head and insisted that it wasn't funny.

Despite their protests, she assured them she'd be sensible, and she didn't fancy her friends tracking her every movement like a parcel on its way from Amazon.

To begin with, Lucille decided to be old-fashioned and wait for the men to make the first move. None of the first batch who got in touch looked attractive or posh, but when she'd read their profiles she judged that any one of them would be an improvement on her ex-husband Jason and his predecessor Luke. And they all claimed to have an income above average or at least to be comfortably off. There was nobody remotely like Walter Farquarson and she tried not to mind.

After they'd exchanged a couple of brief, bland emails and had three quite pleasant conversations on the phone, she went to meet the first one, *Old Curiosity* aka Will Elsworth. He lived in Oxford, but suggested they should meet at a café in Chipping Norton, one of her favourite small Cotswold towns. It made sense that Oxford residents would want their date to be outside the city so as to avoid being seen with a strange woman by people they knew.

She hated the way Will Elsworth eyed her up and down, but

this was something she would have to get used to. "You're even prettier than your photo," he said, and kissed her on both cheeks. She said thank you and commented on the attractions of the town.

"Yes, I often come here for concerts and the theatre, of course." He said this in a special genteel accent that reminded her of what she and Dad called Mum's "telephone voice". "And there are some excellent antique shops."

He talked on—about the deals he'd struck in the antique shops and how selling the items via eBay brought in nearly as much money as his proper job at an estate agent's. She smiled a lot and nodded and was disappointed and sad. He stretched across the table and said, "Give me your hand."

"What do you want it for?" she asked, but he didn't get the joke and just stared at her.

She suggested a walk through the town. It was too early to leave. Out of politeness she'd have to stay and have lunch with him. But this conversation was going nowhere.

They strolled down the hill to the large antiques market. She kept her hands in her jacket pockets in order to avoid all the pawing and clutching. He talked about the Internet dating experience. "I've been inundated." he said. "It's amazing how many delightful ladies want to meet me." And you're miffed because I don't appreciate my good luck, she thought.

"Oh. *I* haven't been inundated."

"To be fair, there are a lot more women than men on these sites." He sounded quite sorry for her.

Going round the antique shops only went to show how incompatible they were. Will Elsworth was looking for deals; Lucille was looking for pretty things, things she could afford, things that reminded her of her mother. Neither of them bought anything.

Lunch was a quick ham sandwich in a pub near the bus stop. Although he had come from Oxford by car, he did not offer a lift. He kissed her again on both cheeks and they agreed that meeting each other had been a pleasure. Then he said, "I wish you luck in the future." She didn't fancy him, but all the same it hurt to be so obviously though politely rejected. She was delighted when the Oxford bus arrived. They waved goodbye with smiley expressions that were really smiles of relief.

Her second date was a farmer. When she told them, her friends started to laugh. They competed with each other to suggest more and more reasons why it wouldn't work. "It's just not you, Lucille." "Wellies." "Driving a tractor." "Out in all weathers. Bad for your complexion." "And what a name! *Farmer Giles!*" Their shrieks of laughter were disturbing the other staff in the canteen.

"Rubbish. I'm talking *rich* farmer. Gentleman farmer. Nice clothes. Posh car—it's in the photos. And he says his income is above average. I can cope with the countryside as well as anybody. I once lived on a farm. And I've even got some green wellies."

Lucille remembered her old black wellies. Cold and smelly things. Squelching through the mud around the cottage. They were hard to run in, and that made you feel unsafe. And you had to shake them out before you put them on, for fear of spiders or wasps—Dad once got stung by a wasp in his boot while he was driving the tractor.

The others went on giggling and Marcia Johnson, passing their table, stopped to ask what was the joke. For an awful moment, it looked as though Jillie was about to tell, but Lucille cut her short with a fierce look and a sharp kick. Annette shrugged. "It's a long story." Marcia didn't stay to hear it.

Lucille and *Farmer Giles* (real name: Giles Brewer) met at a pub outside the city. Giles had a paunch, a big red face and small beady eyes, none of which had been detectable on the computer. A long, evil-looking dog followed him like a shadow. A lurcher, he said, name of Fly. It snarled when Lucille tried timidly to make friends, but settled down under their table and fell asleep.

Giles fetched drinks and when he had finished eyeing her up, sat and smiled at her, clearly at a loss for anything to talk about.

Lucille asked what sort of farming he did. She expected to have a conversation about different breeds of cattle or sheep or about corn or hay or perhaps oilseed rape.

"Chickens."

"Chickens?"

"Yes. I have one of the biggest egg businesses in the county."

"Oh … not battery hens?"

"Started out with battery hens. There's money in that. But the stupid European Union made me change to colony cages. These bleeding heart animal welfare types took away half my livelihood."

"Oh." Lucille always tried to be fair, not to judge people on just one piece of behaviour or just one attitude they held. But she knew there could be no happy-ever-after with a man who liked to imprison hens in tiny cages.

"I'm sorry. Should have said—I'm not able to stay for lunch, I'm afraid." Giles' face fell, and Fly the lurcher awoke and even wagged his tail, but she hurried away.

Next was *JimBoy*, the owner of a boutique in Reading. He said he was sure it was fate—he happened to be on the lookout for a clued-up sales adviser who was friendly and presentable. "You mean a shop assistant?" she asked.

And there was Edmund, who called himself *Prince Charming* and was high as a kite and wore green trousers and a Hawaiian short-sleeved shirt. He was either on something or had mental health issues. She felt sorry for him, but that was no good as a basis for a relationship.

Several who seemed suitable and nice were snapped up before they met her. One of these nevertheless kept the date they'd arranged and then announced that he felt committed to someone else already, but could they just be friends? "I feel we have lots in common and you can't have too many friends." (He wants me for his Plan B, she thought.) She was too polite to say no, but she managed not to say yes either. And when he wrote to her enthusing about a weekend in Barcelona with his new love, she didn't reply.

Finally, she met a sexy, cultured photographer. His username was simply *Michael C*, and he was the first, the only, person to recognise her own username *Sue Bridehead* as the name of the lover of Jude the Obscure. After they had visited an elegant stately home that featured in her favourite TV programme, lunched at a Michelin-starred gastro pub, and attended an exclusive and bewildering private view in a gallery, Lucille was beginning to think she had found a soulmate at last, and she started wearing her best underwear.

But the course of their romance was interrupted. She got toothache. Then she had a horrible experience at the dentist's. After several nasty jabs with the anaesthetic, the dentist set out cheerfully to do root canal treatment. But the pain from the drill was excruciating. She waved her hand and the drilling stopped.

The dentist said, "You have been given as much anaesthetic as you need. Just bear with me for a moment." His nurse murmured something meant to be soothing and patted Lucille's hand. The drill started again. She began to shake uncontrollably. She could feel her heart thumping. Her breathing turned into panting.

The dentist gave up. "You've worked yourself into an awful state. You've got to be sedated and I shall have to refer you elsewhere."

The sedation expert's fee was hundreds of pounds but she had no choice. Her legs were trembling so violently she could hardly walk to the bus stop.

Back home she collapsed on to her bed. The phone rang, and it was her new man. He asked how she had got on at the dentist's. She could have wept for gratitude—it was wonderful to have someone who cared about her like this; no one really had since her mother died. She told Michael the whole story.

An email arrived within minutes. From Michael. Her joy quickly turned to humiliation and then anger. *I have to cancel our arrangement to meet again. I can't cope with people who moan about their teeth.*

CHAPTER EIGHTEEN

Memories and Memoirs

"A lucky escape—you're well rid of him," said Jillie.

"Horrid man! No wonder he's still single," said Annette.

But the sensitive photographer had hurt Lucille almost as badly as the dentist's drill, and she kept wondering, could he be right about her? Was she a terrible whingebag?

It was some small reassurance that dentist number two, the sedation expert, X-rayed her teeth and declared that she was neither phobic nor coward—the first dentist had been drilling into an exposed nerve. But whingebag or no, she was back to square one, lonely and hard-up and losing hope.

The evening after her last dental appointment, Jason Brown rang. She took the call without thinking; she hoped it was one of the more desirable Internet daters who had changed his mind and wanted to see her. When she found it was Jason she lacked the strength to cut him off.

This time Jason persuaded her to meet him for a drink. Sallyanne ("the Slapper" Lucille called her in her head) had done a runner, he said, and he was on his own again. He sounded desperately keen to see her—"for old times' sake, baby girl"—and she desperately wanted someone to feel that way. He said he had something to hand over to her, something important she had left behind in their house when they split up. He refused to say what it was. "But I bet you'll be pleased." She couldn't think what it might be, but she hoped it was something valuable that she could sell.

Jason surprised her by suggesting that in case she was worried, they could meet at a pub, in daylight. She would not have said so, for fear of hurting his feelings, but she was a little afraid of him. It was reassuring that he had read her mind.

The Lamb and Flag was crowded that Saturday lunchtime. Jason had arrived before her and was sitting in a corner looking pleased with himself. He was sipping what seemed to be lemonade. A bag of plain potato crisps and a schooner of sweet sherry were waiting for her—he had not forgotten what she liked. Though it was only two years since she had run away from him, he seemed to have grown thinner, and more distinguished. She'd forgotten how handsome he was—he was nearly as handsome as Walter Farquarson. She liked his expensive new haircut, and his blazer and well cut flannel trousers were a lot smarter than Walter's old jacket and cords.

They talked about their work and their house moves. Jason said, "You must come and see my new place." It was a luxury detached executive property on a new estate, or "village development". Lucille had seen the estate from the bus on the way to Bicester Village and she'd read in the paper that some of those houses cost nearly a million. She did not say much about her own flat.

She already knew Jason's car sales business was prospering, but she listened politely while he boasted how his fortunes had changed since he had taken control of his drinking. She noticed he said "control" not "stop", though he also said he had joined Alcoholics Anonymous, and pointed triumphantly at his pint of lemonade.

If only he would get round to the main reason she had agreed to meet him—this thing she had left in their house. Unwilling to let him see her eagerness, she allowed him to talk on till she could bear the suspense no longer.

"I've got to go, Jason. Wasn't there something you were going to bring for me?"

"Oh, yes. Here's what I found in the loft when I was moving house." He lifted a plastic bag from under the table and took out a large square biscuit tin. The tin was battered and the picture on the lid was hard to make out, but she recognised it at once. Her mother had had it since the time of Charles and Diana's wedding and often it was empty, but in a good week it would contain digestives, sometimes even chocolate digestives. When she earned a fiver from her first job, helping the farmer's wife to pick strawberries, she had bought a new tin of fancy biscuits—custard creams and bourbons as well as chocolate digestives—and begged the old tin off her mother in exchange.

She was conscious of Jason watching her closely as she prised off the lid. His kindly expression reminded her of Christmases and birthdays when he had watched her opening presents from him. Inside the tin was a bundle of blue exercise books tied together with orange binder twine. She undid the bow. The print on the front covers said "*Holly Hill School*". Some were marked "*Property of Miss Mary Carter. Strictly Private and Confidential*" in large red letters, and others had a neat drawing of a noticeboard with the words "*Trespassers will be Prosecuted*." There were ten of them in all.

"You've read them?"

Jason grinned. "Sure. How could I resist? Impressed—you ought to write a book. Poor little cow, you had a tough time. Your dad was a right bastard, wasn't he?"

Talk about the pot calling the kettle black, she thought. "You know I don't like to discuss those times."

"OK, OK, baby, we won't. Don't get your knickers in a twist."

She took the bag, and put the biscuit tin with the notebooks back into it. "I have to leave now."

Jason grabbed her arm. "Please don't go. I haven't upset you, have I? Just one more drink?"

He looked so crestfallen that she felt sorry for him. She sat down again and he fetched more drinks. She asked how he had come to join Alcoholics Anonymous.

"Baby, I was sick of myself. It was the morning after a heavy session. My head ached and I actually flinched when the doorbell rang, and here were these two young men who seemed like twins, in smart dark suits with old-fashioned haircuts, wanting to bend my ear about Jesus.

"One of them gave me the once-over and said, 'You look crook, mate. You OK?' Aussies, you see.

"Missionary Number Two already had his foot in the door and I was too weak and ill and depressed to make a stand, so I let them in.

"Number One said, 'Can I put the kettle on?' and not long after I was drinking a cup of tea and telling my life story to a pair of Jehovah's Witnesses. Number Two kept trying to convert me, the other drew me out on the subject of the booze. He seemed to care what would become of me, didn't judge me, was trying to understand.

"As they were leaving, Number Two handed me a tract about God and when Number Two's back was turned, Number One slipped me a little card: 'Alcoholics Anonymous'.

"Five minutes after they'd gone, the doorbell rang again. It

158

was Missionary Number One. 'I've shaken off that preachy hyp-ocrite,' he said. 'Just wanted to tell you, mate: I'm an alcoholic, too—that's why I carry those cards. True, there's a bit of Higher Power stuff that comes with it, and I guess you won't care for that. But you know what? I used to be a bit of a gambler as well and now I'm just doing the safest gamble of them all. You may think it's kind of unlikely, but if there's a God you'll be quids in and you'll go to heaven. And if by any chance there isn't a God after all … well, you'll just be dead and it won't have done you any harm.'

"So I thought to myself, I won't bother with God, but I might give Alcoholics Anonymous a whirl."

Lucille laughed. She was beginning to remember what it was that had attracted her to Jason when they first met—the tales he told, his sense of fun, and a loveable openness, whether confessing his faults and failures or bragging about his achievements. Like Walter Farquarson, Jason was a great talker.

He proceeded to tell her about the resale value of several makes of car and the outrageous cost of spares, and the moment of fondness passed.

She pretended she was expected somewhere for lunch, and he wheedled a promise to meet him again soon. "Why did I ever let you go, baby?" He appeared to have forgotten that he sent her away with two black eyes and a nosebleed.

* * *

On the bus, Lucille was tempted to start reading the notebooks, but she feared she might start to cry and make a spectacle of herself, so she waited till she was inside her flat.

It was all there. The cottage on the farm. Being given a good thrashing. Her mum being knocked about. Her dog … And the happy moments, too, and the promises and the hopes. Her father meeting her from the late bus; the way he apologised for hitting her and Mum, and vowed it would never happen again; the bags of crisps he brought them from the offie along with his booze. Her mum and dad kissing and making up.

She read all afternoon and she thought how much it would have helped to hear a similar story from someone else. At the time she had believed what happened to her and her mum was their own unique bad luck. Or somehow her mum's fault. Their social workers seemed to agree with this idea. What caused women to hook up with violent men, their first social worker suggested, was some peculiar, unconscious need to be hurt or punished, dating back to their early childhood. The second social worker was more interested in what Mum said or did in the here and now that triggered, or rather provoked, the violence. This one insisted on private meetings with her mum to discuss what she called "intimate matters". Her father had refused to attend these sessions with the social workers, and he wasn't available when she and Mum were in the homeless B and B waiting for their council flat—by then he was gone for good.

The more Lucille thought about it, the more sure she was that there were at least three reasons for men abusing women and getting away with it: a) The men had anger-control issues, and drink made this worse, especially when they wanted to be the boss and believed they were being defied; b) The women had a poor opinion of themselves and thought these men were the best they could get; c) It was hard to leave because they still cared about their men, still hoped they might change, and they often had no money and nowhere to go.

She remembered how flattered she had felt when Luke Higgs asked her to marry him. The same with Jason Brown. Both times she knew beforehand that the man would be difficult to live with, but she believed she didn't deserve to marry anyone better. And she remembered what a struggle it was to make up her mind to get out—all those practical problems to do with money and housing. And perhaps most powerful of all: such stupid, stubborn fondness for the man and the hope that he would change.

Early, clumsy versions of these ideas came up in the notebooks along with her account of the Carters' home life. She had even written down the words of the Cathy Carr hit song her mother recited to her, about a woman who was going to change her man. The song went on to say the man was not really bad.

She didn't know whether her diaries were any good as writing. Probably not. Jason had said he was impressed, but who was he to judge? He was just cosying up to her, trying to make her forget what he had done to her and angling to get her back now that Sallyanne was gone.

But perhaps retelling all this in the right way could help some other person with the same kind of experience to feel less alone, or to deal with similar memories? And maybe make other people more sympathetic towards her mum and mothers like her, and explain the complicated feelings of children in families like hers? Lucille wished she'd had more education. If only she knew grammar and didn't make silly mistakes. If only she could write like … Thomas Hardy, or Sarah Scott.

She read through the notebooks again. The first entry told of waking in the night and being terrified at the sight of a dressing gown hanging on the back of the bedroom door, and hearing a vixen scream and thinking it was her mother. She had jumped out of bed and run to her parents' room to try and protect Mum, but found her parents fast asleep.

In places the writing was moving and quite vivid, she thought—but nearly every sentence followed the same boring pattern. A subject, verb and object: *Dad hit Mum. Dad hit me. I hugged Chips. Dad killed Chips.*

She had learned a little about grammar and figures of speech from Miss Morgan, an elderly lady who came out of retirement to teach English in Lucille's last two terms at school, after the free-and-easy younger teacher had left suddenly. Miss Morgan was strict and dull, and smelt of onions and eau de Cologne, but she was kind and she had tried to persuade Lucille to stay on at school after sixteen. Lucille and her mother had just moved into the council flat and it was hard to make ends meet. The idea of a job in a dress shop and earning her keep at last was more appealing than more exams and the remote chance of getting to uni.

Her writing style had changed after Miss Morgan came, and this could be seen in the later diary entries. Lucille could still recite the rules, Miss Morgan's rules. *1. Never start a sentence with "And" or "But". 2. Always connect up your paragraphs. You can say "However" and if you want to be adventurous, "Nevertheless" or "Furthermore". 3. Put in a nice adjective or adverb wherever possible. Or, even better, think of some clever similes and metaphors.* Reading it now, she could see her writing had become fussy and pretentious. The style was out of keeping with the story. After she came under Miss Morgan's influence, she had dreamt up some dreadful similes, for example, *The sky was as red as blood*; *Mum's face was white as a daisy*; *Dad's nose was like a strawberry*. And one or two metaphors as well: *Our kitchen was a boxing ring with just one boxer punching*; *Dad was a tiger in a temper*; and, in lighter mood, *My dog Chips is a great big pussycat*.

The following Saturday, Lucille went to see Helen and Rod. They were alarmed to hear that she had met up with Jason Brown again. "You should steer clear of that man," said Rod.

All the same, they were intrigued by the notebooks. Until now they had heard very little about Lucille's girlhood. Rod said, "It sounds like you have the perseverance and you certainly have the story. Maybe you could make something of it, a misery memoir? They have two whole shelves of them in Blackwell's."

Helen protested that only horrid cynics—usually men—used the term "misery memoir". "They're a 'memoir' or 'reminiscences'. I've even heard the term 'inspirational memoir'. There's a real hunger for books that help people to make sense of their own lives and the lives of others. A publisher might well be interested."

Lucille did not confess she had thought of this already. It seemed silly and presumptuous to imagine herself as an author, and surely only celebrity memoirs got published? Certainly not the schoolgirl scribbles of a nobody like her.

Helen went on, "Walter Farquarson may be able to advise. Why not show your notebooks to him?"

Lucille tried to hide her sadness. "Impossible. It's not exactly his kind of thing and anyway, we're not seeing each other any more."

"Oh dear ... Well, could you let Rod and me have a look at them?"

"No. Sorry."

"All right, I quite understand. If it was me I'd feel the same. Perhaps you should join a course on writing memoirs?"

"I wouldn't dare. I don't even exactly know what a memoir is. Is it the same as an autobiography?"

Helen fetched a book called *After You*. "Read this. It's a series of letters addressed to the writer's dead husband. It tells what it is like to lose the man you love and the father of your children, unexpectedly, when the two of you are still young. It's very sad, but it's uplifting, too."

On Sunday Lucille read *After You* in one sitting. The author had written it because she knew that many others had been bereaved as she was, and it might help them to know how it had been for her and her boys. Lucille thought, And helpful as well to people like me who have not had the same experience. As she read, she thought about Walter and his children losing Sarah.

CHAPTER NINETEEN

The Cemetery

Later that Sunday evening, Joan Wilson knocked on Lucille's door. "I didn't know what to do. I thought you might have some ideas." Joan had passed a young woman slumped on the pavement with her back against the cemetery gates. "She's crying her eyes out. I'm not sure whether she's ill or just upset about something. I didn't like to ask. I was afraid she might be a drug addict. They can be violent, you know."

"I'll go and see."

"Oh good. Thank you. You're sure you don't need me to come with you?" Joan obviously hoped she would be excused.

"No, it's fine." Lucille hurried down the street and across the main road. The woman was still there, sobbing loudly. A rucksack and a bunch of white roses lay beside her.

She stood up and seemed to be trying to read the sign on the gates, the opening hours.

"Excuse me. Are you OK?" Daft question.

More sobs. The young woman began to rattle the gates.

"My dear, the cemetery is closed for the night. Is there anyone you'd like me to call?"

"No. But thank you." The woman turned her head. Lucille recognised Walter's Rosie.

"Rosie, I'm Lucille Brown. Your father once brought you to my place for lunch."

"Oh. Yes."

"Come home with me. My street is just across the main road."

When Rosie had had a wash and was sitting in the lounge with a cup of tea and a scone, Lucille asked her if she'd like to make a phone call. "Your father, perhaps?"

"No. He mustn't know I wanted to visit Mum's grave—he'd hate to hear that. He never goes there himself and he doesn't like to talk about the grave or the funeral. But I should call John, my brother. We usually talk on Sunday evenings. I haven't got my mobile and I don't want him to start worrying."

When Rosie had finished the call, Lucille said, "Your brother's in York, isn't he?"

Rosie nodded.

"You'd better stay with me if you're not going to your dad's. You can go into the cemetery tomorrow morning."

"I didn't realise it would be closed. I came from Bristol specially. I wanted to put the flowers on her grave and talk to her … silly, isn't it?"

"Not at all. I lost my mum five years ago. When I was in trouble or had a hard decision to make, I used to go to the place where I scattered her ashes and talk to her. Of course, I knew she couldn't hear me or answer me, but it somehow helped all the same. Maybe it was just concentrating on her, remembering her, and trying to think what she would have advised."

"That makes sense."

"Let's put your mum's roses in water so they stay fresh for tomorrow. They're absolutely beautiful."

"Thank you." Rosie burst into loud, despairing sobs and came into Lucille's arms like a child wanting to be comforted.

* * *

Walter tried one more time to reach Rosie on her mobile phone. A man's voice answered. The accent sounded cultured, middle-class or maybe even upper-class. A term he'd heard so often in his childhood, "good family", came into his mind, and Walter for a moment felt reassured. Perhaps he and the boyfriend had more in common than he'd feared.

"May I talk to Rosie Farquarson?"

"May I ask who's speaking?"

"Walter Farquarson. Rosie's father. Please may I speak to her?"

"No. I'm afraid she isn't here."

"When will she be back?"

The voice changed. "Listen up, old chap, Rosie isn't your little girl any more. I imagine all those calls to the mobile were from you?"

"Yes. I've been trying on and off for weeks."

"It's mighty peculiar the way you keep wanting to talk to her."

"What on earth do you mean?"

"Do I have to spell it out? 'Unnatural' is the polite word for it." Before he could reply, Walter was cut off. Tense with anger and a sick feeling of anxiety, he tried to call again. The phone was left unanswered.

The following afternoon, for the first time since Sarah's funeral, Walter went to the cemetery. He couldn't find the grave. He tried in vain to picture himself walking to it for the burial. Sarah's coffin had been in front. Rosie had been on one side, John on the other, both of them silent, gripping his arms, none of them crying. He'd felt hot and uncomfortable in his new black suit. Other people had been with them, but he couldn't remember who they were.

Nor could he remember the funeral, except that St Nick's College chapel was crowded, with people standing at the back and more people outside listening to the proceedings through loudspeakers. John and Rosie had each managed to say a few words during the ceremony, and outside the door the three of them had said "thank you for coming" and shaken all the hands as the long line of well-wishers and mourners filed past. Sarah's coffin went into the hearse and he and their son and their daughter rode in a second car behind it. Then that walk to the burial.

After he had searched around and recognised nothing, he had to go to the cemetery office and find her name on a register and study a plan. When he found the plot he thought at first he must be mistaken; a bunch of white roses lay on the grave. He stared at the headstone. He'd ordered it and paid for it, but he had never seen it in situ. It read simply, *Sarah Scott, beloved wife of Walter Farquarson and mother of John and Rosie Farquarson. 1964-2011.* The roses mystified him. Maybe it was one of her devoted readers or someone who knew her through the rose growers' association? Whoever it was had even got the rose variety right—his own favourite, the one that had been named after her.

"The question is, Sarah," he said quietly, "should I try to see Rosie? Go to Bristol, even though I'm not welcome? Face the intimidating boyfriend?"

And he answered himself, If I don't make the effort to help her, I'll never forgive myself. It was obvious what he must do—he must go to Bristol and see her.

The roses and her books and his memories and their children … they were what remained of Sarah in this world. The flesh and bones under the earth were irrelevant.

CHAPTER TWENTY

The Creative Writing Course

The day after Rosie's appearance at the cemetery gates, Lucille kept worrying about the young woman, and wondered what had gone wrong between her and her father. She wished she could help. If only she and Walter had got together. They could both have been there for Rosie, who was obviously in serious trouble.

But there was nothing more to be done for Rosie, and she was glad of the distraction when Helen called in after work and brought her a brochure. It advertised a course on memoir writing, thirty sessions, on Wednesdays from six till nine. The fees came to several hundred pounds. Lucille decided to apply immediately before she lost her nerve. She had to submit a thousand words and wait to hear whether she would be accepted. Without wasting any time, she began to prepare her application.

She googled the tutor, Andrew Charlton. He was a thirtyish man with both a novel and a memoir to his name. She bought the memoir; it was in the Walton Street bookshop window in a display of books by local authors.

A deprived childhood. Hanging out with a gang on a council housing estate. An inspirational English teacher. Manchester University. A lot of sex. Gradual development of self-confidence.

Like the first memoir she'd read, this book did seem to have something life-changing to offer, some glimmer of encouragement, some holding out of a hand and saying "*You're not alone*" to people whose lives had been similar. And to those whose lives had been different, it said, "*Pay attention. This is what it's like.*" If she could do this for other people, especially young people, it would be the most worthwhile thing she had ever done.

These thoughts, together with encouragement from Rod and Helen, made her force herself to write. She began typing:

Introduction

No please please no. Sorry. So sorry. It feels like those were the first words I ever heard. The first words my parents taught me. Though I maybe wrong. Most babies learn to say Dada first dont they.

However this story begins where it begins in my diaries. After age 9. I've got 10 full school exercise books. So I dont need to have a good memory. Actully I could remember most things without the diaries, but maybe not the right order.

I know you are possibly not a teen ager reading this. However, I pretend you are one. Listen if Dad hits you or Dad hits your Mum YOU ARE NOT ALONE. You are like me. I am like you. I got through it. You can get through it.

However, You are awfully sorry for Dad. He had Frustrasion. anxiousness. Or he was born with a bad temper. Or it was the beer.

Nevertheless you probly feel sorrier for your Mum. I hope you do. You must not blame her. And do not let other people blame her. Its not fair.

After this introduction, she rewrote the first few diary entries, which told of their arrival at the farm and how happy the three of them had been and how her dad seemed to be a new man, keeping off the drink, working hard, and enjoying the fresh air.

She twisted the sentences round and made some of them longer. Soon she had her thousand words, and the computer corrected some spelling mistakes: *actully* became *actually*, *probly* became *probably* and *frustrasion* became *frustration*. The other long words, like *nevertheless* and *however* and *introduction* had been learnt from Miss Morgan. She considered asking Rod or Helen to check her work before she sent it in, but decided that this would be cheating. Anyway, if her writing didn't stand a chance, it would be best if she got rejected now.

They called her in for an interview. The small print had said they would do that in "*some cases*"—presumably candidates like her who might not make the grade. She wore her grey skirt and grey jacket and less make-up than usual, and put on her glasses in the hope they would make her look a serious, bookish person. She was terrified, and when the interview was over she could not remember what they had asked or what she had replied. She was told to wait outside, and soon the course organiser came and explained in a kind voice that if she was accepted she must work her way through a grammar textbook.

Two days later came a formal letter inviting her to join the class. To celebrate, Rod and Helen took her to Brown's restaurant and bought her *Teach Yourself English Grammar*.

* * *

Lucille was nearly late for the first session, because she had tried out three different outfits before she could leave home. What does a writer look like? she asked herself, and the only picture that came to mind was that photo of Sarah Scott in her dull skirt and shapeless jumper. She put on the black bubble skirt and the yellow top but these were already dated and apart from that, she now thought they made her look like mutton dressed as lamb on its way to a disco. Next she tried her velvet trousers and a big loose smock with her Italian silk scarf. Now she looked like someone who wanted to look like an artist; only the paintbrush and easel were lacking. In the end, she kept the scarf and settled for the plain skirt and jacket she had worn to her interview and to Walter's award ceremony. A serious, modest person with a little bit of creative flair frowned back at her from the landing mirror. That would have to do.

Her fellow students were a young male reporter with wild hair and wild eyes and a wide-brimmed leather hat which he never removed; two elegant businesswomen whose ages she couldn't guess; and three university people: a man with a black beard and a wedding ring, and two women, one old and slightly whiskery, and the other thirtyish but dressed like a teenager in tight jeans and a tee shirt with the name of a rock band on the front. They were already chatting to one another and setting up their tablets; several of the tablets were in those deceptive covers made to look like ancient leather book bindings with gilt letters on them. Lucille opened her crocodile handbag and took out her pretty new notebook and her new five-pound ballpoint pen with coloured birds on it. She realised she should have brought her laptop.

The tutor—she called him Mr Charlton and he told her to

say "Andrew"—asked them to introduce themselves and talk about why they had joined this class. Andrew had a northern accent like her own, and this made Lucille less afraid. All the same, she tried to avoid his eye, and she succeeded so well that she was the last to be called on.

Everyone else was well educated and successful, and their self-introductions made this obvious. They had all been published before. And they each already had an outline for their memoir, whereas she had nothing but a general idea, some memories, and a bundle of badly written diaries. But as she listened to them talk about their writing projects she realised there was more common ground than she had first thought. The topics were adoption (the woman lecturer), war (the woman professor), an air crash (the reporter), life with an Alzheimer's sufferer (the bearded academic), and growing up with two blind parents (one business woman). The odd one out was the second businesswoman's story about her late father who was a famous conductor. They all had what they called "a working title"— "*Somebody's Child*", "*Air Raid Baby*", "*Disaster*", "*You and Not You*", "*My Parents' Eyes*", and "*Daddy had an Orchestra*". She missed some of the detail because she needed to scribble a few notes before it was her turn to speak.

"My father had a drinking problem and he used to hit my mother and myself. I wrote about it in diaries at the time and I want to turn them into a book for young people." Unlike the others, she had nothing to say about structure, or tense, or working title, and she wasn't able to list any similar works or talk about her "prospective reader base" or "platform".

Andrew set them an exercise. "Just write a sentence or two explaining *why* you want to produce this memoir."

Lucille wrote quickly. When she raised her eyes from her notebook, she saw that all the others were still typing, or frowning or looking blank. Andrew called a halt and asked them to read out their efforts. Lucille was the only person who had finished; Andrew had noticed that and suggested she should go first.

"I want to reach out to young people who have had the same bad experiences as me. And tell them they're not alone," she read. "And explain why women like my poor mum stick with the men who beat them up and how they shouldn't be blamed."

"Who are '*they*'? The bad men? Or the women like your mum?" asked the reporter, with a sneer in his voice. His name was Marvin Burk and she couldn't help thinking that he deserved it.

Andrew ignored Marvin and said, "Excellent. And I'm sure you are going to do it by *showing* all this, not simply *telling* your readers."

Lucille nodded. She did not know quite what he meant, but the word "excellent" made her go pink.

There was a break at half-time. They went into a small common room with a coffee machine and chatted about coffee machines and lent each other change and complained about the coffee.

After ten minutes they came back into the classroom and discussed memoirs they had read, what they liked and what they didn't. Lucille spoke about *After You* and added that she had enjoyed Andrew's own memoir.

Marvin Burk burst out laughing. "Now we know who's hoping to be teacher's pet."

Andrew seemed embarrassed and said nothing, and it was a

relief when the bearded man said, "I've read your memoir too, Andrew. Can I be teacher's pet as well, or am I too old and ugly?"

Andrew urged them to read as much as they could in the style that appealed to them most or seemed closest to their own. For Lucille, it would be important to study material intended for the age group she wanted to write for, the teenage years.

Before each class, the students—Andrew insisted on calling them "writers"—were expected to email round two thousand words of their memoir and bring a written critique of each other's work to the following session. "And please, please back up your work," he added. "The only tears I've ever seen in this class have been when someone lost their manuscript."

When the class was over, Andrew suggested they all go to The Eagle and Child in St Giles. He said present-day Oxford writers liked to gather at The Eagle and Child, because it was the favourite watering hole of some famous authors of the past including JRR Tolkien and CS Lewis, who called themselves "the Inklings". They hoped to experience something magical, or at least beneficial, in the atmosphere. Besides which, he said, the beer was excellent.

They sat round the very table where the Inklings had sat, and talked about books till closing time. Marvin Burk stayed away, and Lucille was glad of that. The others turned out to be friendlier, and more like herself, than at first she had feared—a little lacking in confidence, excited, looking forward to the course.

Lucille felt much happier that evening, but not completely re-assured. Was signing up for this course really such a good idea? Second to the embarrassment of having to show her work to the tutor and her classmates, her main worry was the expense. She was shocked at the price of the tiny pink memory-stick she'd had to buy for the back-up. Luckily she now had her Kindle, and e-books were cheaper than paper ones, but e-books were harder to study closely. Though a tidy person normally, she liked to make pencilled comments in the margins of books and underline the important bits. Jason had found her doing this in *A Dress for Diana* and said, "Why not write your comments in biro? Then this daft book will be valuable when you're famous and dead."

She calculated she could afford to buy print editions if she did her grocery shop at the cut-price supermarket. After the course she could sell the books second-hand if she removed her pencil marks with a clean rubber.

* * *

Lucille worked with a dictionary and her new grammar book at her elbow, and wrote and rewrote and polished and agonised till the very last minute.

The other people's submissions impressed Lucille so much that she was almost too frightened to go to the second session. She sat up late the night before, struggling to put into words her reasons for liking what she liked, and what she felt was needed to transform her colleagues' good pieces into excellent ones. She dreaded having to give her opinion and hand over her written feedback to each person during the workshop part of the evening. She dreaded that almost as much as receiving their comments on her own work.

On Wednesday evening she was too agitated to eat the burger she'd bought for supper and had to stow it away in her handbag for later. The beefy smell leaked out and embarrassed her.

In the first half of the session, Andrew handed out a passage from Charles Dickens and they discussed why it was considered to be great writing.

Lucille never would have imagined she could be part of a discussion like this, and yet it turned out she was as quick as anyone else to pick out the magic phrases, the references and the echoes, and to appreciate the fine sound of the passage when it was read aloud.

During the break, the two university women and the older man told her how much they had enjoyed her piece. She thanked them and returned their compliments, and did her best to control her anxiety, breathing slowly, squaring her shoulders, and trying to smile. Andrew asked her where her story was set and told her a little about his own childhood in Yorkshire. The excitement of it all made her feel dizzy. If only her mother had been alive to hear about the lovely conversations with all these friendly, clever people.

She wished the break could have been longer. All too soon, they had to return to their places round the big table, and the second half of the session began.

Each person's homework, or rather "submission", was "workshopped"— everyone explained what they liked and didn't like and made suggestions for improvement. At the end, Andrew summed up and added his own comments.

When it was Lucille's turn, five of her colleagues said the same in different words. They admired her plain language, her directness, the way she launched into her story without a wordy introduction. But they all said her work required editing. Somehow it still had spelling mistakes in spite of the computer programme, and her grammar needed attention. Marvin Burk spoke last. He agreed with all their critical comments but he did not repeat any of the praise and he pushed his written critique across the table to her with a look that seemed almost hostile. Puzzled, she thought back to her comments on *his* work and could not understand why he should be annoyed with her, for she had loved *his* writing and said so.

When she got home from The Eagle and Child she studied the written comments on her submission while her burger was in the oven. Apart from Marvin, everyone had put lots of ticks and "*goods!*" in the margins.

But Marvin had written on a print-out of her work, in green biro, *This must be the least believable load of bullshit I've ever read. The child is an idiot and as for the mother who stays with this useless piece of shit, is she a half-wit or what? Plus you can't spell and your grammar makes you sound like a three year old. "I was sat on a wall"!!! And the dog—what's the point of the dog? How on earth did you manage to get accepted on this course?*

Lucille stared at it. She read it again. She reread the others' critiques.

She told herself that Marvin Burk was in a minority of one, that we always remember the bad things most clearly, even when they are just a tiny part of what has been said. She knew this from personal development reviews at work.

But that night she barely slept. She decided she would not have the courage to return to the class and wondered if she could claim her fees back.

The next evening, Lucille took a print-out of her submission and all the critiques to Rod and Helen's. While she pretended to read the newspaper, they worked their way through, reading together side by side, and passing the occasional comment:

"Lovely," "So moving," "Oh, that must have been terrible," and "Nicely put". Reading the complimentary assessments, they said "Spot on" and "Well deserved". Finally, at the bottom of the pile, they arrived at the note from Marvin Burk.

"You can't let him get away with this," Rod said.

"I'm going to leave the course. I can't face him again." Lucille told them she intended to ask for a refund. She asked if they would help her compose a letter to Andrew Charlton and the course organisers.

"Don't do that yet," said Rod. "First you must send this Burk fellow a dignified reply. And copy his comments and your reply to everyone else."

Dear Marvin

Sorry you don't like my work. You may be right about that. Lucille insisted on starting like this, although Rod said, "Don't give him the satisfaction."

But I do take exception to your personal remarks, especially about my mother. Providing feedback is not meant to be a blood sport. I am considering withdrawing from the course because I am not willing to go on sharing my work with you. She copied Marvin's comments along with her message.

Before she left for work next morning she had received emails from all the rest of the class. *Ignore him, He's got it all wrong, Poor you, You didn't deserve this.*

Andrew wrote, *As you know, I have already formed a high opinion of your work. I will speak to Marvin Burk in private and we'll begin our next session with a discussion about how to give constructive feedback.*

She was much relieved, though still nervous of attending the class with Marvin Burk present. That evening, an email from

Marvin awaited her. It was addressed to all the students, to Andrew, and to the head of the department. She thought it was going to be an apology.

I assumed this was a course for writers, not a remedial English class. I'm exceedingly disappointed in everyone's work (though Ms Brown's pathetic effort takes the biscuit. How can this person fancy herself as a writer?!) and I'm not impressed with our tutor's taste or judgement.

Lucille stared at the screen. After she'd read it several times she closed the email and opened her memoir, but she was unable to go on writing.

On Saturday Andrew phoned her. Marvin Burk had "overstepped the mark" and he'd been "invited to withdraw from the course."

She wrote to Andrew later that day to plead with them not to make Marvin forfeit his course fees. It had occurred to her that there must be some unhappy reason for his harsh reaction to her work, and his bitterness. She wondered if he had himself suffered or witnessed abuse.

The course organisers wrote to thank her for her "*measured response to this unfortunate incident*" and Helen and Rod encouraged her to get on with her memoir. This she did. She managed to circulate another thousand words and to read her colleagues' submissions in time for their next session.

While the group was assembling, she received hugs and sympathy and more praise for her work. They held a brief inquest. Andrew assured them over and over that the class was a safe place, that they were to feel supported, that nothing like the Marvin Burk incident had ever happened before. By the time he had run out of things to say he was red in the face. He's a marvellous writer and teacher but he's not a therapist, Lucille thought.

It was a relief to return to their studies. They examined a passage about making breakfast in James Joyce's *Ulysses*.

CHAPTER TWENTY-ONE

Online Dating: Walter and Paul

Walter knew that, like himself, Paul was interested in meeting unattached women. After he'd treated Paul to a splendid St Nick's College dinner, and they were both mellowed with a glass of vintage port from the supply in his room, he felt relaxed and un-embarrassed enough to raise the subject of online dating. It was a relief to learn that Paul had investigated already. Paul said, "If we dare to entrust ourselves to the Internet, I propose we sign with one of the more exclusive agencies. I've found one for Oxbridge and Ivy League graduates only, or if you don't mind slumming it a little, there's another one for graduates of any university."

"Really, Paul, I didn't think you could be such an intellectual snob. You're joking, aren't you?"

"Yes and no. Well, not entirely. I suppose I want to find someone with a decent education and these two agencies ap-parently check out people's degrees. It means one thing less to worry about—there are plenty of other important variables. And, yes, before you point it out, I'm perfectly aware that lots of lovely, bright women don't have a degree. Your Lucille, for example."

"She's not 'my Lucille'. Never was. But all the same …" Walter didn't quite know what point he was trying to make.

Paul continued, "It's like university admissions—a set of good A-levels just acts as a useful, timesaving filter. If we insist on three As, it means we miss some able young people, but at least we are not stuck with unhappy students who can't go the distance."

"I'm not sure I like the analogy, or perhaps it's just the way you put it."

Paul explained that the dating agencies match people according to what they say about themselves and what they are seeking. Paul wanted someone like himself and like his late wife Elizabeth. A wildlife enthusiast, with a sophisticated sense of humour, and well read with a preference for the classics over modern fiction. Paul also wanted her to have the same leftish political loyalties, and a similar level of attractiveness to his own—that is, not a stunner, just acceptable. Not a lot shorter and not taller than himself, close to his own age, and preferably childless. "'Opposites attract'" is a great big nonsense," said Paul firmly. "There's research to prove it."

"Then why did you try to persuade me into a relationship with Lucille Brown?"

"As I'm sure I've said before, Lucille's exceptional."

"Well, anyway, I think the research is wrong," said Walter. "At least for our age group it's wrong. I'll grant you, Sarah and I were similar in many ways, but I'm not searching for another Sarah. I know I'd never find anyone like her again. But what we want at this stage in our lives is the joy of discovery, the thrill of the new. And of course, decency and warmth. And sexual attractiveness."

"That's quite a lot, and it's pointless to *ask* for those qualities—everyone on these dating sites claims to be decent and warm and sexy. But do at least stipulate a university degree. And age forty to fifty, presumably?"

"Yes, all right." Walter's doubts persisted.

"You're still hankering after Lucille Brown. She meets all your criteria."

"Stop talking about Lucille Brown. But it's true—I certainly don't want to be restricted to a particular social class."

"And what do John and Rosie think?"

"I wouldn't dream of discussing this with them. It's none of their business."

Walter shuffled the papers on his desk. Any mention of Rosie reminded him of his resolve to visit her in Bristol and his cowardice in not doing so. He half wanted to discuss this with Paul, but he was too ashamed.

He forced himself to focus on the question of Internet dating and social class. "You remember, we sent them to private schools. Sarah was against, but I insisted. I saw it as giving them the best possible chance in a competitive world. Now I can see that a state school might have served them better."

"Made them less snobbish, you mean?"

Walter was annoyed. He himself might sometimes call his children snobbish (he had called Rosie that after the lunch at Lucille's), but no one else was allowed to. "No. But they've been cocooned, they're unfamiliar with the lives of less advantaged people. They're somewhat naïve, perhaps."

"You went to a private school yourself, didn't you, Walter?"

"Yes. What are you implying? That I've been cocooned as well?"

Paul nodded. "The words 'cap' and 'fits' come to mind."

"Sarah was at a state school, though."

"Walter, this isn't about Sarah, you know."

"Well, yes, it is. I have to face it—this is my problem. Everything is about Sarah in the end … Enough of that! All right, Paul, I'll insist on a degree. Does that satisfy you? But I'm going to use the biggest agency, *partnersforall*. They have thousands more customers on their books than those other two."

Walter signed up with *partnersforall* and Paul chose *camfordblues*, the more exclusive of the graduates-only sites. Both of them were surprised and pleased, then somewhat alarmed, as the messages poured in. "It feels like an invasion," Walter said. The work of examining these and responding to all the eager women threatened to interfere with their academic responsibilities.

Paul, after initial consternation, began to enjoy checking out his matches. He restricted himself to women who lived in or near Oxford, and crafted an untruthful and kindly no thankyou letter to those who seemed incompatible. He wished the woman well and said how charming she sounded and how attractive she was, but he'd just met "*that special person*" and already felt committed. He ranked the rest and held phone conversations with them in order of desirability. Then, without further ado, he began bravely inviting the most promising ones for coffee in Blackwell's bookshop. He reported to Walter that it was great fun and he was meeting a host of delightful, well educated women of his own age.

One day Walter came upon Paul with one of his dates in the café at Blackwell's. Wanting to be tactful, he pretended not to see them, even when Paul beckoned him to join them. Afterwards, Walter remonstrated with him. "Aren't you embarrassed to meet in a place where there's every chance you'll be spotted by colleagues or, worse still, by your students?"

"And why should I be embarrassed?"

Walter didn't really know why and therefore couldn't explain.

Because his criteria were so much looser and his agency *part-nersforall* had many more clients on its books, Walter got more approaches than Paul. He was glad of the agency's ready-made "*courteous refusal*" pro forma. It was two weeks before he dared to email some of the matches and talk to them on the phone, and another week before he arranged rendez-vous, always outside the main university district. He tried not to think of the women as candidates and the meetings as interviews.

Walter experienced a surprising number of no-shows, proportionately far more than Paul. He began to wonder if they were scrutinizing him surreptitiously, peering through the pub or café window and deciding against him without even saying hullo. Walter was baffled. Admittedly, the photo on his profile was indistinct, but surely he looked acceptable, well preserved, even, for a man in his late forties?

"The way you hide your face behind an academic history journal may produce a daunting impression," Paul commented helpfully. "Wouldn't it be more strategic to be found reading the *Independent* or *Private Eye*?" Walter followed this advice, and it did seem to make a difference.

Walter did not receive any explanations from the no-shows and rejected Paul's suggestion that he contact them again to enquire why they had changed their mind.

One whose reasons were clear was Miranda. He liked her profile, which was thoughtful and self-deprecating, with a photo which showed a pretty, slender woman half-hidden behind an extremely large dog. Even over the phone he could tell she was painfully shy. After he said something, she would leave such a long pause that he would speak again and they would end up talking simultaneously. She apologised for this, and for everything else—her late phone calls, her early phone calls, for being out when he rang, and for any gaps in her profile that he invited her to fill in. Whenever he asked a question she apologised for the fact that she hadn't already provided the answer. Miranda phoned to cancel their meeting at the last minute and when he asked why, she said she couldn't go through with it, she had realised that Internet dating was not for her. When he tried to reassure her, she muttered, "Sorry. Goodbye," and he was sure she was in tears.

Another cancelled date was with Jennifer, who was separated, divorce pending. She sent an email. *My husband has reappeared and asked for another chance. It would be wrong not to try.* She apologised.

After seeking Paul's advice, Walter replied, *I don't know you or your husband, so forgive me if I'm being presumptuous—but I do agree with you that everyone deserves a second chance. People can change, I think. And even if your attempt at reconciliation fails, at least you will know that you have tried your best.*

Jennifer wrote back to thank him for being so understanding and he was embarrassed because his kind letter had been entirely Paul's idea.

A third Internet match, with Corinne, did lead to a meeting. But this was after many failed appointments, postponed because of Corinne's duty to provide childcare for her two sets of grandchildren. The woman was quite attractive, but she talked of nothing but the six children, brought a big envelope stuffed with photos, and made him look at dozens more on her mobile phone. After she had gone—she had to rush in order to collect three children from two different schools—he realised she had not asked whether he had children or grandchildren, or indeed anything about him. Apart from comments about the photographs—and all he could do was to repeat bland compliments like "charming!", "how sweet!" or "he looks a tough little fellow!"—he'd hardly got a word in edgeways. He and Corinne did not contact each other again.

After a month Walter was on the verge of giving up. Internet dating helped to mitigate his loneliness and distract him from his increasing worry about Rosie and his failure to go to Bristol and confront the situation. But he concluded that the dating was a waste of his own time and that of the hopeful, decent women he found on the screen of his PC.

CHAPTER TWENTY-TWO

Money and other troubles

The payments to the Internet dating agency were adding to Lucille's money troubles. Having summoned the courage to take a close look at her credit card account—she had almost developed a phobia of accounts, like her phobia of the scales when she'd put on weight in her teens—she regretted nearly every damned thing on the list. She regretted the Greek holiday—all it had given her was a reminder of how enjoyable sex can be and a genital wart. And she regretted the costly components of her two makeovers, the new clothes that Walter hadn't noticed or hadn't liked, and the two sets of expensive cosmetics. The only items she still considered reasonable were the "maintenance" ones, the skin care, hair care, and dental work. She wasn't sure whether the online dating was a good investment or not. So far it had only meant more expense—paying her share of meals, and bus fares to meeting places, on top of the monthly fifteen-pound membership.

She had paid for the memoir writing course in advance, so at least she did not have that to worry about. She was now reading hard and writing hard every spare moment of the day and late into the evenings. She mentioned Andrew Charlton such a lot that her friends teased her about those two old films *My Fair Lady* and *Educating Rita*, where the main characters were a posh, educated man and a working-class, uneducated woman. But Andrew Charlton was not in the least like Professor Henry Higgins or Dr Frank Bryant. He was professional and a little distant, and when he praised her work she was fit to burst with pride and delight.

She had long since dropped out of the Saturday lunches, but she sometimes went to Helen's for coffee on Saturday mornings. Only to Helen could she confide her growing doubts about personal shopping as her career. Sometimes she sensed a kind of emptiness at the heart of her work. And yet again, wasn't fashion an art form like any other?—and wasn't it a joy to show off beautiful clothes, like hanging paintings in an art gallery? And to bring a little more happiness and confidence into women's lives?

These rather idealistic considerations aside, without her salary she would be in terrible trouble. She had begun to suffer money-related nightmares. In one that recurred five times over five nights, she was lost and penniless, walking the streets of a strange city, going from one cash machine to another, and every machine spat out her card.

Although she was usually very down-to-earth and practical, Annette believed dreams could foretell the future. When Lucille told her about the cash machine dream, they were sitting in their room with nothing to do, because their eleven o'clock customers had both cancelled. Annette interpreted the dream as a warning of money troubles to come.

"Money troubles for you, Lucille, and possibly for Richley's as well."

"Why for Richley's?"

Annette said Lucille must have noticed that customer

numbers were down on last year, and the ones they did see bought less than they used to. "You've been thinking about that subconsciously."

Lucille let this piece of nonsense pass. "It's true, that last lady didn't buy anything. I think she comes to us for ideas and then buys similar clothes online."

"I know her," said Annette. "The poppy she was wearing— I'll bet it was recycled from last year. She's the sort of person who saves her poppy to avoid contributing to the British Legion every November."

* * *

In late November Lucille received a summons to an appointment with Marcia Johnson at the Human Resources office. It came in a letter to Lucille's home address, and it began "*Dear Lucille Brown*" and was signed "*Marcia L. Johnson*".

When Lucille arrived at her office next day, Marcia looked solemn. She said "Good morning" formally, as though she had never had Lucille to supper at her house.

"We've received disappointing financial information from Head Office." Marcia had obviously been trained to drip-feed bad news so that the unlucky employee could prepare herself to receive it with dignity, without making a scene.

Lucille said nothing and looked straight at Marcia, who sat behind her desk with her chair pushed back as far as it would go. "Yes," Marcia continued. "As I'm sure you are aware, we've had very poor sales in the last four quarters, and the organisation has had to make some tough decisions as regards staffing. I expect you can guess what this means."

A pause. Marcia shuffled her papers. "Redundancies, I'm afraid. And Personal Shopping has to take its share."

Another pause. Lucille breathed in deeply and tried to relax the muscles throughout her body. She still said nothing.

"So … I'm sorry, Lucille. Your position is one of several that have to go." Marcia hurried on. "After your month's notice has expired, we can offer you a temporary sales position if you're still looking around. Maybe you can find something at one of those big stores in Milton Keynes? We'll give you a first-rate reference. And severance pay, of course. Don't worry, I'll put all this in writing."

"I see. Thank you." ("*Don't worry*", indeed!)

"I know this is a lot to take in. I'm going to let you go now and you can come back and see me when you want to discuss all this further."

After applying to every department store within feasible travelling distance—Milton Keynes, High Wycombe, Reading—Lucille explored possibilities in London. She found several vacancies, but when she saw the salaries and did the sums she concluded that a move to London was out of the question, and so was commuting.

Christmas was spent with Joan Wilson. A repeat of the previous year—same food and drink, same conversation topics, same sadness when she was alone again in her flat. She didn't tell Joan about her problems.

Early in the New Year she lost the sales position at Richley's too. She found a temporary job at a newsagent's.

* * *

The mortgage was no longer affordable. The Citizens Advice Bureau couldn't suggest a solution. She put the flat on the market and it was quickly sold, but for a figure that only just paid off the mortgage.

The sale was conditional on immediate vacant possession. On the day she left, in the early morning, she put a note in Joan Wilson's pigeonhole: *Sorry not to say goodbye. I'll let you have my new address in due course.* And as an afterthought she added, *Would be grateful if you don't mention my move to anyone—I'll explain when I see you.* She was deeply ashamed and did not want Walter to hear what had happened, and she was confident that Joan, though puzzled, would do as she was asked. She was glad Joan had never known that she and Walter had been an item—if indeed they ever were.

And so Lucille ended up at Jillie's one-bedroom flat. Jillie also took in Cleo the cat and eight black bags full of clothes. Lucille sold some of her furniture and rented storage space for the rest, plus five packing cases filled with household effects.

Jillie's routine was disrupted. She was not used to sharing a bathroom with another woman and she needed a long time in the bathroom for the elaborate make-up session in the morning that she said was part of her job. "A beautician is a living advert, you see, just like a personal shopper. They ought to pay me for the time I spend in front of the mirror."

Jillie's latest boyfriend Geoff—her best Internet find, she called him—stayed over several nights a week and now he had to be asked to bring his dressing gown. When Jillie mentioned that she and Geoff liked to roam the flat with no clothes on, Lucille said, "Too much information," and felt embarrassed.

Lucille slept on the couch with Cleo. Although the couch was comfortable, she slept badly. This was mainly because of her worries about the future and grief over the loss of her flat, but another reason was that she could hear Jillie and the boyfriend making love. Lucille herself could be noisy during sex, but it was always intentional, as a way of expressing her appreciation. She'd read that some women couldn't control themselves. When she and Jason stayed with Jason's rather crude cousin Zena, the cousin had said to her after only short acquaintance, "Make as much noise as you like," and actually winked. Had Zena interpreted the silence in the night as meaning that she was frigid?

Now she wondered what was normal and whether Jillie's half-stifled cries were deliberate or not. And she disliked herself for wondering. Was she becoming obsessed with sex, especially her own lack of it and other people's imagined plenty (or not imagined, but real, in the case of Jillie and Geoff)?

She had to move out, and she devoted half her spare time to job-hunting and the other half to seeking somewhere else to live. A vacant bedsitter was impossible to find in this city with two universities, and opportunities to share were few. Her age counted against her.

The first time she managed to get a meeting with potential housemates, it was worse than a job interview. The three women were younger than her, and on their way up the career ladder. They showed her into their stuffy lounge and sat in a row on their couch while she sat in front of them on a hard chair. They looked her up and down as though it was Internet dating, and fired a volley of loaded questions. "Where did you go to university?" "What did you read?" "Have you got a boyfriend?"

They even asked about her car. What make, and where would she park it? "I cycle or go by bus," she said, and tried to sound proud of that fact. "You don't need a car in Oxford, and I try to be as green as I can." Doubtful nods.

And finally they asked about her job.

"I'm a fashion consultant ... between jobs at present." She could see this impressed nobody. "And I'm on a course." They did not bother to ask what sort of course.

"You'll understand we have other people to see. Thank you for coming. You'll hear from us by the end of the week if we decide you're the right person."

She had four similar interviews and never heard back from any of them.

Lucille was in a bad way. She was growing more and more fearful of the future. She suffered from loneliness, and she hated to think she was going to be without a partner for the rest of her life. And Jillie, kind though she was, could do nothing to help. With the boyfriend taking so much of her time and attention, she was not available to listen to Lucille's worries. And both she and the boyfriend clearly wanted Lucille gone.

Where could she turn for a remedy?

* * *

She wondered about Jason, the new improved Jason, and finally agreed to spend a weekend with him in the grand house he had bragged about. Any port in a storm, and at least she'd be out of Jillie's hair for two days. And though she didn't say so to Jason, she thought of it as a trial weekend. Assuming Jason really had got over his drink problem, he could offer at least some of what she needed. Top of her list: a place to live and financial security. She must put aside her silly romantic ambitions.

Jillie's bread-maker broke down and Lucille went to the storage depot to fetch her own. While she was hunting for the bread-maker, she came across *The Singing Butler*. She removed it and donated it to Oxfam. As she took one last look, she realised she hadn't missed it and no longer dreamed of servants or a beach or an elegant man. In fact, she didn't much like the picture any more—it now seemed shallow and crude and more like an advert than a proper work of art.

Jason picked her up in his large black BMW. He opened the passenger door and out leapt the biggest, fluffiest German Shepherd she had ever seen.

"This is Millie. Millie, this is Lucille." The confident, affectionate dog capering around in front of her seemed evidence of Jason's reformation.

After they had greeted one another, Jason opened a rear door. "Back seat now, Millie." Millie obeyed instantly and lay down thumping her tail.

"My deputy got her from the German Shepherd rescue people. They said she would make a good guard dog but it was a lie. She would just wag her tail at intruders, wouldn't even bark. So we had to fire her. But I couldn't bear to send her back—she's my best mate."

Half an hour later they were at the house. Lucille was amazed at the sheer size of it. And there was a shiny cream and black kitchen, a lounge that opened on to a garden with a water feature, a separate dining room, and a TV room with a flat screen that covered most of one wall. "This was the show house," said Jason. "I bought it complete with furniture."

Like a gentleman, he picked up her suitcase and led her upstairs to her room. At first, she was confused—it looked as if it was the master bedroom. It had a double bed and an en suite bathroom, yet it seemed to be unoccupied. "Is this your room?" she asked, and wondered what to say if the answer was yes.

He chortled. "Baby, I can guess what you're thinking. Don't worry. This is one of the spare rooms. I don't want to rush you but if you do feel like sharing my bed, be my guest. It's just next door. I still fancy the pants off you, you know. I'll leave you to think it over. Come downstairs when you've settled in."

As soon as she was on her own, Lucille investigated the en suite, as excited as she was when she stayed in a hotel. The shower was in a "wet room," the first she'd ever seen. No shower curtain or screen. Gleaming green and blue tiles. A bewildering range of sprays at different levels. Gold or gilt taps on the cream whirlpool bath.

Jason had supplied her favourite jasmine gel and talc, and a brand new, real sponge. In the bedroom she found a fluffy blue towelling robe and matching fluffy slippers. There was a TV on the wall for watching from the bed. It was like a posh hotel.

Plain oven crisps and sweet sherry were set out on the occasional table in the lounge. She noticed a photo of their wedding on the shelf above the fire. Supper was served in the separate dining room on a table made entirely of glass. It was Moroccan Spiced Harissa Chicken, a gourmet ready-meal from the freezer-food shop in Summertown, lemon meringue pie to follow, and white wine for her and fizzy water for him. He refused to let her help clear up afterwards. "You're my guest, baby doll."

Jason offered a choice of three liqueurs to go with the coffee. Limoncello she had first tasted on her trip to Italy; it had helped to console her after the break-up with Jason, and the bottle she brought back had been a hit with the guests at her last dinner party, the one that Walter had come to. The Amarula came from South Africa—it was made from cream and a fruit that makes elephants tipsy, Jason told her. And from Canada, whisky and maple syrup liqueur. Jason had been to all three countries since she left him.

Because she couldn't decide between them, he poured her a small glass of each liqueur and while he was doing this she wondered who had drunk three-quarters or more from each of the three bottles. Sallyanne, perhaps. Or perhaps he'd been doing a lot of entertaining. She was about to ask when an unpleasant, jealous thought struck her— had he taken Sallyanne on these trips to Italy, Canada and South Africa?

They chatted about Italy and holidays and Lucille felt increasingly relaxed—almost back to how she had felt when they were happy together and enjoying a quiet evening after a successful day at the car showroom. She said casually, "Was Sallyanne with you on those holidays you mentioned?"

"Only Italy. We finished soon after."

Perhaps he could read the question from her expression, for he went on, unasked, to tell her why. "I couldn't trust the woman. Awful, it was."

"How did you know you couldn't trust her?"

"Late home time and again, pretending she'd been to the movies with her mates. When I tested her on the film she said they'd seen, she never put a foot wrong. Knew the story and the names of all the actors."

"Well, then …"

"Don't you get it? She'd obviously read up about the film in the papers or online, to make sure I wouldn't catch her out."

Lucille was confused. The three liqueurs were muddling her brain.

Jason went on, "When I phoned her girlfriends to check on her they always backed up her story. The last straw was at a party at work—somebody's birthday—and I could see she was smiling at the birthday boy in a special way ... I'm sorry to say I lost it—well, it was the booze made me hit her. She did a runner the next day."

The whole evening Jason did not touch a drop of alcohol.

She got up to go to bed. He had made no moves and she was half-disappointed. He gave her kiss on the cheek. "Goodnight, sleep tight, baby. I'll just watch the end of the footie," he said.

When she was ready for bed, she put on the robe and went to the landing and listened. The football noise was still going on. She went to the next-door room and peeped inside. A room just like hers, big and luxurious. But she noticed a faint, strange smell—some sort of aftershave perhaps? No, a sweet, peaty odour. She brushed a suspicion aside. Probably the smell was her own liqueury breath.

In bed, Lucille intended to go over in her head all the pros and cons of returning to Jason. She dropped off while she was still listing the pros and hadn't got beyond "no need to shop at cut-price supermarkets."

After the weekend—four slap-up meals at grand restaurants and a shopping expedition to Bicester Village, where Jason bought her some red shoes with amazing high, spikey heels—Lucille began to be optimistic about a future with Jason. But she decided she should take things slowly.

On the Sunday evening, less than an hour after he had dropped her off at Jillie's, he telephoned. "Now you've had a taste of what I've got to offer, why don't you come back and share it, baby?"

"Give me time."

"What's stopping you? You've seen how well I have the booze under control. Did I tell you I'd joined Alcoholics Anonymous?" Surely he couldn't have forgotten their conversation in The Lamb and Flag? And AA members were not supposed to take any alcohol at all, she remembered; they didn't believe in "controlled drinking." She knew this from her father's brief, unsuccessful stint as an AA member.

"Can we wait to decide till after I've finished my writing course?" In the meantime she would go on hunting for somewhere to live and another job, and concentrate on her memoir.

CHAPTER TWENTY-THREE

The Bookshop

Lucille went to the bookshop in Walton Street, a place she had grown to love in the few weeks since she began the memoir course. She enjoyed seeing Frank Booth, the friendly bookseller/host, and trying one of his fifty varieties of tea. Frank helped her to select books and often joined her when she sat down at one of his three small café tables.

She had quickly overcome her dislike of wall-to-wall books, and no longer felt intimidated by them. She was reading other people's memoirs, and books intended for teenagers, or "young adults" as they were called in the publishing world. Andrew Charlton had explained that she needed to get a feel for the sort of writing she herself aimed to produce.

* * *

Walter met Paul at their favourite bookshop for their weekly tea and browse session. They showed each other their finds. Frank Booth had located two books on the Civil Wars that Walter did not know of, and a collection of eighteenth-century prints that Paul had been seeking for months.

They were quiet, munching Frank's chocolate fudge cake and leafing through their purchases. Frank could be heard talking in low tones to a customer at the back of the shop. The other voice was a woman's. The woman suddenly shouted, "Oh Frank, thank you. And here's another one—"

There followed a series of thuds, and a tower of books came cascading down and skittered across the floor. And here was Lucille Brown, scarlet in the face, muttering apologies, bending to pick up the fallen books and dropping some again because she had tried to lift too many at once. What on earth was Lucille Brown doing in a bookshop?

Paul, who was sitting opposite Walter and facing the street, said, "Is that who I think it is?"

Walter whispered, "Be quiet. I don't think she's seen us. Do you mind if we go?"

But they couldn't go because they hadn't paid. Paul, annoyingly, ignored Walter's embarrassment and called, "Hullo, Lucille. Come and join us. Help us finish the chocolate cake."

She said, "Oh yes, thank you. I'd love to," finished piling books on to Frank's desk, and went to choose her cup. An original tradition at Frank's—some thought it charming—was for customers to pick their own cup from a selection as eclectic as the bookstore itself. Walter observed that Lucille chose a dainty bone-china cup and saucer with gilt rims and delicate painted roses.

* * *

Frank took her usual order for Earl Grey tea, and Lucille smiled at Walter and Paul and asked how they had been. Walter still said nothing. Lucille saw his mug had "*TS Eliot The Waste Land*" on it and Paul's had "*The Pickwick Papers*."

Paul replied for them both. "Last term was tough. The powers that be reviewed the History Department and Walt here had a lot to do with our brilliant showing. As well as that prize-winning book, he's published a torrent of articles and got absolutely glowing reports about his teaching. Hard to believe—but his students adore him." Lucille smiled at Walter, but he seemed to be avoiding her eye. Paul chattered on; she could see that even he was finding it hard to cover for Walter's unfriendly silence.

Walter went over to Frank, who was building a new tower with the books Lucille had knocked down. "Can I pay you now?" He returned to the table and spoke to Lucille for the first time. "Please excuse me. I have to go back to the department. I'll leave Paul to entertain you."

Trying to smile as if she didn't care, Lucille said goodbye and turned to Paul again. He asked about the books she had just bought and she told him about the memoir writing course. She hoped he would pass her news on to Walter. Even though they were no longer seeing each other, she longed for Walter to know she was improving herself.

She asked if Paul had any news of Walter's children. "They're OK as far as I know. Rosie's doing a master's now—but you knew that, I expect. She causes Walter a fair amount of worry, sometimes doesn't ring him for weeks—she never used to be like that. At least John keeps in touch regularly. He will graduate next summer. First-class degree on the cards, like his sister."

Paul suddenly remembered he was due to lecture in fifteen minutes' time. He leapt to his feet and bundled a pile of loose papers, his reading glasses, his scarf and his new book into his overstuffed briefcase.

After he had left the shop, Lucille picked up a single sheet of paper which had fallen under the table beside Paul's chair. She rushed after him but he had disappeared. She hoped it was not part of his lecture notes, and glanced at the top of the page. It was a woman's profile from an Internet dating agency, one with a name she did not recognise. If Paul was doing it, was Walter doing it too?

When she got home, she sat miserably in front of her computer for an hour. She googled the name of Paul's dating agency, *camfordblues*, and tried an experiment with this agency's search options. She specified a desired age limit of fifty-three; then she entered an improved version of her own profile, awarding herself an imaginary BA in English Literature from Newnham College, Cambridge. Walter did not turn up; nor Paul, for that matter—but Paul, she remembered, was ten years older.

She logged in to her own dating agency, *partnersforall*. She adjusted her profile details—a long shot, for there were so many agencies, but *partnersforall* was one of the biggest, best-known ones. This time the computer delivered profiles of some twenty pleasant-looking men, and among them was Walter, calling himself *Leveller* and smiling out of a blurred photo which betrayed the presence of another person with an arm round his neck—Sarah Scott, no doubt. According to his profile, his one "*non-negotiable criterion*" was a university degree; this put him officially out of her league. It gave her no pleasure to discover that he was doing Internet dating. He would not want this information to be spread around, and, rather than crowing, she felt sorry she had snooped on him and invaded his privacy.

At least he wouldn't discover *her* on the *partnersforall* site. She changed her own profile back to how it was before. With no mention of a degree, the computer would not place her in Walter's line-up of suggested matches.

So Walter was in fact in the market for a partner. It made her failure to attract him harder to bear. Saddened, she thought how much she missed their talks and outings. She had tried her best, but her best had not been good enough.

Even though she had given up her flat, she still faced pressing financial problems. She checked her accounts and they confirmed what she already knew—the dentists' bills had almost emptied her savings account and her credit card interest charges were mounting up. Lucille cancelled her subscription to *partnersforall*.

That same evening, Jillie asked again what progress she had made towards finding a place to live.

"Still nothing to report. I'm sorry," she said.

After Jillie and Geoff had gone off to the bedroom—it was only nine o'clock, and if she hadn't been there, they would surely have stayed in the lounge and watched TV—Lucille dialled Jason's number.

CHAPTER TWENTY-FOUR

Back with Jason

"Jason, could I stay with you for a bit? I'm not talking about getting married again, but could I come for a sort of trial period?"

First thing next morning the big car was outside Jillie's building, and the black bin bags full of clothes were going into the boot. Geoff was clearly trying to keep a pleased expression off his handsome face. Jillie was apologetic. "We didn't mean to drive you out. Please don't feel you have to leave." Lucille guessed that her friend was worried about her. Jillie knew how the marriage to Jason had ended.

"Don't worry, Jillie. I'll take good care of her," said Jason. He was sharp when he was sober, quick to work out what other people were thinking.

"You mustn't forget Cleo," said Jillie.

"As if I would."

"Who's Cleo?"

"My cat … Oh, God! Jason, I'd forgotten you were allergic to cats."

"I'm so sorry, baby. It has to be me or the cat." He sounded confident that she would choose him.

She looked at Jillie. She was relieved to see Jillie's face light up. "Does that mean I get to keep Cleo?"

Lucille spoke to Cleo. "Cleo, would you like to stay here with

Jillie?" Cleo turned away from her, and went to the corner of the kitchen where her food was served and began to beg for it, noisily.

Jillie smiled even more. "There's your answer. That's cats for you."

Jason had won. It was him, not the cat. Annoying, but the allergy was real – she remembered that now.

In the car, the welcome from his dog Millie made her feel happier, though she would miss Cleo, and Jason seemed to guess at her feelings, for he said, "Millie has quite taken to you." When they arrived at his house, he said, "From now on you must think of this as *our* house."

He took the day off work to celebrate, and after another of his delicious meals they went up to his bedroom and made love. Her body remembered what to expect and she remembered what to do to please him. It was like when they first made love, before they were married. "A perfect fit," as Jason put it. "Perfect sync."

Later, she realised his bedroom still had that strange faint odour she had noticed before. Jason himself smelled of pepper-mints and aftershave.

After that, every night was like a honeymoon night.

She resigned from the newsagent's and continued job hunting. Jason gave her lifts into Oxford, since the new estate had as yet no bus service. But he insisted there was no hurry and she should concentrate on her writing, so she was able to make progress on the memoir. She worked through several text-books on creative writing and English grammar, and after a couple of months she felt confident that her written submissions looked just as "educated" as her classmates'.

Jason paid off her debts and arranged for a generous sum to go regularly into her bank account. He seemed to like having her as a stay-at-home, kept woman.

On St Valentine's Day he presented her with a new silver, top-of-the-range Honda Jazz. "Sorry it's not your favourite colour, baby. I couldn't find a yellow one." She was glad it wasn't yellow—if it had been yellow she would have thought of Walter Farquarson's Jazz every time she saw it.

On Saturdays Lucille drove into Oxford and had lunch with Helen and Rod or her friends from Richley's. Whenever she'd been out, Jason asked lots of questions. Sometimes it annoyed her, because she had already told him where she was going and he made her repeat herself, but at the same time she was touched by his concern. He wanted to know exactly where she had been, who with, how long and what they'd talked about. Apart from her mother, Lucille had never had anyone show so much interest in her. Her first husband Luke certainly didn't, and neither did Jason while they were married.

Jason attended AA meetings on Thursday evenings. One Thursday he skipped the meeting and came home unexpectedly. She was watching TV with Millie beside her, and he walked in so quietly that she let out a cry of fright.

"Oh, Jason, you're back early. You scared me."

"Did I? Did I, now? Why?"

"Well, just because I wasn't expecting you."

"Were you expecting somebody else?"

"No. Of course not."

That episode bothered her, mainly because of what he said, but also because he had missed his meeting, and she was afraid he was going to give up AA. She was unwilling to ask him directly, but she tried to encourage him to talk about the meetings and how he was coping. He seemed reluctant to tell her.

The next Thursday she said, "I must check the TV schedule. Just me and Millie again this evening while you're with your mates at AA."

"Well, I may go and I may not. It's a bit like those awful chapel services, you know. Everybody confessing their sins and all. 'My name is Jason and I'm an alcoholic.' I'm not really. I can control it, like I told you."

While he was out, Lucille went to the tool shed to get a flowerpot. Millie had knocked over a pot of orchids with her tail.

The tool shed was Jason's special place, his "den", he called it. Under the workbench she found several bottles of whisky. Had Jason stashed the stuff away in order to avoid temptation? Or to hide it from her? She was looking at the bottles with her torch when the shed door suddenly opened, and she screamed.

"Came home early. What are you doing out here? What are you staring at? If I still had a problem, all those bottles would be empty, now wouldn't they? Why can't you trust me, baby?"

He grabbed a bottle of whisky and opened it there and then and began to drink. He followed her indoors. She left him in the lounge and went to bed. When he came up three hours later he was drunk.

"Don't you worry … not to worry, lovely girl," he mumbled. "Had a good night. Sober again tomorrow. Never fear." He slumped on the bed without undressing and rolled towards her, and she got up and removed his shoes. He fell asleep holding her tight, too tight, and his whisky breath made her feel sick. She wriggled free of his clutches and lay awake till it was nearly daylight.

Next morning, hung over, Jason phoned the showroom and asked his partner to hold the fort. By afternoon he had recovered and their life went back to normal for a few days. Neither of them mentioned the booze in the shed or the events of that night.

On the evening of the fifth day, she found him in the utility room rummaging among the contents of the laundry basket spread out on the bench. Hastily, he gathered up the things and said he was trying to find a missing sock. It made no sense. She saw that he had separated out her knickers from the rest of the laundry, and she guessed what he was about. "Are you looking for signs that I'm cheating on you?"

"No, I'm not. And what if I was? Have you got something to hide?"

"No, of course not. You have to trust me, Jason."

No more was said. But Lucille remembered one of her mother's social workers: "We make it a rule never to interfere or give firm advice. There's just one exception to the rule—if your husband seems to be jealous for no reason. It's a danger sign, and in that case we would strongly advise you to leave as a matter of urgency." But were Jason's suspicions entirely unreasonable? He was usually so good at guessing other people's feelings; this was part of his attractiveness and the reason for his success as a salesman. Had he realised that though she was fond of him, she didn't really love him, and there was another man she still missed?

Next day her contraceptive pills had disappeared. After a search in all the obvious places, she contacted the surgery to ask for a repeat prescription, thinking she must have finished the pack and had a strange memory lapse.

When she scraped some burnt toast into the food compost bin, she caught sight of the foil package and fished the pills out. Jason was at the breakfast bar, finishing his coffee. Though she was beginning to be afraid, she knew she had to confront him. She held up the pills.

"Why did you throw them away, Jason?"

"Maybe I'd like to have a kid with you."

"Then we need to talk about it like grown-ups." Lucille tried not to listen to the tick of the clock—she would have loved to have a child, but not with Jason, not now. She was too old, anyway.

Jason took another tack. "And of course the pill makes it all too easy for you to put it about."

"Jason …"

He turned away, and left for work without kissing her goodbye.

After Jason had gone out, Lucille rang the domestic violence helpline. A counsellor called Janet answered. Lucille did her best to explain the situation. "My husband has a drinking problem. Last week I discovered that he hides his whisky in the shed, and he got drunk. But he's trying to cut back. He doesn't drink every day. He cares about me, I know he does." She could almost hear her mother's voice talking to the social workers who had tried to help them.

Janet said little at first. Then she asked about violence, and Lucille said that since she'd come back to him, Jason had not hurt her. It was quite different from when they were together before; during their marriage he'd attacked her several times.

"So he's binge drinking, but you say he doesn't hit you … and you're willing to try and support him in his efforts to give it up?"

"Yes. I divorced him because of the violence. Now he seems to have changed."

"Is there a reason why you got in touch with us, rather than your doctor or Alcoholics Anonymous? They have a section for relatives as well, you know—Al-Anon."

"Yes, I've heard of Al-Anon." Lucille hesitated.

The counsellor must have picked up the hesitation, for she asked, "Perhaps you've something else you'd like to tell me?"

Then the rest all poured out—the incidents with the underwear and the pills, and the grilling whenever she'd been out without him.

The counsellor's reply was exactly what she feared and did not want to hear. "Lucille, do you know what is meant by 'paranoid jealousy'?"

And the advice was what she expected. "These are danger signs and I must advise you to consider leaving."

"I'll think about it," she replied. She promised to ring the helpline again—or the police—if she needed urgent help.

In the daytime, when he was not hung over, Jason coped with the business. But the bouts of evening binge drinking got more frequent and his colleagues had to take on more and more of the work at the car showroom. All the questions and the snooping and spying continued. Lucille told herself "Every cloud has a silver lining" and "It's just because he loves me." She knew it was comforting rubbish.

CHAPTER TWENTY-FIVE

Kingston College and The St Frideswide's Centre

Walter despaired of Internet dating and continued celibate. He could not emulate Paul's sociable, optimistic and adventurous approach to the dating experience. His was a different sort of personality from Paul's, he told himself. Besides, he'd been widowed much more recently, and it was natural to feel that everyone he met compared unfavourably with Sarah. One evening when they had both been drinking, he explained this to Paul. Paul ventured to suggest Walter might have been comparing his Internet dates to Lucille as well as to Sarah, and missing Lucille too.

"That's outrageous."

"I'm sorry. I shouldn't have said that."

Paul went home immediately, and rang next day to apologise again. "Please don't think I meant to play down the importance of Sarah. She'll always be the most significant person in your life, and rightly so."

"Forget it." He was still angry and he had no wish to talk about this with anyone, not even with Paul. He changed the subject quickly, and they arranged to meet for lunch at Kingston College the following week.

Paul was waiting for him at the porters' lodge. Since he usually had to go and find Paul in his room, Walter wondered if this touch of formality was an attempt to compensate for the previous week's upset.

After they had collected their food at the canteen-like counter, they took their trays to a corner of one of the long tables of pale wood, which were already crowded with students and Fellows. Since this was a postgraduate and defiantly democratic college, they had no high table, and it was hard to distinguish who was a don and who was a student. There were even people with young children at some of the tables. The noise was almost intolerable. Walter had a theory that postgraduates' voices sounded all the louder for including so many that were American. He looked out of the plate glass windows at the newly built family flats and glanced up at the plain modern ceiling, set in a pyramid roof, such a contrast to the Elizabethan ceiling in his own college hall. He often thought Paul's membership here, rather than at one of the older, more traditional colleges, might account for his friend's youthful outlook on life. As if to confirm this hypothesis, two exuberant young Americans took the seats next to them and proceeded to greet Paul and exchange banter with him as though he was an intimate friend. The young men devoured their lunch at speed and Paul and Walter were soon left by themselves.

"I've met a lovely widow," Paul announced without preliminaries. Since they'd started Internet dating, Walter had heard these same words several times before, but on this occasion Paul's voice had a different tone—solemn, portentous, thick with emotion. When he mentioned his dates previously, he had gone on to list their attributes and qualifications: age, shape, education, job, hobbies. But this "lovely widow" was not further described, and Paul had not brought a print-out with photo and profile for Walter's opinion. This time, thought Walter, Paul's serious. He wondered what this presaged where he himself was concerned. Would he see less of Paul in the future, or would he gain a new friend in the lovely widow? How selfish I have become, he thought.

Paul seemed to be expecting a reply. Walter asked what the lady was called.

A pause. "It's unfortunate—her name's Elizabeth too."

At least it won't matter if you call out your wife's name by mistake, thought Walter.

"We're trying out some different versions of 'Elizabeth'," Paul continued. "We'll probably settle for 'Beth'—that's what her school friends called her."

"So soon? It seems awfully early to be deciding on a change of name. You sound serious."

"I believe we are."

A few days later, Walter joined Paul and Elizabeth for lunch at the brasserie in Jericho. They had arrived before him, and as he approached he observed signs of a beginning love affair— Paul's hand on hers as she held the menu, Paul gently moving a lock of her hair that obstructed her view. The "lovely widow" even looked like Paul's wife Elizabeth. She was a similar age to Paul, and as they talked it emerged that she was an English teacher, enjoyed classical literature, and went birdwatching every weekend. The gods who operated through the exclusive dating site had granted Paul's wish to meet someone like his late wife and like Paul himself.

When they stood up to leave, Walter saw that Elizabeth was just a little shorter than Paul, and pleasantly plump like him. Yes, he thought, this will last.

"It's been lovely to meet you, Walter," she said. "Paul speaks so highly of you."

After this, Paul and Beth (as he was now to call her) kept asking Walter to accompany them on trips and evenings out. But Walter feared he would be intruding; it was important to allow them time to themselves, especially so early in their relationship. He recalled how he had urged, even bullied, Paul to come out with him and Lucille in order to protect himself from Lucille's advances. He'd used his friend as a sort of human shield. By contrast, it was obvious that Paul, with Beth's encouragement, invited him to join them out of friendship and kindness.

* * *

The St Frideswide's Centre had been open for some time. Now that Walter was seeing Paul less often, had less contact with Rosie and John, and had given up Internet dating, he had more time to study the reports that came to him as chair of the trustees. All seemed to be going well, but he ought to see for himself. The fact that he was the founder and main benefactor did not give him a licence to turn up unannounced, so he had written a polite request to Louise Curtis, the officer in charge.

Her reply was a welcoming, friendly phone call. Yes, they'd love to see him. Yes, the residents would love to meet him. After that he couldn't cry off.

He stood outside the St Frideswide's Centre and wished he hadn't come. This place was inimical to his interests and his experience. He was here out of some indistinct sense of duty, even though Mike had made it clear that he was under no obligation

216

to visit and indeed, he might not even be welcome in spite of what Louise Curtis had said.

He rang the bell. Louise, whom he'd met only once, seemed to think it appropriate to take his hand and hold on to it far too long. She led him inside and he was assaulted by noise and smells. He'd been told that there were only ten women and seven children, but it felt like at least twenty large families. Laughter, loud voices, children's squeals and babies wailing. The smells of chips and cleaning fluids and baby powder. To his relief, Louise ushered him into the small office and closed the door. But the relief didn't last long. After quick introductions to a couple of other women, she led him out again for a guided tour of the downstairs rooms. Then he was given a seat in the kitchen, a mug of tea was thrust into his hand, and four of the residents joined him.

"What would you like to ask us?" said the tall fortyish woman who seemed to be the most confident of the group. He was struck by her educated accent and her smart clothes. At first, he did not know what he could ask without being intrusive or sounding ignorant. Eventually he managed, "Are you quite comfortable here?"

"Yes, thank you. We have all we need. An excellent kitchen, as you can see. And the bedrooms are very nice. Yes, it's clean and comfortable—like a five-star youth hostel," said another educated voice.

"I gather we have a lot to thank you for, professor," said the first woman.

This made him more embarrassed than ever. "Call me Walter, please. It was the wish of my late wife that we should do something to help … people like yourselves."

"Battered wives, you mean?"

They all smiled good-naturedly while he tried not to look shocked when he heard the expression that Mike had censored so firmly.

Another woman came to his rescue and continued the conversation.

"Of course we're happy it's so clean and warm and friendly, but even if this was just a barn with straw to sleep on, we'd be glad to get in. We're here because we had nowhere else we could feel safe.

"We four all felt we'd like to tell you a bit about our lives before, why we came here, what we've escaped from."

Walter didn't want to hear. But how do you say to people who have suffered that you don't want to know their story?

"Can I go first?" said the youngest woman. "I'll have to leave you in a minute because I've got two toddlers being looked after by someone else, and they're probably driving her crazy. My husband—he's an ex-soldier—served in Iraq, and he just couldn't settle back into ordinary life. He had anger control issues before, but when the twins arrived not long after he came home for good, that was the start of it."

She went on to tell of rapes and beatings and her husband's determination to control her every movement. She was punished for not having his dinner ready, not finishing the washing-up, leaving toys on the kitchen floor. When she'd run away to her friend's and again to her sister's, he came after her and things got worse. Finally she had called the police and taken him to court, and he was on an order to leave her alone. But still he had found her again. He was out on bail at present, and she needed to get right away. Here at the refuge she was at last making proper plans. His solicitor said her husband was being treated for post-traumatic stress disorder. She hoped they could cure him, but until then she and the children had to stay out of his reach.

The other three told their stories too, each one appalling, each one different.

Walter listened in silence. He wished he could leave. He was sickened by what he heard, and though he knew it made no sense, he felt ashamed to be a man.

They asked if he had questions. He just shook his head. "No questions. Thank you for talking to me."

As he walked towards the front door with Louise, he noticed some children in the play area. He tried to speak to them but the first one he approached shrank away, and the others hid behind the women.

There was a general bustle and a lot of laughter, but he could sense the pain and the fear still present below the surface. He thanked Louise, and they shook hands. She said, "Thank *you*, Walter, for all you have done for us."

"No, it's my wife—my late wife—Sarah, who ..." His voice trailed away.

He hurried out into the street. Back to my comfortable home and my comfortable life, he thought. He summoned a taxi.

CHAPTER TWENTY-SIX

Rosie

Walter's loneliness increased. Naturally, John and Rosie needed to make the most of their university years without having to give up time during term to see their father. He relied more and more on their emails and phone calls, and if he came home and found he had missed a call he was disappointed and sad. Rosie seldom phoned now, and when they did speak, she seemed to be without news of any kind and kept turning the conversation back to him and Oxford and John. Whatever he asked about was "OK", and she'd been doing "this and that" or "nothing special" or "nothing that would interest you." If he mentioned her work or her boyfriend, she clammed up completely. He was bewildered by this change in Rosie, for she was the chatty one of his two children and used to relish telling him every detail about her life at university. He dreaded becoming estranged, but her unwillingness to communicate and the thought of coming face to face with the hostile boyfriend still deterred him from going to see her.

Reluctantly, he turned to John for explanation and advice. At first, John said, "Give her time, Dad, give her space."

When he got this answer for the third time in a row, Walter lost patience. "John, I want you to tell me what you know. I believe the two of you are keeping something from me."

He heard John take a deep breath. "Dad, I wanted to shield you, and Rosie was scared to tell you herself." John paused.

"I already know she's living with the boyfriend. I've spoken to him on the phone."

"That's not all, Dad."

Walter felt himself go cold with fear.

"She's dropped out of uni."

Walter was almost relieved. In those moments far worse possibilities had raced through his mind—illness, an accident, some dreadful news concerning the unpleasant boyfriend ...

"I've got her address. I'm going to see her. I made up my mind to do that some time ago, but I've been unable to summon the courage."

"Dad, she doesn't want to see either of us."

"I realise that, but I'm going."

* * *

In Bristol, Walter took a taxi from the station. Rosie's street consisted of tall terraced houses, built in the early twentieth century, he guessed, or possibly for merchants in the nineteenth. The rows of tightly parked cars and the rabble of wheelie bins suggested multiple occupancy. Obsolete election posters were stuck in many of the windows, with torn curtains, and here and there a cracked pane.

The house where Rosie lived appeared especially defeated, tired, unloved. "*Farquarson/Griffiths*" was scrawled on a scrap of paper in a slot above three vacant slots by the front door. The door swung open when he tried the handle. He hesitated and then went in without pressing the bell beside their names.

As he neared the top of the stairs, the reek of cigarettes mixed with alcohol made him feel sick. A distant memory from smoky

Oxford pubs when he was a student. He could hear two voices. One was male, loud, and angry, the other was shrill and pleading—his daughter's voice.

Rosie came out to the landing just as he reached it. She had grown more like her mother; but not her mother in the good years, rather her mother after the cancer had spread, haggard and shrunken, as if trying to disappear from view. When she saw Walter she gasped and backed away. He moved towards her, wanting to take her in his arms.

"Dad, why didn't you phone to say you were coming?" She let him hug her, but she felt stiff and resistant.

A shabby, distressingly thin young man emerged. He wore a string vest and a pair of stained grey jogging bottoms and he looked as pale and unwell as Rosie herself. He bared yellowish, uneven teeth in a smile that was without warmth. "Who have we here? Not darling Daddy, surely? I don't remember issuing the invitation."

"You must be Nigel," said Walter stupidly.

"Oh, must I?" Nigel's manner changed without warning. "Come on, girl, invite your daddy into our lovely home and give him a cup of tea."

Rosie pulled herself out of Walter's embrace and led the way into the flat. The place stank of unwashed clothes as well as alcohol and tobacco. Walter sat in the only armchair and Nigel and Rosie sat on cushions on the bare floor. At first, no one spoke, and the tea did not materialise. Walter noticed a faded bruise on his daughter's face.

"I've come to ask if there's anything I can do," he said carefully. "I know you've dropped out of your course, Rosie. But you could go back to it. I could help with that."

Nigel said, "Professor Farquarson, would you be able to increase Rosie's allowance? Otherwise we can't afford for her to give up her job. I'm sorry, but there it is."

Rosie still said nothing.

"Job? What job?"

"I've got a temporary job in a supermarket."

Nigel snapped, "Never mind telling him about the job."

"What do you think, Rosie? Would raising your allowance make it possible for you to go back to university?"

"No, Dad, that wouldn't work. No amount of money is going to fix it." She gestured round the room, at the ranks of empty cans and bottles, and the saucers full of cigarette butts. Walter understood—Nigel was drinking and smoking their money away. He wondered, Were drugs involved as well?

"Don't listen to her. Of course we could do with some help. Surely you can afford it?" By turns wheedling and aggressive, Nigel continued to plead. When Rosie tried to interrupt, he silenced her with a long look filled with threat. Rosie's fists were clenched white and her hands trembled.

Ashamed, Walter admitted to himself that he longed to get away, but first he needed some time with Rosie on her own.

"Rosie, could you walk me to the bus stop?" He had intended to call a taxi, but this seemed a better idea. Nigel would not insist on accompanying them, for he was barefoot and half-dressed. Rosie agreed, and she sounded relieved.

In the street, Walter said, "Rosie. Tell me what I can do."

"There's nothing you can do."

"Darling, John told me, and I can see for myself—you're in a terrible state. How can you possibly deal with this? Why not come home with me now?"

"No, Dad. I can't leave him. I'm committed to him, and … "
Her voice faltered. "I don't drink or take drugs, but he does both
and he can't help it."

"Drugs?"

"Yes, cocaine. That's why he looks so ill. I wish you had met
him before—if you had, you'd understand. You might even have
liked him. He was different then, and he could be again. People
can change."

"I wish I could believe that."

"And there's something else … But no, it doesn't matter.
Thanks for trying—I know you meant well—but don't come
here again, it only makes things worse. I can sort this out myself
and when I have, I'll get back in touch, I promise.

"If I don't stick with him, I think he would kill himself. On
purpose or by mistake. Mixing coke and booze is terribly dangerous. I'm all he's got—his parents won't have anything to do
with him, though they're as well off as you are. So I have to stay;
somehow I've got to make him see he needs medical help. It's
not something he can tackle on his own." Her sad, defiant face
caused Walter so much pain that he feared he would break
down and cry.

They had reached the stop and a bus was due in five minutes.
Walter took sixty pounds from his wallet, all the cash he had,
and pressed the notes into her hand. "At least buy some proper
food."

"Don't send any more, Dad." She looked at him pleadingly.
Her blue eyes were just like Sarah's.

"If I address it to you and you keep it for groceries …

"He'd guess and make me hand it over."

"If your mother could—"

"Dad, don't play that 'if your mother could see this' card. It's not fair." Walter was silenced. They hugged and parted.

On the bus he brushed away tears of sorrow and frustration. What had become of their bright confident girl? At least Sarah had not had to see this.

On his return to Oxford, Walter rang John.

"I'm sorry, Dad. Yes, I went to Bristol to see her last term—got the address from one of her university friends. I should have warned you properly, but I was trying to protect you, I suppose. It's no use sending money—Nigel takes everything. And he's sometimes aggressive into the bargain. I suspect he hits her or at least threatens to."

"Yes, he hits her. I saw a bruise on her face."

John went on to give Walter the whole story. "She met him at a sort of community for people who have dropped out of conventional mental health care and their fellow travellers—I'm not sure which Nigel was. She'd visited as part of her research for the novel she was writing."

"The sort of set-up that was fashionable in the sixties?"

"I suppose. They claim there's no such thing as mental illness and it's all the fault of the bourgeois parents. Or Society with a capital S. That kind of thing."

"Psychiatrists are part of the conspiracy and medical treatment is evil?"

"Right. They won't touch prescribed drugs. But they use illegal drugs and alcohol to keep their demons at bay."

"And it was Nigel who persuaded Rosie to leave university?"

"Yes. He was on the English course with her and stayed on to do a foundation art diploma, but he dropped out. He filled her head with romantic nonsense about them being a pair of artistic lovebirds who'd live in a garret and produce wonderful literature and art. Now he sits at home in their garret and she works at a supermarket."

"What can we do?" How strange to seek advice from his younger child. He needed Sarah more than ever. He stood up and ran his hand along the books.

"Dad, right now I don't think we can do anything. We just have to wait. And be there for her when she sees sense."

Walter could not bear to accept the wisdom of John's words. He resolved to try again with Rosie.

* * *

He knew he should not have come back to Bristol. Walter squeezed the Jazz between two badly parked cars, and got out and opened the boot. One by one, he removed six cardboard boxes and placed them on the pavement. Then, thinking better of it, he put five of these back, closed the boot and locked the car, glanced around anxiously, and carried the first box along to Rosie's house and up the steps into the porch. He repeated the procedure with each of the others. Inside the boxes were tinned foods and biscuits, and fruit and vegetables that might last a few days, and yoghurt and cheese and honey. He had tried to choose foods that would not deteriorate quickly and would contribute to a healthy diet such as she had once had. In the porch he stood wondering, should he simply place a note on top of the groceries and leave? Rosie would find them, surely. If he was going to leave, he had best do so soon, before Rosie or Nigel came upon him there. He calculated that Rosie might return from work any time now, and as for Nigel, he was probably upstairs in the flat and if he wasn't in some sort of stupor, he could appear at any moment and make trouble.

He decided to leave. He began to scribble a note, but found it hard. *I know you asked me not to come, but …*? *Just passing through Bristol and thought you might like these*? Not plausible. And then he thought, how could he be sure the food would not be stolen in a neighbourhood like this before Rosie or Nigel found it? He pressed the bell. It didn't work, but the front door was unlocked.

He lugged the boxes up the stairs one by one. He planned to leave them outside their flat and go away without knocking. Just as he turned to go downstairs for the last time the door opened. Rosie. He'd miscalculated. She saw the boxes and said in a whisper, "Oh Dad you shouldn't have."

He tried to make light of it. "It's nothing. I wish you would let me do more. You've heard of the Bank of Mum and Dad? Well, think of this as the Food Bank of … Dad." His feeble joke had come out badly and Rosie gave not a glimmer of a smile.

"That's not what I meant. I wasn't just being polite. I mean it—I wish you hadn't come and I'd rather you didn't come again. Or at least not for a while."

He now saw that she was utterly serious. "Just take these, Rosie. Please." To his relief, she dragged the first box into the flat.

As he was about to follow her inside with another box, Nigel appeared. He was staggering. When he saw the groceries he said, "We're not a fucking charity case. It's cash we need, not your health food rubbish." He glared at Rosie. "Did you tell him to bring this stuff?" She looked scared and denied it. Walter knew he was defeated. Nigel took a step towards Walter. Walter's fists clenched, but he leaned to one side to avoid the expected blow. Nigel seemed to lose interest and returned to the living room.

Before Walter left he gave Rosie one last hug. He could not speak. He couldn't think what to say and his throat felt dry. He walked slowly down the stairs. A moment later she came running after him and when they were in the street he said, "Please, Rosie, come and talk to me properly. We can sit in the car."

She agreed. "But only for a few minutes."

She said, "It looks bad, I know. But Nigel really is cutting back."

"Cutting back because he has to, because he hasn't the money for his drugs and alcohol?"

"It's not just because of that. He's making an effort for both our sakes."

"So are you telling me all's well now?" He realised he sounded angry and sarcastic.

She burst into tears.

He remembered that last time he saw her she had mentioned "something else" and clammed up. "And there's something else, isn't there?"

He had got through to her at last, the confiding daughter he thought he had lost. Crying noisily like a child, she grabbed hold of him. "Oh Dad, I'm pregnant. Oh I wish Mum was here."

He did not say the first thing that came into his head, which was to offer to take her away and give her a home and take care of her and her baby. He too wished Sarah was here.

"When is the baby due?"

She stopped crying. "I'm not going to have the baby."

He stared at her.

"It happens," she said.

"What are you going to do?" he asked, afraid, although he understood what she meant.

She dried her face on her sleeve. "Get rid of it, of course," she said in a cold, still voice. He tried not to think—my grandchild, Sarah's grandchild.

He began to speak but she spoke over him. "No ifs and buts. Please believe me, I've thought this through. I've talked it through, too, with a counsellor, but not with Nigel. Nigel doesn't know.

"I'm booked in next week. No need for you to worry: I've got a friend to come with me, and I'll be staying with her for a couple of days afterwards. Nigel thinks I'm going to York to see John. He's hoping John will give us some money. I didn't intend to tell you and you mustn't say anything about this to John. Please."

He agreed not to tell John and made her promise that after the termination she would let him know she was all right. As an afterthought he persuaded her to give him her friend's phone number. She refused to divulge the friend's address, and he knew it was to prevent him from turning up again in Bristol and trying to see her. She got out of the car and hurried into the house. He waited a minute or two, then drove off, taking several wrong turnings, hardly able to find his way to the motorway. He stopped at the first service station and wondered whether to go back to her and try again. Try what? There was nothing he could do. He forced himself to continue his journey to Oxford.

When he got home he went immediately to the phone, intending to break his word and ring John. But he thought better of it. John was in the midst of exams and in any case, what could John say or do that would change Rosie's situation for the better?

What would Sarah have said? He could not imagine. This was a state of affairs they had never discussed, far less expected to face in their own family. Looking back, he saw that they had an irrational belief in their own immunity. True, Sarah had visited a women's refuge, but they had never known an abused woman personally—except their cleaning lady, and at the time they didn't realise she was being abused. Neither had they known addicts of any description. And he could not recall ever having talked with Sarah about abortion.

The evening after the termination he rang the number Rosie had given him. Rosie's friend answered and told him Rosie was in bed asleep. "She's tired, but she's fine." The friend sounded sympathetic, and Walter asked her to keep him informed. He explained that Rosie was unwilling to stay in contact and had asked him not to visit. The friend was in the same position as Walter: Nigel made it impossible to call in or even to phone, and he never left the flat except when he went out to replenish his supplies of cocaine and alcohol, and he did this at unpredictable times. Rosie was at work most days. Nigel had taken possession of her mobile phone— useful for arranging rendez-vous with drug dealers. And anyway, Rosie had made it clear she did not want to talk.

Walter grieved. For the baby, for Rosie, and, as ever, for Sarah. Next morning he contacted his department to cancel some lectures, on grounds of ill health. Joan Wilson phoned him. He was evasive, but confessed to feeling under the weather.

The phone rang a few hours later. He snatched it up, hoping it might be Rosie. But it was Lucille Brown. "I met Joan Wilson and she told me she was worried about you. Joan says you would never cancel lectures unless you absolutely had to. Are you on your own?"

"Yes." He had begun to listen to some Mozart, but what he needed was human company and he had been thinking of ringing Paul.

"I'd like to come round and bring you some supper."

"There's absolutely no need."

"What are friends for?"

Too dispirited to invent an excuse, he could not say no. Though as soon as he'd accepted her offer, he wished he had refused. He hadn't seen her since that awkward encounter in the bookshop, and in spite of their agreement to keep in touch and stay friends, he hadn't meant to see her again.

* * *

When she went back to the flats to collect her post that morning, Lucille had met Joan Wilson in the hallway and heard the news of Walter's illness. She thanked her lucky stars she had made a lamb casserole earlier. After the phone call to Walter she went straight home, picked up the casserole and left a note for Jason with an apology. She said she'd arranged to go to Jillie's for a girls' night in, and had forgotten to tell him. She took a steak out of the freezer ready for Jason to grill for his supper.

She hoped Walter would not be too ill to eat. He was thinner, she thought, but she soon guessed that he was deeply troubled rather than physically ill.

She waited till their meal was nearly ready. They'd agreed to eat in the kitchen, and he was laying the table and she was sautéing potatoes to go with the casserole. She knew it was best not to sit face to face when you wanted to encourage someone to confide in you. She was ashamed to think how badly she had handled that conversation about his bereavement the first time they met. Then, she had been all too eager to impress him and make him like her—now, she just wanted to comfort and help a friend who was suffering.

She said simply, "Walter. Stop me if I'm out of order. To be honest, it looks to me as though you're worried about something. Do you want to tell me about it?" At first, Walter did not answer. He had his back to her. He was taking cutlery out of the sideboard drawer and instead of turning, he stopped, holding the knives and forks and still facing away. His head was bowed so low that she could not see his face in the mirror above the sideboard. She felt a wave of sympathy, and an urge to put her arms around him, which she knew she must resist.

"Well, yes, but nothing you could help with," he said.

"Tell me anyway. You never know."

"I don't think ..."

"Another serving spoon, please ... Is it to do with John or Rosie?"

"Rosie."

"It must sometimes be tough having to cope with a young daughter without your wife."

"That's it exactly."

"We need serviettes. Now sit down and eat, please." He told her then, about the disturbed, domineering boyfriend, his fear that Rosie was being abused, and finally, about the abortion and Rosie's refusal to accept his help.

Lucille hesitated. She decided it was not her place to inform him of Rosie's visit to the cemetery. She understood now what had prompted that visit.

Should she tell him about her own past, and about her parents?

No—this was not about her. But she could make use of her own experience. She knew what it was like to talk things through with a social worker. A social worker would try to help Walter see the other person's point of view, but make sure he arrived at a conclusion in his own time and in his own way. Even if the problem and the solution seemed obvious to any sensible outsider, a social worker wouldn't advise him what to do or what to think.

She persuaded Walter to tell her slowly, in detail, everything he knew about Rosie's situation. Whenever he stumbled she engineered a little pause, offering more wine or potatoes. They went over all that had happened and every course of action available to Rosie and to himself. She got him to imagine himself in Rosie's position, and to face the fact of the abortion.

Lucille herself had felt dreadfully ashamed, responsible somehow, and unwilling to tell anyone about the abuse from Luke, and then from Jason. And she had so much wanted to forgive, to help each of those two to change. And she'd wanted to decide her own future in her own time, to feel in control, however stupid her delay might seem to someone else.

Step by painful step, Lucille guided Walter through, till he had considered the situation from Rosie's point of view and examined Rosie's options.

Walter said finally, "I have to try and see it through her eyes. She loves this wretched man and she believes she can help him. Even if it ends in failure—and I'm sure it will—she needs to feel she's tried her best, and that she's made her own decisions. I suppose I have to accept she's a grown woman."

"Yes, I'm sure you're right. And remember, she knows you and John will be there for her when she's ready to take your help."

* * *

Walter felt exhausted, still deeply sad, but more at peace with himself. He had not expected so much wisdom and compassion from Lucille, even though he had come to appreciate her more fully by the time they parted. After that regrettable sexual encounter they had agreed to remain friends—Lucille, he now realised, was good at friendship.

It was only later that he began to feel ashamed. And somewhat resentful, though that was irrational. How had he not been able to work through his problem himself? Grateful though he was, he did not want to see Lucille again. He would throw himself into his work and wait for Rosie to get in touch.

Why do we turn against people who help us? he wondered. Is it because we've let them see how weak and foolish we can be, and we don't wish to be reminded of it?

Next day he tried to ring Lucille, just to thank her for her kindness, and discovered that she was no longer at her flat. The man who answered said he was the new tenant. Mrs Brown was the previous occupant, and he did not have a forwarding address.

Lucille's mobile phone was disconnected. He phoned her department at Richley's and learned that Lucille had been made redundant. The woman who answered said one of Lucille's closest friends worked at Richley's, someone called Jillie. He should ask to speak to her, she suggested. Jillie would know more.

He was touched that Lucille had been able to push her own troubles aside and focus on his. But he did not want to talk to Jillie, whom he had heard of but never met. Surely he had done enough to try and contact Lucille to say thank you? She had certainly had some bad luck, but he didn't wish to feel obliged to feel sorry for her. Losing her job at Richley's and leaving the little flat she was so proud of must have been a disappointment, but troubles like those hardly compared with his own, and he had very little compassion to spare. Anyway, his family came first.

CHAPTER TWENTY-SEVEN

Lucille in Crisis

When Lucille got home after her visit to Walter, she found Jason sprawled on the couch. He struggled to his feet when she came into the lounge. On the floor beside the couch, an empty whisky bottle told how he had spent his evening. The steak, defrosted and bloody, still lay on the kitchen table. She said nothing.

She started up the stairs. He followed unsteadily and grabbed hold of her. Although he was swaying and looked about to fall, his grip was firm and his nails dug into her arm.

"Let me go to bed," she said.

At that he confronted her. Jillie had phoned. "Your mate Jillie said she just wanted a chat with you, nothing important. So if you weren't at Jillie's, where were you, baby?" Lucille was found out in her lie—she wished she had had the sense to ask Jillie to cover for her.

Jason answered his own question. "You've been with him, haven't you? Fucking that man who sent the postcard from Ecuador? You're his bit of rough, I suppose. Or he's your bit of posh. That postcard you keep in the back of your knicker drawer, the picture of some fairy queen—you thought I wouldn't find it, didn't you?" He tugged her arm and made her come back down the stairs.

Lucille turned and faced him. "I did pop in to see him this evening, but it's not what you think."

Without warning he smacked her hard across the face. She tottered back against the wall and he smacked her again, and punched her, and she slid to the floor. He reeled forward and kicked her in the stomach. Millie came out of the lounge and stood by, whining softly, confused. Jason staggered out, cursing. Millie looked back once at Lucille and then followed at his heels. She heard the front door slam.

Lucille lay on the floor, in too much pain to pull herself up. It was dawn when she crawled across the hall and reached for the telephone.

She rang the domestic violence helpline. She was relieved to find Janet on duty, the counsellor she had spoken to before.

"My husband has just given me a beating. I'm too scared to stay with him any more and I've nowhere to go."

"Do you need a doctor?"

"No, I don't think so." She dragged herself upright. "Nothing's broken. Just a cut lip and a few bruises."

"Have you called the police?"

"No, I really don't want to. And anyway, he's left the house." She was confident Jason would not return for a few hours at least. On previous occasions he had gone to sleep off his drunkenness in his car. She was not sure why, but she thought it was to avoid being found in the house if she did call the police.

"Can you make your way to a refuge? You're near Oxford, aren't you? We can ring round and see which of the local refuges has a vacancy."

"But I'd prefer to get right away from here."

"If you're sure." After a few minutes Janet called her back with the address of a refuge in Bristol. "They'll be expecting you."

It was full daylight now. She scribbled a note for Jason.

Please don't try to find me. And please, for yourself, for your own sake, see if you can get some more help. Perhaps you should talk to Dr Bradley. At least get yourself back to AA—haven't you a buddy you could call?

I have not informed the police.

I hope everything turns out well for you in the end.

Lucille

P.S. Don't forget to cancel your payments to my bank account. Sorry, but it is all over now.

Lucille packed a suitcase and took her laptop and phone; most of her clothes had to be left behind. She looked around the house for the last time. I will never live anywhere like this again, she thought.

At the garage she hesitated but then turned away—it would not be right to take her car. She pushed the house keys and the car keys through the letterbox. She went shakily out into the street and lifted up her suitcase so as to make no noise; she did not want to rouse the neighbours. Painfully, slowly, she made her way towards the main road. In a cul de sac not far from the house, beside the unfinished community centre with roof beams still showing like the ribcage of a skeleton, she passed Jason asleep on the back seat of the BMW with Millie curled up beside him. She knew she would miss them in spite of everything, and she was sad for them both.

She summoned a taxi to take her to Bicester station; she hoped Jason would not guess where she had gone and try to follow her. She bought a one-way ticket for Bristol.

Lucille was not used to travelling by train. How different this was from the time they went to Blackpool when she was ten—the only holiday she could remember with both her parents.

Her face was a greyish blur in the dirty window, and her eyes burned from lack of sleep and the harsh carriage lights. The click of computer keyboards was interrupted by mystifying phone conversations, ending sometimes with "Love you!" Otherwise no one spoke. Above their heads, a sign said, "*Consider those around you.*"

When they were stopped in a station and another train went by, she felt an odd sensation of movement. Like when you think you're making progress, but in actual fact you're stuck, and it's Time and your life running past.

By the time she reached the Fairways Refuge, the throbbing ache from her bruises had grown worse, and she felt faint and sick.

She rang the bell and almost fell into the arms of the woman who opened the door. "I'm Lucille Brown."

"Come on in, love. You're safe now."

When she saw her face in the bathroom mirror she felt a rush of shame. She had travelled from Oxford looking like a boxer who had just lost a fight. And under her own bloodied face with the bruises now turning purple, she saw the ghost of her mother's face, pale, tired and defeated. Her cream shirt was stained with blood. She wondered what her fellow passengers had thought. No one had given a sign that they had noticed.

She had a soothing shower and soon she was sitting up in bed with a bowl of soup, wearing a clean nightie, and a doctor and a social worker were with her. They provided painkillers for the injuries and advice about benefits. Most important: they urged her to change the number of her mobile phone.

Later she rang Jillie, and found that Jillie already knew roughly what had happened. "Jason has been round here looking for you. He said you'd had a tiff and he was really sorry. He brought your clothes and said maybe you could forgive him after you'd had a bit of a break." Lucille explained that it was more than a tiff.

"I thought as much," said Jillie. "He's a horrible man."

Lucille just said, "Poor Jason. You know something? I'd rather be me than him."

She asked Jillie to pass her news on to her other close friends but made Jillie promise not to give her new number to anyone. She did not say where she was. "This address is only temporary, and it'll be easier if you don't know in case Jason tries to get it out of you."

Even harder was the phone call to Andrew Charlton. She told him she'd had to move away at short notice for family reasons, and would have to drop out of his memoir class.

Andrew suggested she should continue to send her work round by email as before, and he'd ensure that everyone would send feedback to her. "And you can do the same for them. The 'Review' facility is a doddle."

She doubted that, but agreed to try.

"You're doing so well, Lucille. Don't give up now. I'm sure you are going to produce something really worthwhile."

CHAPTER TWENTY-EIGHT

At the Fairways Refuge

Although she was exhausted, that first night at the refuge Lucille lay awake for a long time and thought about her new situation. She was safe. Andrew Charlton believed in her, she could go on writing her memoir, get a job, find somewhere to live. She would make a fresh start in Bristol.

The routines of the refuge, talks with the staff, sessions with advisers, socialising with the other residents—it all helped to comfort her and to strengthen her determination to sort herself out. Her bruises healed, both on her body and in her mind, and soon she was sharing chores and making friends. When she heard the stories her fellow residents had to tell, she began to see herself as—not fortunate, certainly not that—but as someone with a set of obstacles to overcome more manageable than theirs. Most of them looked pale and ill, and their children were frightened and clingy. Some seemed to rely on tranquillisers and cigarettes to keep going. On paper many of these women had no skills to offer an employer.

The community meeting took place every morning. To her own surprise, she found herself making suggestions, and being consulted on everything from finding a job in a shop, to washing bloodstains off a white shirt, to coping with other people's bad temper.

She also attended a smaller group focused on beating depres-

sion and building self-esteem. The leader, Tania, was a psychologist who came twice a week. They examined their
thinking—what they said to themselves, and how that made
them feel. At the end of the session, each group member agreed
to do a homework task which she reported on at their next
meeting.

Lucille couldn't get much writing time. She shuttled back and
forth between the office desk and the kitchen table, or perched
cross-legged on her bed. She pressed on with the memoir and
for two weeks managed to send in her submissions to Andrew
and the class and to write comments on her classmates' work.
But too much else was going on, and too much noise—children
shouting, babies wailing, women's chatter and laughter, phones
and doorbell ringing.

Also, she was becoming more and more involved in the life
of the refuge. Not only did she take on more than her share of
the chores, she soon found herself in demand as a confidante
and adviser.

Janine Bailey became a particular friend. But Janine had a
temper. She flared up at unexpected times, so it was difficult to
feel relaxed around her and she was shunned by most of the
others. Lucille soon gathered that Janine had often been in-
sulted and hurt throughout her life, and she was hypersensitive
to any remark that could be interpreted as racist.

Early one morning, while in the kitchen eating toast and
writing on her laptop, Lucille was disturbed by shouts. The
louder voice was Janine's. The other person was Clare, the
officer in charge, who was trying to explain that she was not
picking on Janine because she was black, she was merely asking
her not to forget the door entry code again. It appeared that

Janine had for the third time rung the doorbell after midnight and woken up the staff member on duty.

"All she said was 'Please try to remember the code next time you're out late.'"

"But she wouldn't have talked like that to a white person."

Clare pointed out the worker in question was black too.

"But you're white and you're having a go at me as well."

Janine stormed into the kitchen. Lucille poured a mug of coffee and offered it to her.

Janine yelled, "And you stop patronising me!" and knocked the mug out of Lucille's hand. Coffee splashed over the table and over Lucille's laptop. The laptop gave up the ghost. Lucille stared in horror at the dark blank screen and clicked uselessly with the mouse. Janine grabbed a tea towel and dabbed frantically at the keyboard. It was hopeless.

Lucille told herself this was by no means the worst thing that had happened to her recently, not by a long shot. Janine was now in floods of tears and Lucille tried to console her, but she was soon in tears herself.

Then she remembered—she had backed up her memoir on that little pink memory-stick, and it was still safely in her handbag. All the same, the accident was a major setback. With no insurance, she could afford neither a new machine nor a repair. Clare allowed her to work on the second office computer when it was not in use. But it nearly always was in use, by people searching for jobs and accommodation, checking benefits, writing official letters. "I can't put my hobby ahead of all that," she said, and Clare had to agree, though she added, "Don't call your writing a hobby, Lucille. It's more than that."

But after a lot of discussion, and trying to think where she

243

could find the money for a new computer, Lucille gave up, rang Andrew Charlton to say she had to drop out of the memoir course, and returned to notebook and ballpoint pen. She resolved that once she was earning again, her first purchase would be a new laptop.

She told Clare she intended to leave as soon as she could. Clare helped her to find job opportunities online and in the local paper, and she contacted the big Bristol department stores direct. Once her bruises had disappeared she began to go out to job interviews. She explained the gap in her CV by saying she'd been made redundant, and moved to Bristol and taken some time off for family reasons. With a kind reference from Richley's, signed by Marcia Johnson, she was taken on as a personal shopper by a large store in Bristol city centre. Next, she found a tiny furnished flat. She could just afford the deposit out of the last of Jason's payments into her bank account.

The Friday she got the flat she went to talk to Clare. "I can move out on Sunday. I just have to fetch some of my stuff from Oxford. I've taken tomorrow off work."

Clare said, "You're so resilient, Lucille. I've spoken to the other staff and we wondered if you would come back and take part in the group work programme, as an official volunteer. If you agree, we'd like you to be co-leader with Tania in her next self-esteem group."

CHAPTER TWENTY-NINE

A Return Visit to Oxford

Lucille hired a small van and drove to Oxford. Helen and Rod came to the storage depot with her, and she was grateful for their company and support. They went up in the lift and made their way through the big echoey building. All those compartments holding so much sadness behind their bright yellow doors, she thought—the loved possessions of people who like her had lost their home, and couldn't bear to part with their things, hoping they would be needed again some day. She unlocked her compartment and sifted through her remaining belongings.

Into the box for Oxfam went *The Green Lady*. Lucille apologised silently to her dead mother, who had loved that picture, and she promised she'd always keep the little gold cross, even though she couldn't accept what it stood for. She took away linen and cutlery, and left most of the clothes. She left her furniture, too; she was determined that one day she would again be able to afford an unfurnished flat and from there fight her way back on to the homeowner ladder.

As they travelled down in the lift and pushed the trolley to the van, she felt a small increase in hope and a sense of a new beginning.

Helen and Rod gave her lunch at their house. She told them about the Fairways Refuge and the new job and the memoir and her ambitions. Telling it all to old friends who cared made what was past seem more bearable and her hopes for the future seem more realistic. "I've heard it said that everything happens for a reason, and I think that's rubbish. But all the same, if you are very lucky—and I have been lucky—you can turn your life around even when you're an old lady of forty-four. You two are part of my luck—I owe you such a lot."

When it was time to go, Lucille said to Helen as casually as she could, "Have you heard anything on the university grapevine about Walter Farquarson? We lost touch after I went back to Jason."

She thought she saw Rod catch Helen's eye and Helen shake her head ever so slightly.

Helen answered. "Just that he got an award, an OBE, in the New Year's Honours, for services to the domestic abuse charity and the refuge he set up … Oh, and he was best man at the wedding of that other historian, Professor Paul Wright."

So Paul's Internet dating has paid off, she thought. "That's good to hear." It seemed an awfully long time since she and Walter and Paul had been eating chocolate cake and drinking tea in Frank's bookshop.

Helen riffled through a pile of papers on a kitchen shelf. "I've kept the cutting from the *Oxford Times* for you."

The photo showed Paul grinning from ear to ear and a little too portly for his obviously hired morning suit—she remembered him complaining that he came out where he ought to go in. Next to Paul stood a smiling sixtyish woman in a floaty cream dress, and on his other side was Walter, a surprisingly elegant, tall figure half-turned towards the bridegroom, as proud and affectionate as if he'd been Paul's father.

"Do keep it if you want," said Helen. Lucille folded the cutting carefully and put it away in her handbag.

On the way into town she wondered what was the meaning of that glance Helen and Rod had exchanged after she asked for news about Walter. There was something they hadn't told her. Had Walter, like Paul, found himself a new partner? If he had, they wouldn't have wanted to mention it, for fear of upsetting her.

Lucille's next stop was the coffee shop near Richley's. Marigold, Jillie and Annette joined her when they came out from work. They all beamed and hugged her and soon, each in her own way, commented on how Lucille had changed. Not surprisingly, Jillie noticed how little make-up she was wearing. And Annette recognised the sober outfit she had bought at the time of her second makeover, and had worn to work for only a few days before being advised that these clothes weren't fashionable enough for a personal shopper.

"I'll be back to normal for work on Monday," she assured them.

"You do seem a bit more serious, pet," said Marigold, "somehow not so happy-go-lucky." I never really was happy-go-lucky, she thought, I was just pretending.

They moved on to The Eagle and Child. "We used to call it The Bird and the Baby," said Marigold. Lucille thought sadly about the evenings here after the memoir class. She was glad it was not a Wednesday because she felt ashamed of having dropped out, and she did not want to run into Andrew and her old classmates. She managed to put that out of her mind, and soon she was enjoying the catch-up with her friends. It was a good antidote to the hurt she was feeling at the idea of Walter with a new woman.

She described the larger, grander department store where she now worked, and the nice part of Bristol where her flat was located. The area reminded her of Jericho, she said—trendy, lively, but quite a village atmosphere. And after some hesitation she let on about her new career ambitions—her writing, and another plan she had started to form. "If my volunteer work goes well, I may try to get some social work or counsellor training. I'd be what they call a mature student, and I should be eligible for some sort of grant or loan." Once she'd shared her own big news, the others followed suit. She could not remember a conversation when the four of them had confided so much and felt so close to one another.

Marigold was soon to retire and would spend two days a week taking care of her grandchildren. "And my better half says we're to celebrate our fortieth anniversary with a cruise round the Greek islands."

Lucille grinned. "Don't do anything I wouldn't do." Though she couldn't visualise Marigold and Bill making love in the sea as she and that Yannis had done.

Jillie had important news as well. "Geoff and I are getting married. We want to start a family before I'm too old."

Now it was Annette's turn. How could she cap that? Lucille felt quite sorry for her. But Annette's news turned out to be the biggest bombshell of the lot. "I tried Internet dating after all, but I kept it to myself because I knew you'd all tease me after I'd been so sniffy about it. Anyway, I've met somebody, and I think he may be The One." Lucille wished she could join them in the boozy toasts that followed, but she made do with diet Coke because she had to drive the van back to Bristol that night.

During the journey a touch of envy crept in alongside the joy for her three friends with their successful relationships. She wondered what Walter was doing, where he was, who he was with. She felt certain he had found a new partner. She thought about Jason, too, and hoped he was getting help. She cared about Jason still, but it was Walter she thought about most. That photo of him at Paul's wedding had re-awakened the feelings she had worked so hard to forget.

CHAPTER THIRTY

Walter in Crisis

The day after Paul's wedding, Walter sat in his college room waiting for his next tutorial. He hated having to teach the students in pairs or even threesomes in order to fit in with the so-called reforms, which simply meant that the college made more money, the student experience was less rich, and the tutor's life was more stressful. Younger colleagues, and those who had come to Oxford from newer universities, did not mind this, and there was much pompous talk about students learning from each other as if this was a new idea. We learned from each other in our day too, he thought, remembering the long talks with Sarah about history and literature, in punts and pubs and even in bed. He recalled trying to make love to her while she read aloud from *Paradise Lost* and pretended to be unaware of his caresses—the memory of that afternoon always made him smile.

Perhaps it was because of those vivid memories that when his student Sharon Brennan came in wearing a plain blue dress he almost gasped, she reminded him so much of Sarah. Then he thought, No, not Sarah—Rosie. Not the Rosie he had seen in Bristol but the lively, healthy, merry young woman she had been before Nigel entered her life. Except that this Sharon Brennan was quiet and solemn, and when she spoke she sounded like Lucille Brown.

Her tutorial partner had a cold, and sent his apologies, she said.

Walter was glad of the chance to see Sharon by herself. Her work was meticulous, but this essay was the third he had read that barely reached the standard of a pass. It was properly referenced, grammar and spelling perfect, but dull and laconic. The facts were all there, neatly summarised, but the only ideas in it were paraphrases of parts of his lectures or books on the reading list. Nothing of her own. She's afraid to express herself, afraid to take risks, he thought.

She read the grade he had given her, C+, and looked at him with fear in her eyes. "I'm sorry," he said.

Before he could begin to explain the grade, she started to cry. She scrabbled in her handbag. Embarrassed, he handed her some tissues and tried again. "I'm sure you have ideas of your own on the question. I know you read widely, and you have soaked up quite a few facts about those wars. But you must have noticed that not every historian explains the facts in the same way. So what do *you* think, Sharon? I wanted your own opinion—backed up by evidence and argument, of course."

"I'm going to fail, aren't I?" She began to cry again. He remembered some details about her. The reference from her school, somewhere up north, had said her mother was a single parent and they lived on a "sink estate". Somewhere up north—that was why she sounded like Lucille Brown. The college had been delighted to receive Sharon's application, since they had been criticised in the newspapers for social class bias.

She got up to go, muttering between sobs, "Sorry. There's no point."

He rose and put his arms round her and she pressed her face

into his shoulder and cried some more, and then he felt her grow tense. He released her and motioned her to sit down again. She remained standing.

"All right, Sharon, I won't keep you today, but can you come back tomorrow and we'll have a longer conversation. I know you are perfectly capable. It's just a matter of loosening up, I think. I'm sure I can help you if you'll only try to do what I ask."

He watched her as she walked across the quad; she was still crying. She met a female friend and said something to her, and the friend put an arm around her and led her away. Walter was glad she had someone to comfort and take care of her.

Sharon did not keep the appointment next day. Two days later one of the women Fellows sent a note asking Walter to come and see her in her room. She was at her desk and she asked him to sit down.

"Why so formal, Margaret?"

"We've had a complaint about you, I'm afraid. I have to talk to you in my role as Chair of the Harassment Complaints Committee. One of the first-year undergraduates, Sharon Brennan, claims you touched her inappropriately and offered to help her pass the exams in exchange for sexual favours."

Walter was silent for a moment. He tried to make sense of what he'd just heard. He stared at Margaret. "It's only three days ago. I can remember every detail of our meeting. I can't have forgotten. When she saw I'd marked her essay C+, she started to cry and I tried to comfort her and I promised to help her with her essays. I planned to give her practice in speaking her mind in her answers to what one might call 'opinion' questions."

"You're saying she's made this up?"

That nice young woman? She had no reason to want to hurt him. "Why would she do that? No, this must be a misunderstanding."

"I'm afraid I'll have to convene the Complaints Committee. In the meantime, I must ask you not to communicate with Sharon Brennan. We'll let you know what the next step will be as soon as we can."

Walter had no idea who spread the story around. Oxford University was a very leaky institution. It could have been college staff, or students—Sharon Brennan herself or one of her friends and mentors. It even reached a student newspaper: *Well-liked History Don accused of Sexual Harassment*. At least he was not named and nor was his college, and the word "*alleged*" appeared several times in the report.

The Complaints Committee recognised that it was his word against Sharon's. An informal meeting was arranged. Sharon attended with her "supporter". The latter turned out to be a consistently angry young woman who ran a women's group and had a track record of leading protests against the college authorities. Walter recognised her as the person Sharon had met in the quad after the tutorial.

Paul came to the meeting as Walter's supporter. Before they went into Margaret's office he said, "Now Walter, just keep your cool and tell the truth. The poor girl's got the wrong end of the stick and that so-called friend of hers has probably told her that if she doesn't complain she'll have let the side down and she'll be shamed."

Walter spoke directly to Sharon. "I'm so sorry I gave the wrong impression. What I meant to say was that I would help you to produce better essays, encourage you to express your own ideas. All I asked was that you should follow my advice, nothing more."

He turned to the Committee. "It makes no sense to say I offered to fix her exam results. I couldn't do that even if I wanted to—the candidate's name wouldn't be on the answer paper, and anyway I'm not an examiner this year."

"That's correct," said one of the Committee members.

Sharon's companion said, "You touched her."

"But you were crying, Sharon. I've got a daughter of my own, your age ..." His voice trailed away and he felt close to tears himself. He addressed the others. "I would hug my daughter if she was crying."

Sharon said in a small voice, "I'm so sorry." She paused. "I haven't got a father."

"And I'm sorry too," said Walter.

There was silence.

"Professor Farquarson. Does your apology mean you accept that you did what you are accused of?"

"No, absolutely not. But I'm deeply sorry to have given Sharon the wrong impression."

"Ms Brennan?"

"Please can we drop this? I was muddled. I got it wrong." Sharon's companion whispered something to her, and she shook her head.

The committee members went outside to confer. The opposing parties were left to sit together in silence, trying not to look at one another.

When the Committee came back, Margaret said the matter must now be considered closed. However, the Committee had decided Ms Brennan should be transferred to a woman tutor.

Walter and Paul went to Walter's room. "Cheer up, old man," said Paul as he poured the whisky. "Naturally you must feel a bit bruised. And I know you're sorry for the lass, but she's young and the young recover fast."

Walter gulped down his whisky, and needed a second glass before he could reply. He castigated himself for all the times he had mindlessly believed rumours about men who were accused of harassment and, if the accusation turned out to be false, he had joined in the angry backlash against their female accusers. And he thought about Sharon Brennan and all the obstacles she had overcome in her life.

"I'm still ashamed. I keep wondering what Sarah would have said."

"Sarah would have told you to stop blaming yourself."

"Sometimes I feel as if we are both dead, not just Sarah. Perhaps that's how it ought to be."

"What do you mean?"

"I don't know what I mean. Let's drop the subject. Shouldn't you be going home now? Beth will be wondering where you've got to."

"I won't leave unless you come with me." Paul took Walter home to Jericho for a scratch supper with Beth.

Afterwards they drank coffee and ate shortbread. Walter had little to say and left it to Paul to tell Beth about the meeting in College and how the harassment complaint had been resolved.

Their attempts to console him were touching but ineffectual.

"Poor girl. And poor you," said Beth. "But all the same, you must be relieved."

"Not entirely. I can't understand how it happened. How could I have misjudged the situation so badly? And the students will probably mistrust me from now on. No smoke …"

"'No smoke without fire' is a stupid, nasty proverb," said Paul.

Walter tried to smile, and with an effort asked about their week. They had been to an exhibition in London, and spent one afternoon making bread and another preparing the garden for summer. Next week it was Beth's birthday and they had booked a weekend in Paris.

Paul said, "We're making up for those years alone before we knew each other."

"Yes. The one life we have. Making every moment count," said Beth.

Walter blurted out, "I've had enough."

"Of what?"

Walter ignored Paul's question. "I ought to be going home."

Paul tried again. "What have you had enough of?"

"Oh … the college, the students … and Rosie and John don't need me any more. But I tell myself to get a grip. You have to go on living till you die."

"There was never a truer word spoken, my friend," said Paul. Even Walter had to smile at the mock solemnity of his tone.

Beth asked about Rosie and John.

"John's made arrangements to go to Peru for a year. I blame you, Paul. You bought him that book about a teddy bear. It came from 'Darkest Peru' and John has had a fixation about the place ever since."

"Surely that's not the only reason?"

"There's a dig—well, an enormous excavation—at a site called Chan Chan. Built in the ninth century. A huge pre-Inca city. Marvellous decorated adobe walls. Grave goods in burial chambers. Canals."

"Yes. I've read about it," said Paul.

Walter wanted to block the question he knew was coming

next. He rattled on. "I wish we could have continued south after our trip to Ecuador. Did you know about all these other fantastic sites in Peru? Not just Machu Pichu. Though we must go to Machu Pichu, of course. I think there might be an alumni holiday we could take, the three of us … It's very high, involves a lot of strenuous walking. We ought to go while we are still reasonably fit."

"Yes, OK. We'll think about it … But you still haven't told us how Rosie is doing."

Walter shook his head. "I haven't anything to tell you. I just wish I had." He rose and said an abrupt goodnight.

Back home, Walter went straight to Sarah's books. Nothing. He slumped briefly in the chair, then hauled himself upright and walked slowly out of the drawing room, past the study, across the hall and up the stairs to their bedroom. He stood beside the chest and peered at the two lines of photos. Nothing. He felt … not distraught, not tearful, but as though everything had become bland, grey, empty and pointless. Utterly pointless.

He phoned Rosie. As he expected, he got no reply. John. No reply either. It was almost as though they too had turned against him.

He thought about Paul and his happiness with Beth, and his own aloneness and his failure as tutor and parent.

The sleeping tablets on the bedside cabinet caught his eye, and he remembered the painkillers in Sarah's bathroom cupboard—they had been forgotten, along with her few jars of simple creams and lotions, on that terrible day when he and Rosie had cleared away her things.

The doorbell rang. It was so late he assumed it must be a mistake, or someone who meant to burst in and rob him. He looked out of the window and recognised Paul's rickety bicycle with its big old-fashioned basket.

"Beth made me come. I think she picked up vibes that I missed this evening. Walt, old man, are you OK? Really? And Beth said I was not to pussyfoot around but to ask you straight out—are you feeling suicidal?"

"No, it's just the worry and tiredness," he began. Then he confessed what he had planned to do. "I need sleep—I was going to take some tablets … I suppose I don't much care whether I wake up or not."

"You haven't taken any yet, have you?"

Walter shook his head.

"Some whisky would be nice," Paul said. "I'll just go to the loo while you pour it out for us. I'll take mine neat, with maybe a few nuts or a biscuit."

After Paul returned, the two of them sipped their drinks and again talked over everything that had happened. Paul said he couldn't leave because he had drunk too much to be able to cycle in a straight line. He took a sponge bag out of his jacket pocket. "I brought my toothbrush just in case."

When they turned in for the night Walter found that the sleeping tablets and painkillers had disappeared.

* * *

The fact that Walter's name had been cleared did not make the student newspaper. "That's always the way," said Paul. Walter passed many restless nights mulling over the harassment accusation. He thought about John and Rosie and missed them dreadfully, and he missed Sarah more than ever.

258

And though he tried to convince himself that gossip didn't matter, he noticed a change in how the students related to him. At first, there was a buzz whenever a group of them saw him, followed by a silence when they came closer. After a day or two this stopped happening, but they did not greet him as they used to.

Walter's next lecture after the harassment meeting was as well attended as ever. Over fifty young people, some trying to record his every word, tapping on tablets, scribbling in notepads, and others staring at him the whole time as if mesmerised. He looked in vain for Sharon Brennan. No one lingered behind to chat or ask questions.

In the tutorials later that week both men and women students were cool and formal. The young man who had been Sharon Brennan's tutorial partner sent a note to ask if he might make a third with two of his female friends whom Walter also tutored.

"Writing and research is all that's left to make my life meaningful," he said to Paul. "Rosie has cut herself off, John has a very full life, and now I can't seem to connect with the students any more."

They were drinking tea in Walter's college room. In the dusk outside, students were hurrying past in groups, laughing and chattering, returned from tutorials or sports and on their way to end-of-term parties.

"Term's nearly over. This too will pass. And in the meantime, focus on the other part of your job, your writing and research." Paul waved at a line of books by Walter Farquarson. "What's next?"

"Women."

"Oh, that's excellent news. We'd be so pleased if ..."

"That's not what I mean. I've given up the Internet dating. What I meant to say is that I'm working on a book about seventeenth-century women."

Paul's disappointment was almost comical. "That's interesting ... And talking of women, what's happening with your women's refuge?"

The refuge was up and running, Walter said. He chaired the meetings of the trustees. "And I'm carrying on with the fund-raising. Also, I've come to realise how complicated it all is."

"In what way?"

"One shouldn't make easy assumptions, I suppose. When I went to visit the place, I met some of the residents. I hadn't expected to find so many different background stories. And different social classes, too—even people like us, if you know what I mean.

"And such a range of disadvantages and obstacles overcome. What a lot it takes to get out from under. The courage they need to leave their abusers. And the touching faith so many women have in their man's ability to change. I used to think it was just a matter of having the gumption to walk out and start over.

"To be honest, I'd rather despised them for choosing the wrong men and being weak, though of course I kept that to myself. It was Sarah who really cared."

"But, Walter, you went to such a lot of trouble setting up the refuge. And I know you gave them much more money than was allotted in Sarah's will. Your own money."

"That was all for Sarah's sake. Now I'm determined to do a bit more. I'm going to increase my financial contributions. And I'll try to be more active. I know I'm not qualified to help the victims of abuse directly, but I'm good at administration. The staff have so many ideas for expansion, especially about education and training for workers and clients both. They're particularly interested in some sort of group therapy, I think."

CHAPTER THIRTY-ONE

Group Work and Counselling

In the first few sessions of the group, Lucille said little, and left it to Tania, the psychologist, to guide the discussion. The members told their story and learned to take note of their achievements and the hurdles they had overcome, the battles they had fought and won. She could see evidence of self-confidence boosted through getting and giving help. Despite Tania's efforts to bring everyone in, and even after she had tried to parcel out the talk time more evenly, the group came to be dominated by those who felt comfortable to speak in front of others. So not everyone benefitted equally.

In her supervision with Clare after the fifth session, Lucille suggested that all the members, but particularly the quieter ones, might gain from some non-talking activity. Lucille's idea was to tackle the self-esteem issue from another angle.

"I'd like to try something new. As a personal shopper, every day I see women come into our department looking awful, and miserable, as though they hate themselves, and leave the store with a bit of a smile and a spring in their step."

"Yes, and it costs them an arm and a leg. You may know the business, Lucille, but you can't replicate that in here."

"I'd like to try."

Lucille bombarded the fashion departments of every store in Bristol and persuaded them to donate garments that were destined for their next sale.

Helen went to the storage facility in Oxford and drove to Bristol with the bin bags full of clothes from there, and others that Jason had delivered to Jillie's. She also brought the tall mirror that once stood on the landing outside Lucille's flat.

Lucille wheedled free samples from beauty counters—tiny pots of coloured creams and powders, and tubes of fawn and brown foundation, and lipsticks in every possible shade from palest pink to wildest orange. She discovered a website where you could sign up as a "tester" of new products from big name manufacturers. With her own money—it was the money she had saved towards the new laptop—she bought a cheap sewing machine. Finally, she brought in a stack of fashion magazines.

After two weeks she was ready to start. Tania offered to be her assistant.

"Honestly, Tania, I don't mind if you say 'supervisor'. I really need your feedback and advice. I've never done anything like this in my life."

"Here's the plan," she told the group. "Each person will get a new outfit, good enough for job interviews, and new make-up. A makeover. We'll aim for everybody to have a turn over the next few weeks. We'll have to learn to sew and alter the clothes. I'll try to remember what my mother taught me. She was expert at make-do-and-mend."

"What shall we call our group?" asked Tania.

"'Make-Do-and-Mend?'" someone suggested.

"That sounds a bit depressing. Anything more cheerful?"

Tania said "Dress for Success", and Janine proposed "Style Yourself Stronger" or "The Makeover Group". They voted, and "The Makeover Group" won.

A colleague of Tania's, another psychologist, got them to fill in a questionnaire, a "before" test of self-esteem. She said she'd come back after eight weeks and test them again, to see if they felt any different about themselves.

They dragged a bench and two tables into one of the larger group rooms. They hung dresses and skirts on hangers along a rail, and next to them on the bench the other clothes were folded and laid out in neat piles like in a store. On one small table lay the cosmetics, shiny and tempting, and on the other was the new sewing machine. The tall mirror stood near the window.

"Who would like to be the first guinea pig?" said Lucille. There was silence and everyone seemed to be avoiding her eye. She realised she was asking a great deal; no one wanted to be the centre of attention – they were all very short on self-confidence and optimism.

Lucille looked across at Tania, hoping Tania would come up with some professional ploy to draw a volunteer out of a group of reluctant, unhappy people. Then suddenly Janine spoke up and said she would do it if nobody else would. Lucille knew she was trying to make amends for the computer accident.

Together the group selected a new outfit for Janine, a slim black skirt that had once belonged to Lucille, and a draped top in soft blue jersey. Over the next few days, three of the best needlewomen altered the garments—an inch off the hem, a little easing at the waist, a little more modesty at the neckline. Another member of the group trimmed Janine's hair.

The following Saturday Jillie visited from Oxford with a colleague who specialised in make-up for dark skin. While Janine received her expert treatment, Jillie and Lucille helped the others experiment with lipsticks and foundations. Friendly laughter and compliments drowned out the occasional protest and a few "Oh my God!"s as people saw their faces transformed.

At last Lucille called the group to order. Janine came out of the next room where she had put on the skirt and top. Everyone started to clap. Another member led her to the mirror, which was covered with a sheet. Janine was told to pull off the sheet. It was like Her Majesty the Queen unveiling a portrait of herself.

"A miracle!" Janine exclaimed.

"No. It's not a miracle," said Lucille. "It's just you, Janine, with different clothes and cosmetics and a little help from your friends."

Janine said, "Thanks so much, to all of you. We're a talented lot, aren't we?"

After that there was no shortage of volunteers for a makeover.

* * *

"How about a part-time counselling course?" Clare suggested. Lucille's dream was coming true far sooner than she had expected. She applied to a College of Further Education.

With Clare's help, she wrote her personal statement. She touched lightly on her own relevant life experience and mentioned that she had been accepted on to the creative writing course in Oxford but had to drop out when she moved away. She described her work as a personal shopper and how some of the same skills should help her to become an effective counsellor—listening, and drawing people out, and helping them to feel better about themselves. She tried to put into words how much she had learned at the refuge, and how much she had gained from her work as a volunteer. Clare and Tania provided references.

A gruelling interview followed, which focused especially on the question whether her recent experiences and her unhappy childhood would interfere with her ability to see other people's problems clearly. Might she over-identify with them? She answered that she recognised the danger but she believed she could cope; on the plus side, she was sure she would be able to empathise with her clients all the more accurately through having suffered loss and hurt and humiliation herself.

She got a wait list place and someone dropped out, and so she started the counselling course earlier than she'd planned. It was necessary to take on one client in her first term, and she needed a supervisor. Clare suggested they might find a client among the callers to their domestic abuse helpline and Clare herself would supervise. Lucille joined the helpline volunteer team.

So now she was running a group, working full-time at the department store, writing her memoir, attending classes in the evenings, answering calls to the helpline, and might soon have her first client.

"It's like I'm starting a new life," she said to Clare. "Do you think I could go back to my real name? I called myself Lucille because I wanted to sound alluring and sexy and special. My parents had me christened Mary, and now that seems more suitable somehow."

"Mary Brown it is." There were a few forms to fill in, but it was no more complicated than the change of surname after each of her marriages. She still thought of herself as "Lucille"—after twenty years it was hard to shake off the habit—yet when people called her "Mary", she felt more grown-up, more dignified and more sensible.

It took a while for her client to materialise. They waited for a Bristol-based woman to ring the helpline, someone who might benefit from counselling and who didn't need emergency help.

At last they heard from a young woman who seemed suitable. She refused to give her name. Lucille had taken the first call. The caller was living with a man who tyrannised her and hit her occasionally, but who could be kind and even romantic and inspiring. She said she couldn't leave him. She hoped he would change—in fact she was sure he would. All she needed was someone who would listen to her worries and help her to cope until her partner got over his problems. She rang again a few days later and asked for "Mary" again.

"We could talk regularly if you like. On the phone, or here at the refuge if it suits you better."

"It would be easier to come and see you. My partner makes it difficult for me to talk on the phone."

"Do you feel you can give me your name now?"

"Rosie."

Lucille struggled to stay calm. "It's Rosie Farquarson, isn't it? I thought I recognised your voice. But when you said you work at a supermarket, I assumed I must be mistaken, as you were at university when we met. Rosie, this is Lucille Brown speaking."

Rosie seemed puzzled. Lucille explained that she was a friend of Rosie's father, though they'd lost touch since her move to Bristol, and mentioned the two occasions when she and Rosie had met—when Walter brought Rosie and John to lunch and when Rosie came to Oxford to visit her mother's grave.

Lucille wished she had found out earlier that this caller was Rosie Farquarson. It was frowned upon as unprofessional to take on people you knew as clients. Besides, she did not want to betray Walter by admitting that she knew more than Rosie confided to her, in particular about the abortion. Feeling guilty and foolish, she apologised for her name change. "Mary's my real name. I changed it to Lucille for work reasons." She added, "It might be preferable for you to talk to one of my colleagues."

"Oh, no, Mary. Please let me go on talking to you."

Lucille explained that she would have to discuss this with her supervisor.

Clare helped to sort out the dilemma. It was for Rosie to choose whether to continue with Lucille or start again with a different counsellor. As to what Walter had told her about Rosie—Lucille must simply wait for Rosie to reveal that herself, if she wished.

The next evening Rosie rang the helpline and again asked for Mary Brown.

"I've talked it over with my supervisor. It's up to you, Rosie. If you want to stick with me, that's OK. But if you'd prefer someone else that's OK too."

"I'd much rather continue with you, Mary. You seem to understand, and it would be awful to have to explain everything all over again to another counsellor." Lucille started to say that one reason why she was able to understand was because their experience was similar, but she remembered in time that this was about Rosie, not about her. Rosie had been told that many people who worked for the charity were themselves survivors of abuse, and this was enough.

"A couple of other things. Everything you say to me is in confidence. But you realise I'm a trainee? I guarantee I won't talk about you except to my supervisor. And if you happen to mention me to John or your father, would you mind not telling them who I am? Please just refer to me as Mary." Lucille wanted to spare Walter the awkwardness he might feel if he knew. And she didn't want Walter to guess that she herself had been abused. She did not want his pity; she still cared what he thought of her.

After these preliminaries, Rosie attended weekly one-to-one sessions with Lucille at the refuge. She had to invent excuses to give to Nigel, such as overtime at the supermarket, a doctor's appointment, or a visit to a friend to borrow something, usually money. Lucille felt for her as she declared tearfully how much she hated to tell these lies.

Lucille put to use what she learned on her counselling course and in the group work sessions with Tania, ways of building self-esteem and fighting depression and making decisions.

She arranged for an expert on addictions to see Rosie and explain the kind of help that might be available to Nigel, and all the difficulties involved. The main problem was that Nigel refused to seek help. And even if he agreed, recovery would not be an easy process, although medication would help to conquer the withdrawal effects which tormented him when he tried to cut down on his own. The consultant emphasised how danger-ous it was to mix alcohol and cocaine.

CHAPTER THIRTY-TWO

Rosie in Crisis

Without his phone conversations with Rosie and John, Walter felt bereft. John was now in Peru. He had spent part of the summer in Oxford, and like Rosie, collected his bachelor's degree in absentia. Walter received emails from him at weekly intervals. Every time he wrote back, he asked John for news of his sister and week after week John repeated that he had none to give.

At last that changed. John wrote:

Dad, forgive me. I've been claiming I hadn't heard from Rosie, but it wasn't true. She made me promise not to tell you and even threatened to cut off all contact if I did. At long last she's given me the go-ahead to tell you what has been happening.

I should start by saying her situation has improved a lot. Now here's what led up to that, and to her change of heart. I'm hoping she'll contact you herself soon and fill you in better than I can.

As well as taking her mobile phone away and spending most of their money, Nigel has hit her more than once. Each time he was sorry afterwards and insisted he could cut back on the drinking and the drugs. And each time she believed him. She still does, it seems. And she absolutely refuses to involve the police.

One particularly bad attack left her so severely bruised that someone at the supermarket noticed and persuaded her to get in touch with one of those helplines. After two or three phone conversations, she started going to sessions with the person she'd talked to, a counsellor called Mary.

Now this Mary has somehow got her to be more open with me and we've managed a couple of phone calls and more emails. Rosie says her discussions with Mary are helping her to sort out what is going on, what her goals are, what she could do to turn her life around.

Mary arranged a meeting with an expert on "double addictions" and this expert gave Rosie a clearer picture of Nigel's problems and how they might be tackled if he could only be persuaded to stop his denial and accept help. She hasn't given up hope of persuading Nigel to seek treatment, but at least she knows now what she and Nigel are up against.

So that's the position at present. It's great to know Rosie has found someone she can confide in and who can help her find her way through this mess.

Hang in there, Dad. My guess is that after coming clean with her baby brother she'll soon be back in touch with her old dad as well.

Walter read John's email over and over. He tried to ring him, but there was no signal in the area where John was working.

He walked to Jericho to see Paul and Beth, partly to prevent himself from trying to contact Rosie, partly because he so badly wanted to share his news.

All Paul and Beth had known up till now was that Rosie was out of touch. He told them about Nigel, and Rosie dropping out of university, and showed them the email from John.

"I know Paul's very fond of John and Rosie," said Beth. "I'm looking forward to meeting them. We are very happy with each other, but we do sometimes wish we had a daughter or a son to sort of complete us. Paul has always envied you that, you know."

"Well, here's proof of the heartache and worry that comes with being a parent."

"I wish you had felt able to talk to me about Rosie instead of bottling it up," said Paul. "I do care, you know."

"I know. It's my stupid pride, I suppose. Sarah and I told each other everything, and since Sarah died I've tried to keep my troubles to myself."

He asked them what he should do now, and they both insisted he should do nothing.

"This counsellor seems to be helping her to sort it all out," said Paul.

"Yes. It sounds like exactly the right kind of support. Rosie must reach her decisions herself," said Beth. "And if she fails with this Nigel, at least she'll know she has done her best." Echoes of Lucille's wise counsel when he'd told her about his longing to help Rosie after the abortion, and his own advice, prompted by Paul, to the woman on *partnersforall* who was trying to rescue her marriage.

Calmer now, Walter stretched out his legs before the open fire. The fire was one of several improvements to the little house in Jericho since Beth had come to live with Paul. There were new, scarlet rugs on the plain dark floor, bright cushions on the chairs, and the delicious aroma of recent baking pervaded the open-plan room.

"Is that shortbread I can smell?"

* * *

It was some weeks before Walter received the longed-for email from Rosie.

John has told you, I expect … She began with the information he had already received from John—he knew it by heart. He read on rapidly, hoping something might have changed.

A few things had. Rosie wrote that she regretted her long silence, her unwillingness to confide in him, her "*ungrateful and unkind*" rejection of his offers of help. Now she had rehearsed with her counsellor, Mary, what she should say to him, and she had realised he would forgive her. Mary had helped her to see she was not worthless or stupid or a disgrace to her father and mother, and that her decision to abort the baby was not wicked. To stick with Nigel and try to help him was not wrong, either, though she now accepted that her efforts might be of no avail.

Nigel doesn't change, unfortunately. Mary suggested I keep a record of drug- and drink-free days. And I've been shocked to find they are getting fewer—I hadn't realised, or maybe I just didn't want to face facts. On his better days he can still remind me of the Nigel I once knew, but I'm beginning to see that staying with him simply means I am supporting his habit and shielding him from the worst consequences. He is no longer drawing benefits and so I have to pay the rent and buy all our food.

I daren't nag him. He hasn't hit me for a while, though sometimes I can see he wants to. Mary has helped me to take note of the signs and signals and either distract him or get out of his way.

As I said to Mary the other day, things may have to get worse for Nigel before they get better. She said crisis intervention theory would predict that. (Every now and then I can pick up what she has been studying on her course. I gather the main approach is called cognitive-behavioural therapy.)

Other news—I'm still working at the supermarket, and they've promoted me to deputy manager. Better wages of course, but I half-miss being on the till. I met every sort of character, and in quiet times I dreamed up stories and novels to put them in. Though I can't guarantee I'll live up to Mum's standard, I'll be a writer one day, I promise you, Dad. I'll make you proud of me again.

By the way, it was Mary who advised me to add that last bit.

with much love
Rosie

Straightaway Walter rang Paul and Beth with his news about Rosie.

Next, he rang Mike. He asked Mike what else he could do for the St Frideswide's Centre. He could find some more money. He'd been thinking, he said. How were the extra services working out? What about the training opportunities and the groups Mike had talked about? Was cognitive-behavioural therapy available?

"CBT? Of course." Mike sounded amused and surprised to hear Walter talking like this. "They probably could do with more group work, but nobody can decide what approach would be the most useful."

"Is there any way to choose between them?"

"An up-to-date review of the research literature would help. And a meeting with some other domestic abuse charities. A seminar. Could you finance that? I can organise it, and maybe you could chair it? We could hold it at that hotel next to the Park and Ride."

Once they had agreed a date, Walter left Mike to arrange the seminar.

He waited for John's advice as to whether he should reply to Rosie and if so, what he should say. He was afraid an email or a letter might be intercepted by Nigel and for the same reason he was unwilling to phone.

John said, "Write. Just be careful what you say. If Nigel does get hold of it, make sure he won't find anything to upset him."

Walter wrote:

Dearest Rosie

So happy to learn that you are OK. If you need anything you know you can always turn to me and I'm here for you no matter what. I miss you very much.

Life goes on here much as usual. I'm working on the Levellers again and a new book on seventeenth century heroines is with the publishers. They're thinking of entering it for another prize—but this time round it doesn't seem important.

At College I've been elevated to Tutor for Admissions. A lot more paperwork, but it isn't boring. As I read through the applications, I think of you and John and all those family conferences when we talked about which universities would suit you best. Your mother was pro Bristol and I was pro York, I remember. Old-fashioned snob that I am, I'd secretly hoped you would opt for Oxford or Cambridge, but in the end your mother and I agreed you both chose well.

I've saved the best news till last. John has probably told you that Paul has remarried. I can add that his new wife is a kind,

clever, loveable woman and they are very happy. I do hope you
will meet Beth soon. I know you two will get on splendidly.
   with much love
   Dad

Walter hoped and waited, but for two weeks no reply came. He was lying awake trying to decide whether to write to her again, when at last he received a phone call from Rosie. It was after midnight. Before she had finished her first sentence, he started to grab his clothes with one hand.

"Dad, Nigel has beaten me up, but I'm OK—just a few bruises. I've left him and I'm coming home tomorrow."

"*Coming home tomorrow.*" He tried to focus on that, and not think about her being hurt. "Where are you? I'll come and fetch you."

"You needn't set out right now. Mary's brought me to a refuge. I've seen a doctor and I'm OK. Really. I just need some sleep. But if you'd like to come and collect me in the morning—" She gave him the address.

He said he hoped he might meet Mary when he picked Rosie up, but Rosie explained that the counsellor would be at work by then. "She has a day job as well."

Knowing he would not be able to sleep, Walter finished getting dressed. He rang John to give him the news. It was evening in Peru. Walter pictured John relaxing outside his tent in his dusty jeans. Once assured that Rosie had not been seriously hurt, John sounded overjoyed. The line kept breaking up but Walter caught the words "bastard", "great", "brilliant", "love" and "Mum". Finally, they got connectivity again and John said, "I wonder if we'll ever get the chance to thank this Mary."

"I hope so," said Walter.

* * *

Lucille let herself into the department store early. She was the first person on the premises. The place felt awe-inspiring but rather creepy, like an empty church. She used the extra time to sort out paperwork, wander round the fashion floor, and try to turn her mind to the requirements of the customers booked in that day. One lady had told them she wanted a dress to wear at the ball following her wedding. The customer's name began with "The Hon."—the daughter of a Lord or an Earl or some such. Probably it was because Lucille was over-tired—as she looked at the beautiful gowns in jewel-like colours and sumptuous fabrics, she had an overwhelming feeling, almost like a religious experience, like people in the Bible who saw visions or heard voices. Suddenly she knew she could not continue to lead two lives. She would have to find another way to make a living until she could become a full-time professional counsellor.

She had been up till two a.m. at the refuge, settling Rosie in, and debriefing with Clare, who happened to be on duty that night. Clare had persuaded her to sleep in a spare room rather than hire a taxi back to her flat on the other side of the city, but she'd left the refuge at seven, not wanting to be present when Walter Farquarson arrived to take Rosie home to Oxford.

In the weeks leading up to this latest attack, Rosie had de-scribed how Nigel's behaviour was becoming more and more erratic. His mood changes were sudden, and less and less pre-dictable, so that the strategies they had devised for avoiding slaps and punches no longer worked so well. And Rosie re-ported danger signs that Lucille recognised from her own experience as well as from the textbooks. Some days Nigel prevented Rosie from going to work, saying he needed to keep an eye on her. Another time he prevented her from coming to their session. Rosie had said she had a doctor's appointment, and he didn't believe her. And he accused her of having sex with other men. "Just because I'm temporarily incapacitated in that department is no excuse," he said. Once he made her go out to meet a drug dealer and pick up supplies on his behalf.

Lucille could hardly restrain herself from begging Rosie to leave him. But Clare insisted she must listen and wait, and simply reflect back to Rosie what Rosie was telling her. "In due course," Clare said, "she'll take a step back and see the situation for what it is. She'll listen to herself. Just keep helping her along with the decision-making. And, Mary, do make sure she knows what to do in an emergency." Though she knew it was against the rules, Lucille gave Rosie her private phone number and urged her to use it in an emergency.

Rosie did at last make up her mind to leave. She told Lucille that she'd explored all the alternatives and the pros and cons, and concluded that she did no good by staying, no good to Nigel, nor to herself, nor to those who loved her.

She had been planning to tell Nigel in advance, work out her notice at the supermarket, and arrange to go home to Oxford. But before she could summon the courage to broach the subject, Nigel beat her up badly. While he was in the bathroom she managed to ring Lucille at home. She said she was going to run away from him. She refused to call the police.

"I'll come and pick you up as soon as I can. If it's possible, grab some clothes and any important stuff, and go out on to the street." Lucille had difficulty getting a taxi. The ten minutes she had to wait allowed her time to call the refuge and check they had a bed available.

When the taxi reached Rosie's street, Lucille caught sight of Rosie standing in the bus shelter a few metres from the house where she lived. "There's the person we have to pick up."

The taxi slowed down and came to a halt beside the shelter, but when she saw it Rosie turned away and started to run in the opposite direction, back towards the house. Lucille realised that Rosie was afraid the driver was a kerb-crawler. A couple of cases had been reported in the local press, and one of the offenders was a taxi driver. Besides, it was natural to expect Lucille to arrive in a private car, not a taxi.

Lucille asked the driver to make a U-turn and go back the way they had come. When they had drawn level, she called to him to stop, and she jumped out and hurried across the road towards Rosie.

Just before Lucille reached the pavement, the front door of a house opened and a man ran down the steps. Rosie was running straight towards him, holding her rucksack in one hand and her shoulder bag in the other. Lucille yelled, "Rosie! Stop!", but it was too late.

"So you've changed your mind, have you? So you've decided to come back to lover boy?" Nigel grabbed Rosie and punched her in the stomach. She doubled up and fell. He began to kick her as she lay whimpering on the pavement.

Lucille threw herself upon him from behind, and tried to pull him away, but he was too strong for her. He turned round to face her and raised a fist to punch her instead of Rosie.

The next moment Nigel went crashing down under the impact of a small, dark figure who leapt on him out of nowhere and knelt on top of him, muttering what sounded like curses in a foreign language. The taxi driver. Lucille had forgotten all about him.

Soon Nigel seemed to be recovering and the driver was struggling to restrain him. The driver turned his head round. "You help please." Nigel's contortions were lifting the small man up and down; he would be unseated at any moment. Lucille crouched and seized Nigel's legs. Rosie took hold of the railings and hauled herself up. She was weeping, and Lucille guessed she was weeping for Nigel as much as for herself.

While the driver was saying something in heavily accented English, there came the sound of sirens. The driver had summoned the police and an ambulance. The paramedics confirmed that no one had been seriously injured; the police took statements from all of them and arrested Nigel.

When Nigel had been driven away, the two women got back into the taxi and Lucille asked the driver to take them to the address in Fairways. "Certainly, madam", said the driver. He spoke in a formal, courteous manner just as if he had not been involved with them in a violent, horrible scene and risked his own safety to help them.

On the way to the refuge, Rosie began to fret about Nigel. "Will he be all right, do you think?"

"It may sound strange," said Lucille, "but this could be the crisis, the turning point, that Nigel needs. With three witnesses no way could he escape a guilty verdict. I'm sure he'll plead guilty. He'll probably be given probation with a treatment order and he'll get help with his problems at last."

They shook hands with the taxi driver. "You saved two women tonight," said Rosie.

He gave her a lovely gappy smile. "Very happy. I too have a daughter. And is this lady your mother?"

Rosie shook her head. "No, but she's a very dear friend."

As soon as they were inside the refuge, Rosie telephoned Walter.

Then she hugged Lucille. "I don't know how to thank you, Mary. I'm going back to Oxford tomorrow, to live with my father. I just hope we'll see each other again some day."

CHAPTER THIRTY-THREE

Back in Oxford

Walter was so happy and excited he could scarcely concentrate on his driving. It was no use reminding himself of the dreadful events that led up to Rosie's departure from Bristol, or of Rosie's worries about Nigel's wellbeing—he could feel nothing but relief and elation. He had no room for anger toward Nigel, and though he tried to summon some sympathy when Rosie said she was sad for Nigel and she hoped the authorities would treat the man properly, he was soon smiling again and thinking only about Rosie. Safe now, and coming home with him at last.

Once again, he had trouble finding his way out of Bristol. For the rest of the journey, he tried to restrain himself from asking questions, though he longed to know what Rosie planned to do next, whether she would remain in the family home, or whether she would want to go back to her master's degree and her friends in Bristol. He chattered inconsequentially about his work and the College, about Paul and Beth, and about John, and when he saw Rosie stifle a yawn and start to nod off, he went quiet for the rest of the journey.

Rosie's room was ready for her. In the early hours of the morning, he had dusted and hoovered and made up the bed with his nicest sheets. He'd put a little posy of white roses on the chest next to a framed photograph of John in Peru and one of Sarah from the selection in his own bedroom.

For lunch he brought out a bottle of St Emilion, a frozen sliced loaf and some cheese and apples. "You always liked cheese on toast."

"If you'll let me live here rent-free I'll be your cook," she said. "To start with, we need to put the toaster on the frozen setting. Dad, what are you like!"

"Oh … I thought the microwave …"

Rosie began to laugh. Walter felt giddy with happiness. "We've got to ring John," he said.

There was no signal. "It's five hours earlier in Peru, but perhaps he's already out digging somewhere. Never mind, Dad. We'll have to send an email."

Their lunch was interrupted by a phone call from Paul.

Before Paul could speak, Walter burst out with the news that Rosie had come home at last. He summoned her to the phone and she said hullo and congratulated Paul on his marriage. She handed the receiver back. "Uncle Paul has something to tell you."

"Oh Paul, I'm sorry. You obviously rang for a reason."

Peter Corwood had died and Paul wanted Walter to attend the funeral. "I know you haven't seen as much of them as I have, but I gather you went out to Bournbrook once or twice with Lucille. It would mean a lot to Liz to see a good turnout, and I'm afraid many of their friends fell by the wayside as Peter's Alzheimer's progressed. Frankly, I'm trying to twist as many arms as I can."

"But I hardly knew him. Not at all, really. And he didn't know me, either. I don't see the point. If I came I'd feel a bit of a fraud."

"But the funeral's not for your benefit, nor for that matter is it for Peter's. It's for Liz."

Walter agreed to go to the funeral with Paul and Beth.

* * *

Peter Corwood's funeral took place a week later. Around a hundred people were packed in the crematorium chapel. A few elderly friends and neighbours, a cousin, some Fellows from Peter's college, and a number of middle-aged men who turned out to be ex-students of Peter's. Liz Corwood sat by herself at the front. Walter remembered having Rosie and John on either side of him throughout Sarah's funeral, and he was sorry there was no one for Liz. Paul whispered that Liz and Peter's son, who lived in Australia, had not been well enough to undertake the journey.

The humanist service was brief. Samuel Barber's *Adagio for Strings*, a poignant message from the son read out by the celebrant, tributes from the college and the Department of Pharmacology, and finally a short address. The celebrant had prepared with care. She had interviewed Liz and studied Peter's career. She concluded with words of consolation, "Peter Corwood did not believe in God or Heaven. But we are here to celebrate a life well lived. His was a rich life, an ethical life. This man did good in the world and made his family and friends proud and happy to have known him. Peter Corwood made a difference." Against his own expectation, Walter felt deeply moved.

Liz had arranged a wake at the Bournbrook village pub. The landlord was still in a black suit; he and his wife had been present at the funeral. "We called him the Prof," he said. "He was a regular, and everyone had a good word for him."

As Paul had predicted, Liz Corwood was delighted to see Walter. "It's so kind of you to come. Thank you." Then, to his dismay, she asked about Lucille Brown. "I wonder if you have any up to date news? Those Sunday visits of hers meant so much to Peter. The two of them got on beautifully, and her company would brighten up my own day as well. She explained about you being too busy to come with her, and I quite understood."

Walter nearly confessed that he had not even known of Lucille's visits, and stopped himself just in time. He had an urge to apologise for not coming himself, but decided Lucille's explanation was adequate, and more tactful than any other excuse he could think of. "By the way, I should tell you Lucille and I have … well, I'm afraid we've lost touch."

"Oh dear, it's always sad when friends drift apart. It happens such a lot these days—people seem busier than they used to be. Peter and I got quite isolated after his illness became obvious. But Lucille somehow managed to find time for us. She said it was easier for her because she only had an ordinary nine-to-five job. Such a lovely person. She gave me a lot of support, and practical help too, when Peter was so ill. We were upset when she had to leave Oxford. She said it was for a better job when Richley's had made her redundant. After her move she offered to come back and see us, but by that time I wasn't able to make arrangements. Peter was in hospital and it was near the end.

"I asked her to come today, of course, but she does volunteer work as well as a full-time job, so it just wasn't feasible."

"That's a pity," said Walter. He was half-glad and half-sorry.

"I'm so disappointed to hear you've lost touch. I hoped you might tell me more. She'd taken up writing, you know, and got accepted on to that prestigious creative writing course, but she had to drop out after she left Oxford."

Walter did not reply. He was struggling to process the news about Lucille's writing.

Paul and Beth came over to them.

"We were just talking about Lucille Brown," said Liz.

"Ah yes. Lucille Brown," said Paul. "As I've told Beth, Lucille Brown was—" Walter moved away to avoid having to hear more. After that unlucky chance meeting in Frank's bookshop, he had forbidden Paul to mention her. He sat down by himself and picked up the lunch menu, although they had already been well supplied with sandwiches and cake. Then he perused the details of Peter Corwood's life in the *Order of Service*: fifty years of happy marriage to Liz, the birth of their son, the long list of scientific achievements, Peter's love for his garden and wildlife. The photo on the front showed Peter smiling, an unforced smile of affection and happiness. Liz joined Walter again. "Lucille took that photograph the last time she was here," she said. "Just look at his smile. That's how she made Peter feel."

When he got home, Rosie told him she had just been talking to her counsellor Mary on the phone. "I wanted to thank her one more time."

CHAPTER THIRTY-FOUR

Another Award Ceremony

"Good. We can record this case as closed," said Clare. Lucille disliked the expression "this case", especially when it referred to Rosie Farquarson. Clare continued, "And I can tell you now, Mary, you are going to get an excellent report, even though you broke our 'no private phone number' rule. Next, you must concentrate on passing your exams."

Christmas intervened. Lucille spent Christmas Day at the refuge. She was delighted to find a card addressed to her there, from Rosie Farquarson. Enclosed was a letter:

Dear Mary

Thank you again for everything. My father and brother join me in wishing you all the very best for Christmas and for 2016. It's lovely to be back at home and I'm thoroughly enjoying the creative writing course.

I'm in charge of Christmas dinner, with a little help from my father—he's hopeless at cooking—and my brother, who at least knows how to make a white sauce. We'll have guests this year: my father's best friend Paul and his new wife; an older lady called Mrs Corwood who has recently lost her husband—Dad and Paul met them in the Galapagos; and an elderly lady colleague of Dad's. Dad says we're to invite anyone else we know who'd otherwise spend Christmas alone, and I think we

*may find ourselves sharing the feast with crowds of foreign
students who can't get home. Dad says we've been altogether
too cosy and cliquey as a family.*

   Wish me luck!
   With love from
   Rosie (Farquarson)

*Below Rosie's message Walter had written: Although we have
never met, I hope you will accept my heartfelt thanks for all
you did for my daughter.*

*PS from Rosie. And in case you are wondering: I have kept my
promise not to tell John and Dad your real name. Wrote this
PS after Dad had written his!*

* * *

After the holiday, Lucille worked hard on the counselling
course. But she also managed to complete her memoir in time
to enter a writing competition that asked for short memoirs
concerning domestic violence. A specialist charity had hit on
this as a way to raise public awareness, and the prize was pub-
lication. Clare and Helen acted as "beta readers" and helped her
to polish the grammar and spelling.

Weeks went by. Then came a letter which changed everything. Lucille had been shortlisted for the prize and she was
invited to the award ceremony and a dinner at a London hotel.

For the first time in over a year, Lucille bought a new outfit,
a calf-length linen suit in a soft shade of pale gold. When she
tried it on again at home, she smiled at herself in the mirror.

Though she was well into her forties, her face still looked nice and she was not dissatisfied with her figure. But she wished she had a loving companion to share this experience, someone to cheer if she won and comfort her if she didn't. This thought cast a shadow over her happiness. The invitation only said she could bring a "partner", so she assumed it wouldn't be acceptable to invite a friend.

The event was held in the hotel ballroom, a huge room with big bright chandeliers and elegant waiters and waitresses standing to attention. The scene reminded her of important award events she'd watched on television, and she couldn't help thinking it was rather out of keeping with the subject of the books in this contest.

Lucille was escorted to her place at one of the large round tables. Her companions were four couples and another single woman. The conversation was bland and repetitive: "Where do you live?" "What do you do?" "Have you a family?" The dinner dragged and she began to wish she hadn't come.

As the conversation went on, she discovered that not all the guests at the event were memoir writers or their partners—some were social workers from domestic abuse charities and others were sponsors and donors. So Walter Farquarson might be present. She got up and stared around the vast room. She could not see him and she did not feel brave enough to walk round in search of him. Anyway, if they did meet, what on earth would they find to say?

At the end of the meal there were three long speeches. It was like that award ceremony in the Sheldonian Theatre—the powers that be seemed to want to make the five hopefuls wait and suffer as long as possible. At least they had not been made to sit on a platform at the front. She didn't stand a chance of winning, she knew that, but the wait was horrible anyway.

After the speeches about the various charities and the need for greater public awareness and more public funding, the competition judge began to talk about the five shortlisted entries. The judge was a university professor whose books were on the reading list for Lucille's counselling course. She was more considerate than the previous speakers, was brief, and spoke fast. She said Lucille's memoir was deeply moving and sharply observed.

Soon the judge came to the announcement of the winner. There was no slow, agonising build-up because there was only one winner.

It was Mary Brown.

Thank goodness she was sitting near the front, so she did not have a long walk to the lectern where the judge stood. Everyone was looking at her and clapping. The judge said, "Very well done," handed her a big rolled-up certificate, and whispered, "Do you want to make an acceptance speech?" She shook her head.

More than ever, she wished she was not here alone. She went back to her seat. The other people at her table congratulated her, and after she had said thank you, she pretended she was going to the ladies' and did not return. She wanted to get home to Bristol as soon as she could, to her computer, so that she could email her friends in Oxford and Andrew Charlton and Clare and her tutor at the College of Further Education. She was sad that she had no family and no partner to share her pleasure. She had no one she could ring up at this time of night.

* * *

Walter attended the award ceremony with Louise Curtis from the St Frideswide's Centre. As the speakers droned on, he thought back to the event in the Sheldonian Theatre when he had received the Charles Hudson History Prize. How anxious he had grown as the announcement of the winners came closer; how lovely it had been to have John and Rosie to celebrate with him; how he had wished Sarah could have been present as well.

When the competition judge began to speak, he tuned in again. At the preliminary reading stage, he had read a number of the entries without their authors' names. He had liked *Survivor* best and he was delighted when it was placed on the longlist. And now it was through to the shortlist. He hoped to get an opportunity to meet its author, Mary Brown, but the room was so crowded he had not yet succeeded in finding her. He had no idea what she looked like. He hoped she would win. If she did, he would see her go up to accept her award from the judge and he'd be able to seek her out and congratulate her after the presentation.

"… and the winner is Mary Brown, for *Survivor*." Walter craned his neck to see her, a small distant figure in a long, pale yellow dress. He could not make out her features. She appeared only briefly, did not make an acceptance speech, simply took her certificate and walked briskly back to a table near the front.

When he had said goodbye to Louise and the other people he knew, Walter threaded his way through the crowd to the table where Mary Brown had been sitting. She was not there. Her dinner companions told him she had been gone a long time and she had taken her award certificate away with her. Nevertheless, he waited till the room was empty. She did not return. Walter felt frustrated and annoyed with himself. He should have made more of an effort to locate her. All he'd needed to do was to walk from table to table and ask for Mary Brown. He had been too lazy, or too diffident, and now it was too late.

CHAPTER THIRTY-FIVE

Finale

"And to conclude our seminar, we have a presentation by Mary Brown from the Fairways Women's Refuge in Bristol." Walter paused, and the secretary brought her in.

The attractive, elegant woman was Lucille. She looked different, but Walter knew her at once. Her lovely face showed delicate lines round the eyes, and her thick dark hair was here and there threaded with silver. Walter glanced at Mike. Mike was staring at her, puzzled, but he did not recognise her. That supper party in Cowley was a long time ago.

She took her seat at the far end of the long table. Walter could tell she was trying to avoid looking at him directly. She clasped her hands tightly together, the same slender, well-groomed hands, but her nails were no longer bright red and strangely shaped. There were no rings on her fingers.

Walter picked up his notes and continued the introduction. He managed to keep his voice steady.

"Mary Brown is a counsellor and she has been doing innovative group work at the Fairways Refuge in Bristol, a highly original take on self-esteem courses, I'm told. And in addition to that, she has won the Leslie Clark prize for her memoir, which tells of her childhood with a violent father. It's written for the teenaged reader and it's called *Survivor*. Ms Mary Brown."

He laid down his notes but continued to stare at them. Mary Brown stood up.

Still the same soft northern voice. He could not concentrate properly on her words, but he grasped that she was telling them about the "Makeover" group she had run so successfully over the past year. To his surprise, she used PowerPoint and presented data and talked about statistical probabilities.

When at last he forced himself to pay attention, she was drawing to a close. "We have to build our strength in any way we can. If a woman looks her best she can feel that little bit more confident. Many people judge us by our appearance, by what we wear. Of course they're wrong to think like that, but it makes sense for us to conform in the unimportant things, and put up a fight where it really matters.

"'There but for the grace of God' applies even if you don't believe in religion. What's that song? *There but for Fortune*— Joan Baez." Two older members of the meeting nodded. "If only the fortunate women and their men would remember that."

Walter recalled Sarah's words after she had visited a refuge, "I'm no more loveable than those poor women. How fortunate we are, you and I." He had argued then that being cherished by your partner was entirely a matter of deserts, not a matter of luck. Now he knew better.

Lucille finished, and for the first time met Walter's eyes. A serious, thoughtful look. He glanced away, fiddled with his papers, and thanked her warmly but formally—he longed to talk, but now was not the time. While the others were complimenting her on her presentation, he scribbled a note: *Lucille: could you possibly wait till after the meeting and come back to talk to me?* Ignoring the curious glances from Mike and one or two others, he moved round the table to give it to her. She read it quickly, hands trembling, before she left the room.

He brought the meeting to an end. One by one the other trustees, the social workers, the charity representatives and the managers began to leave. He tried to control his impatience and hide his nervousness. He thanked the participants individually for attending. When he came to Mike, he said something had arisen and he would not be going home till later.

After they had all gone, he came out into the hotel lobby. She was sitting on a bench with her hands folded in her lap, staring straight ahead. At first, she appeared composed, but then he saw her hands were still trembling and she was biting her lip.

"Lucille … Mary … could you come back in now?"

They stood quietly looking at one another.

"Walter … I've missed you."

"Me too. Lucille, how are you? Could we—?"

Lucille didn't wait for him to finish. "Is it true that you have a new partner?"

"No. Where did you hear that?"

"Oh, I somehow thought … A misunderstanding … So you're still on your own?"

He nodded. "Yes," he said. "And you?" He was crossing his fingers like a fool.

"Yes, I'm still on my own as well." He detected a hint of a smile.

"Your life must be very different now. Two new careers."

She told him about her new life of writing and counselling. He told her about his latest book on seventeenth-century heroines and his new college post as Tutor for Admissions.

"I hope you would let Jude the Obscure into St Nicholas' College if he applied today," she said with a grin.

She asked about his children.

"John has done brilliantly. He's back from Peru and doing research at Cambridge."

"And Rosie?"

"She's been through a lot—of course, you knew that, I told you all about it the evening you came round to see me, when I was feeling so low—but she seems to have come out the other end. She did finally leave that boyfriend. She's living with me again, and doing a creative writing course in Oxford."

"Yes, I know, and I'm so glad for both of you," said Lucille.

There was a pause. She went on, "That is, I mean to say …". Lucille had obviously said more than she intended.

And he realised. "I get it—how stupid of me not to guess—you're the same Mary, aren't you? Rosie's counsellor? Rosie didn't mention your surname. You're the person who helped Rosie so much. She never told us it was you."

"I asked her not to."

"When I saw in the notes that you ran your group at the Fairways Refuge, I wondered if you had seen her there, but she only stayed a few hours overnight. And I was even at the event where you received the memoir award! But I wasn't sitting close enough to see you properly. Lucille—or do you prefer to be called Mary now?"

"Mary, if you don't mind."

"Mary. I'll try to remember. We have so much to thank you for, Rosie and John and I. I'm trying harder now to give something back, to you and all the other people who counsel and give sanctuary to women who become trapped like Rosie. And I'm making more effort to help the women themselves, and their children, of course. I've read your book. It's bad enough to be abused without being made to feel ashamed as well. I didn't fully understand that before, and I had no idea of the effect it could have on the children."

"It seems to me you've helped a lot already."

"All I did was to hand over some of Sarah's money, money I didn't need, and I only did so because Sarah had suggested it."

"Stop beating up on yourself. Now, are you free this evening?"

He nodded.

"As you know, there's an excellent Italian place in George Street. Could you possibly afford to buy me some dinner?"

"I might just manage that, but aren't you going to insist on paying your way?"

"No, Walter, I'm not."

"You've changed."

"I think we both have."

* * *

Walter said to himself, Yes, I'm a little wiser now. If she will allow me, I want to get to know this woman all over again. How fortunate and rare to have a second chance.

* * *

Mary said to herself, This time I mustn't go after him like an old-fashioned vamp in a silly novel. I never deserved a second chance.

The End

ABOUT THE AUTHOR

Barbara Lorna Hudson grew up on a farm in Cornwall. She studied languages at Newnham College, Cambridge and trained in social work at the Universities of Chicago and Newcastle. She was a psychiatric social worker and relationship counsellor for several years before becoming a social work lecturer, first at the London School of Economics and then at Oxford University.

When she retired she took up fiction writing and completed the Guardian/University of East Anglia Certificate Course in Creative Writing. She began with short stories, including *Click to Click: Tales of Internet Dating*. Her first novel *Timed Out* (Driven Press, 2016) is about an older woman who tries to turn her life around via Internet dating, and looks for a meaningful way to spend her retirement years.

Barbara Lorna Hudson lives beside the Thames in Oxford, and spends a lot of time eating and talking at Green Templeton College, where she is an Emeritus Fellow.

Her website is www.barbaralornahudson.co.uk

If you have enjoyed this book, please consider leaving a review for Barbara to let her know what you thought of her work.

You can read about Barbara on her author page on the Fan-tastic Books Store. While you're there, why not browse our other delightful tales and wonderfully woven prose?

www.fantasticbooksstore.com

16943951R00164

Printed in Great Britain
by Amazon